"You are lovely."

There was a sudden deep note in his voice which seemed to throb through the air between them. Her fingers clung to his; her breath came quickly from between her parted lips; and then she lifted her face toward him and the glory in her eyes was almost dazzling.

They stood spellbound, looking at one another, forgetting the world around them. They might have been alone on top of one of the silent, snow-capped mountains. For a moment it seemed as if even their heartbeats were stilled—and then the spell was broken by another voice. . . .

Later, Hugo thought, "She's just a child."
He did not guess that her unspoiled beauty hid a woman's heart, waiting to offer him love!

WINGS
ON MY HEART

•

Barbara Cartland

PYRAMID BOOKS • **NEW YORK**

WINGS ON MY HEART

A PYRAMID BOOK

Pyramid edition published April 1973
   Third printing, March 1974

Copyright 1954 by Barbara Cartland

All Rights Reserved

ISBN 0-515-02996-3

Printed in the United States of America

Pyramid Books are published by Pyramid Communications, Inc. Its trademarks, consisting of the word "Pyramid" and the portrayal of a pyramid, are registered in the United States Patent Office.

Pyramid Communications, Inc., 919 Third Avenue, New York, New York 10022

1

"Damn and blast!"

The man put out his hand to where the ski attached to his left foot sprawled awkwardly in the snow.

"Damn!" he swore beneath his breath, knowing only too well that this meant that his holiday would be ruined.

It was always the same leg that let him down. He had broken it as a boy, skiing at Mürren one winter when there was not enough snow, and ever since he had had to take care of it.

He cursed again as with fingers that fumbled a little he started to undo the straps.

A moment before he had felt as if he were winged, travelling swiftly through the air, almost godlike, as he sped down the mountainside. Now, with stabs of pain coming from his ankle he felt very human and very impotent.

He freed his foot from the ski, started to unlace the heavy leather boot. His ankle was hurting almost abominably. Then, as he moved in an effort to get into a more comfortable position, he looked across the beautiful valley to the peaks beyond, and his face was suddenly grave.

It was getting late in the afternoon. There was that soft, luminous glow in the sky which preluded the swift coming of darkness.

It would be damnable indeed to have to spend the night on the mountainside. Already, as he thought of it, he could feel the icy winds rising—winds blowing off the glaciers that could bite into a man's bones and paralyse him.

St. Moritz lay below. How far in actual mileage he was not certain. It was a long time since he had undertaken this particular run. To reach the warmth and brilliance of the hotels would take perhaps twenty minutes

5

if one had sound legs and skis, like wings, upon one's feet.

With a leg which hurt, which was to all intents useless, it might take a century of time to reach shelter.

Yet it was no use waiting here. Something had to be done and quickly. He tried to struggle to his feet using the loose ski as a crutch; and then, as he struggled, he heard a voice behind him.

"You have hurt yourself?"

It was the most welcome sound he had ever heard. He turned his head swiftly and saw that a girl was standing a little behind him. She was very small and, for a moment, he thought she was little more than a child. She was wearing black skiing trousers and a red windjammer with a hood which framed a tiny, piquant face with a clear, transparently white skin and eyes which seemed surprisingly large and dark in contrast to the fair curls which played around her forehead.

"Thank goodness you have come!" he exclaimed. "I'm afraid I need help. My ankle is badly sprained, if it isn't broken. I have had trouble with it before."

"I am sorry," she said. "How did it happen?"

"I suppose I took the turn too sharply," he answered grudgingly. "It is a long time since I have been on this particular run."

"It proves disastrous for many people," she answered.

"It would have been more disastrous for me if you hadn't come along," he said. "We had better not waste time talking if you are to send me help before it gets too dark."

He looked up at the sky as he spoke. Her eyes followed his and she nodded gravely.

"It will be dark before anyone can come to you. There is a hut a little further on. If you can get there, it will not be so cold for you while you are waiting."

"A hut!" he said; "that's good news."

"If you could put one hand on my shoulder," she suggested, "and lean on me, I can help you there."

"Do you think you really can?" he asked. "I am no light weight and you—you are . . ."

"Très petite!" she said with a smile that had something mischievous in it.

He raised his eyebrows a bit.

"You are French?" he asked. "I thought you were English."

"I am Swiss!" she answered firmly; "but hurry, Monsieur, we must start if we are to reach the hut before it is dark."

She held out her hand to him as she spoke. As he took it, he found, surprisingly, that she was stronger than he thought. Small though she might be, there was something wiry about her and a strength that he would never have suspected from her small and frail appearance.

Slowly, with difficulty, they proceeded side by side down the mountain, until finally they reached a small log-built hut perched precariously on the side of the mountain.

It contained nothing but some rough planks, but the man was happy to sink down on them.

It had been hard going, moving on only one leg with the other one hurting abominably, striving to keep his balance without resting too heavily on the frail shoulders of the girl who had assisted him.

She stood now in the doorway, silhouetted against the deepening sky; just behind her head the first evening star was twinkling.

Looking at her, the man had a sudden, absurd notion that she was not human, but a sprite such as the ignorant peasants believed in, attributing all their difficulties or good fortune to the good will or ill-humour of the immortals of the mountains.

"You will be out of the wind here," she said. "I will be as quick as I can."

"I am extremely grateful," he replied.

"But I have done nothing yet," she smiled. "I will send back men with a sleigh and they will get you down safely, you can be sure of that."

She turned to go and as she did so the man cried out:

"One minute! You have not told me your name."

She smiled at him again. There was some unmistakable fairy quality about her.

"My name is Utta!" she answered, and then she was gone.

Hugo Roxburton lit a cigarette and sat staring out into the gathering darkness. He began to calculate how long Utta would take to get down the mountainside and then send help.

However optimistic he might be, he could not imagine there was any chance of being rescued under two hours. He knew by that time he would be very cold and very bored. And Hugo Roxburton was not used to being bored.

Intelligence, wealth and good organisation assured for him that everything he desired and wished for should be obtained with the minimum amount of difficulty.

"You know, you are very spoiled, Hugo!" his sister Pamela had said to him only a week ago.

"Why not?" he enquired. "People who do not get what they want in life are usually fools or weaklings."

"Sometimes you frighten me, you are so ruthless," she sighed.

He shrugged his shoulders and walked across the room to stand looking out of the window on to the formal rose garden. Frost lay heavy on the ancient sundial and on the yew hedges which had been planted several centuries ago and which had seen nearly a dozen owners of Rox come and go.

"You have always been so lucky, Hugo," his sister went on. "When the fairies attended your christening, they must have given you good fortune as a gift, though I have a feeling they forgot gratitude."

"How do you know I am not grateful?" Hugo asked.

"If you are, you keep singularly quiet about it," Pamela replied. "I always remember your face when we heard that Andrew had been killed mountaineering. It meant that you were heir—to Cousin John's title, to Rox, the money, the estates, to everything—and yet you didn't even look surprised. It was just as if you had always known that you would inherit."

"You are talking nonsense!" Hugo said a little sharply; then he turned from the window to smile at his sister.

"My dear Pamela, I had no idea you were so imaginative. Is it married life that has taught you to make a drama out of so little, or does being the wife of an eminent Cabinet Minister need imagination to make it tolerable?"

Pamela had only sighed again and gone from the room; but now Hugo Roxburton found himself remembering her words, the expression on her face.

Why had she chosen that moment to reproach him with ingratitude? And yet why should he be grateful to anyone in particular for what had been, it seemed to him now, an almost inevitable train of events?

The previous Lord Roxburton had been his father's cousin. He was a clever, distinguished man, who had married late in life an extremely beautiful, very wealthy American. They produced one son, Andrew, who was ten years older than Hugo, with whom, therefore, he had very little in common.

Andrew had been wild; even as a little boy he was always in trouble, always in danger. Twice he was nearly drowned in the lakes: once in the summer when his canoe capsized, and another time in the winter when he would go on the ice long before it was strong enough to hold him.

He had always wanted to climb to the top of the tallest tree in the park or scramble on the slanting perilous roofs of the house, however treacherous the slates and gutters might be from frost or rain.

If he drove a car, it was at eighty miles an hour on roads on which no one prudent would venture at more than fifty. He was wild, he was impetuous, and he had no sense of danger whatsoever.

It was almost inevitable that Andrew should be killed one way or another.

What Pamela had been intuitive enough to guess was true, that Hugo was not surprised.

Somehow he had always known that Rox would be his. Known it even in the days when his father, the

9

second son of a second son, talked about the need for planning his future, the financial difficulties he would encounter in his life. It was as if he had always been certain that such precautions were unnecessary.

One by one the lives between him and the title disappeared. By old age, war and accident—one after another they went, until Hugo found himself the seventh Lord Roxburton and a very rich man.

His cousin's American wife had died before her husband. Her money had been left to him and when Hugo inherited he found himself owning not only one of the finest houses in England, but also a fortune in American real estate, which had come to him unconditionally.

"Grateful! I am grateful for that," he said to himself, knowing that while his contemporaries were bowed under crippling taxes he had American dollars to spend and to spare.

Hugo's cigarette was finished. He chucked the stub away. Taking out his cigarette-case he saw that there were only three left. He must ration himself, he thought, wait half an hour at least between each smoke.

It was getting very dark; soon he would be able to see nothing. He slipped his cigarette-case back into his pocket and felt for his matches. A full box, fortunately.

He wondered if he dared light himself a fire, but decided against it. It would be awkward if he burnt the hut to the ground and still more uncomfortable from his own point of view.

It was very cold. He had taken off his gloves for a moment while he searched for his cigarette-case and now he put them on again. His fingers were numbed even in that brief encounter with the air.

In an effort to keep warm he swung his arms across his body to his sides, as he had seen taxi-drivers do, and remembered how his mother had told him that when she was a girl cabbies had always performed the same action while they waited on the ranks with their tired horses. The brisk movement got his blood circulating, but it seemed to make his leg throb even more unbearably; and to forget it he lost himself again in his thoughts.

10

He thought of Rox, with its gracious grey pillars and winged front, which had been designed by Robert Adam. How lovely it was, with its terraces encircling it like a necklace, with its lakes, silver beneath the grey skies!

Yet remembering he recalled how irritating Pamela had been on the last morning before he left for Switzerland.

"I hope you will have a good time, Hugo," she had said. "I hear that Carole is in your party. When are you going to make up your mind to marry her?"

He felt, for no particular reason, extremely irritated at the question.

"My dear Pamela," he replied, a trifle pompously, "is there any particular reason why I should make up my mind to marry Carole, or anyone else for that matter?"

She laughed at him because he appeared to be affronted.

"Don't be ridiculous, Hugo!" she said. "You know as well as I do that Carole has every intention of marrying you. She will manage it by fair means or foul. She is as used to having her own way as you are. Besides, it is all so suitable. Do you realise the last three Lord Roxburtons have married American heiresses? You would be true to the tradition, and Carole is very attractive."

"So are a large number of other women," Hugo prevaricated.

"My dear, it is time you married," Pamela said softly. "You have sown a large harvest of wild oats and Rox needs a mistress as well as an heir."

"Dammit! You women are all the same—not content unless you are match-making. I don't think I want to get married and that's all there is to it."

"Oh well, there's always Eddie!" Pamela retorted.

She meant to be irritating and she succeeded. She knew, better than most people, what her brother, and for that matter most of their relations, thought of their cousin Eddie, who was heir presumptive to the title until Hugo should marry and have a son.

He was a middle-aged, boring little man, fastidious and effeminate in his ways, who collected Ming china.

11

He lived in a flat in London where everything was as precious and as spinsterish as he was himself, and he had lately published a slim, elaborately bound book on the history of the Roxburton family.

"Eddie was saying only the other day that he would love to inherit Rox, if for no other reason than that he would have room for his china," Pamela said mischievously.

Hugo was about to reply angrily; then he met his sister's eyes and they both began to laugh.

"All right, you win!" he said. "I will get married if only to spite Eddie."

"I really think it would be a good thing, darling," Pamela said. "Your reputation has really begun to stink a little, you know that, don't you?"

"Who cares?" Hugo asked.

"I do, for one," Pamela answered, "and Walter for another."

"Walter!" Hugo made a little grimace. There was no love lost between him and his brother-in-law, as Pamela well knew.

"Walter is doing very well," she said. "There is every chance that he may be Prime Minister one day, and it is embarrassing for him to listen to all the things his friends say about you."

"If you want to know what I think, he's jealous," Hugo answered. "If Walter has never put a foot wrong in his life, it is because he has not had the gumption to do so."

"Now, we are not going to discuss Walter," Pamela said firmly; "we are talking about your getting married, and the sooner you do so the better for all of us—including Walter."

Hugo had groaned at the time; he groaned again now. He supposed everyone, however they were born, were cursed by their relations; but he found both Eddie and Walter almost intolerable—the former with his mincing, feminine spitefulness; Walter with his narrow, dogmatic manner of laying down the law and not admitting any argument except his own.

He had planned to have a holiday away from both of

12

them and from his friends. But Carole had come with him and he had found himself not alone and free, but one of a party.

That was Carole's doing; as Pamela had said, she always got her own way. She would be worried now, he thought suddenly, wondering why he had not returned to the hotel.

She would be waiting for him in the bar at Suvretta House wearing one of those ridiculously expensive dresses labeled *"après ski"*, which looked so simple and which were in reality a complicated product of brains and daring.

He had a sudden vision of Carole as she had appeared last night in trousers of black wool, with a jumper of midnight blue velvet trimmed with white mink. She wore dozens of charm bracelets dangling from her thin wrists and her ear-rings were a cascade of tiny bells.

She used a strange oriental scent which was somehow characteristic of her. It made him feel almost a little intoxicated after the sharp, bracing air outside.

And when they danced together he had felt her warmth and animal magnetism and he very nearly said the words which he knew she was waiting to hear.

"Hugo, I love you so much!"

Her cheek was very smooth against his as she whispered the words in his ear.

Yes, she loved him; he was sure of that—as sure as one could be of anything where Carole was concerned. She was so rich, so beautiful; there were so many men who desired her, and she had flittered from one love affair to another—even as he had done.

It was that feeling of similitude about them and of talking the same language which had first drawn them together.

He had heard so much about Carole Munton before he met her that he had felt certain that he would dislike her on sight. Apparently she had felt the same about him.

"So you are the Don Juan of St. James's Street," she had drawled in her soft Southern American voice.

13

Instead of feeling annoyed he had found himself smiling.

"I am delighted to meet the Cleopatra of Broadway," he replied, and she had laughed at that.

"I have heard of your many love affairs," he told her a little aggressively.

"And I of yours," she answered. "How else does one gain experience?"

The question had been unanswered; then somehow they had both felt that the answer was there. This was what they had been looking for—each other—she on one side of the Atlantic and he on the other. And yet Hugo had waited.

"Why?" he asked himself now. "Why?"

What was the reason? Heaven knows he had given up being idealistic and absurd years ago. Women were all the same, more or less! You loved them, or thought you did, for a short while, then they faded out of your life or you walked out of theirs.

He thought back over the women he had loved and made love to and who had loved him. He was not ashamed of their number. As Carole had said, it was all experience.

What was horrifying was to realise how little they had meant. For a few hours, days, weeks his heart beat faster when he saw them . . . excitement rising to desire . . . a hunger of the lips . . . an aching need for the softness of their bodies . . . and then the inevitable feeling of disappointment.

Yes, he had to be honest with himself. How remorselessly, inexorably, he had been disappointed. Had he expected too much? And if so, what had he expected? What could he have had more than he had actually received?

Hugo felt himself sigh. There were moments when he had thought that he had found something wonderful beyond compare, but always the reaction had set in.

Women! women! He could hear himself reiterating blithely that there were too many of them in the world. But the next moment he would be intrigued by yet another. He would be chasing after some woman because

14

the sweetness of a smile, the glint of an eye or the faint gesture of a hand had made him feel excited all over again.

Now he had come to the end of his philanderings. Carole was the person he had been looking for and her wealth should add to the treasures of Rox, as her predecessors' had done before her.

He could imagine Carole walking down the Long Gallery; standing at his side to receive their guests in the State Drawing-Room. The Adam Dining-Room, with its green walls, would frame her dark loveliness.

Her long fingers would touch the yellowing keys of the spinet in the Music Room, and her little feet would dance on the polished floor of the great Ballroom with its crystal chandeliers and Queen Anne mirrors.

Yes, Carole would make a beautiful chatelaine for Rox and they could re-open the house in London which he had closed because it was too large for a bachelor.

"I love you, Hugo."

He could hear her voice saying it. Yet even while his arms had tightened instinctively round her, he knew in some cold, critical part of his mind that she was making it too easy for him.

"Man must be the hunter!" He tried to remember who had said those words, then remembered that he had found them inscribed in an old leather-bound volume in the library at Rox.

"Man must be the hunter!" Carole was used to hunting her own prey. Hugo felt himself smile in the cold and darkness of the little hut.

It was ridiculous to think of himself as being the prey of Carole, and yet there was enough truth in the idea to make him feel irritated and antagonistic at the very suggestion.

He took off his gloves, pulled out his cigarette-case and then, as he felt in it, realised that his last cigarette had gone. He had smoked them almost unconsciously, his thoughts far away in England.

He was suddenly aware of being chilled through and through; then, as he felt himself shiver, he heard voices.

He shouted loudly:

"Hallo there, I am here."

He spoke in English, and then, as he wondered if he should repeat the words in French or German, someone appeared in the doorway of the hut and the light of a lantern flashed into his eyes.

"You must be very cold!" a soft voice said. "Hans has brought some blankets—you must wrap yourself in them."

"Why have you come back?" Hugo asked. "It is too far for you."

"Hans and Ludwig might not have found you if I had not been there to guide them," she answered. "They have brought their sleigh."

She moved into the hut as she spoke and now at last, as his eyes got accustomed to the light, Hugo could see her face. She was smiling and her eyes seemed to dance like stars in the shadows.

"If we had been much longer, you would have been frozen to the ground," she said. "Poor Monsieur! But now we shall soon be back at the hotel and the doctor will see to your poor leg."

She turned her head as she spoke and shouted to the men outside.

"Be quick," she said in German. "Lift the gentleman very carefully and wrap him in the blankets. Hurry, there is no time to be lost; he is cold!"

The two men seemed galvanised into action by Utta's voice. They came into the hut and almost before Hugo had a glimpse of them, big and rough in their dark windjammers and knitted caps, they lifted him gently in their arms and carried him to the sleigh outside.

Almost before he had time to get his breath to speak to Utta or ask a question they were away. The sledge seemed to cut its way through the night air and the darkness, the men guiding it by instinct down the mountainside. Utta came behind, holding the lantern in her hand.

The journey took longer than Hugo had anticipated. It was rough going; more than once he had to bite back a cry of pain which rose to his lips. It was not only his ankle, but his whole body which was tortured by being bumped and shaken and rattled.

And then at last, when the journey had become almost intolerable and he was wondering how much longer he could stand it, he saw ahead of him the brilliantly lit windows of Suvretta House. He was back in civilisation.

The men drew the sleigh up to the door of the hotel.

Hugo turned his head to thank Utta for rescuing him, but she was no longer with them—she had vanished as if she had been, in reality, what he had first suspected, a sprite from the mountains!

2

Hugo lay in bed and watched his valet open the shutters and let in the morning sunshine.

It was a very pale sunshine as yet for it was still very early in the morning and less than an hour ago the white peaks of the mountains, now radiant against the transparent sky, were shrouded in darkness.

Every morning of his life Hugo was called at six-thirty. He had got used to rising early when he was in the Army, and he found now, as he grew older, that however many secretaries he kept or however many people there were to look after his interests, there was always a vast amount of correspondence, papers and documents which had to be dealt with day after day.

Those who considered him merely a rake, a man with too much money and far too much time on his hands, would have been astonished if they had seen how many details of his farm, estate and fortune Hugo dealt with himself—and usually while those who criticised him were still asleep.

Although he had gone to bed very late as he had been playing cards with his friends, he had been awake for some time before Smith came stealing into the room.

His valet had an almost feline stealth about him, in

17

fact he had a habit of turning up unexpectedly so that Pamela and many of Hugo's friends swore that he listened at keyholes.

"You mark my words," Hugo's grandmother had said—a formidable old lady of nearly eighty—"that man of yours is up to no good. Nobody can tell me at my age that I am not a judge of character. If you ask me my opinion, he is either collecting evidence with which to blackmail you, or material to write his life story and sell it to a Sunday newspaper!"

Hugo had laughed.

"I was a Valet to a Nobleman?" he queried. "Or do you think *The Secrets of Society* would be more his line?"

His grandmother had not been amused.

"I am warning you, my boy," she said solemnly. "Not but what it's your own fault. The way you go on is an absolute encouragement to blackmailers and the like."

Her words were scathing, but there was a twinkle in her eyes which Hugo did not miss.

"It must be in my blood, Grandmother," he answered. "I wonder how you managed to get away with it all these years!"

She pretended to be outraged at his impertinence; but he knew that she delighted in being teased by him and that he was her favourite grandchild.

Nevertheless, Hugo continued to employ Smith, to like and to trust him. He had been with him for over ten years; and whatever else he might be, Smith was a most efficient valet.

He turned from the window now and began tidying up the clothes which had been thrown carelessly on the chair.

"Come and help me up," Hugo commanded.

"You had best have your breakfast in bed, my lord," Smith replied. "It's chilly this morning."

"What do you think I am—an invalid?" Hugo enquired. "I rested most of yesterday to please you and the doctor. Today my ankle is much better and I am going to do what I want."

Smith looked disapproving, but he helped Hugo from

18

the bed into his dressing gown and across the room to where a french window opened on to a small balcony.

If the journey hurt Hugo's ankle, he made no sign of it. When he was seated in the chair, Smith fetched a stool and lifted the bandaged foot gently on to it.

"Have you ordered breakfast?" Hugo enquired.

"Yes, my lord. Eggs, cold ham and coffee. It will be here at any moment."

"Good. Now give me the letters which came last night."

Smith had anticipated the request and had already fetched a huge pile of correspondence from the writing-table in the corner of the room. He placed the letters by Hugo's side and brought, at the same time, a tray containing pens and pencils and a large blotter on which he could write.

"Thank you, Smith, that will be all I want for the moment."

Hugo put the pile of letters in his lap and for a moment he did not open them. The sun was warm on his face and he turned to look out of the window at the beauty of the view; the valley was white and gleaming; the sky palely translucent, the mountains peaking into the distance.

It was as delicate as the first unfolding of a spring flower; and though he would not have confessed it even to himself, Hugo felt a sudden catch in his heart at the utter loveliness of it.

Then, as he looked at the trees which surrounded the hotel, heavy with snow and frosted until they glittered like an American Christmas card, he became aware of a movement immediately below him.

Casually he glanced down and saw that on the ice rink of the hotel someone was already skating. This was unusual. Hugo was used to seeing no one abroad at this time of the morning.

Later there would be attendants in uniform and crowds of smartly dressed guests from the hotel, skating or watching from the seats which were arranged round the rink. At twelve o'clock there would be a band and waiters in white coats would be in attendance with cocktails and sandwiches.

But at six-thirty in the morning Hugo, until now, had had an empty, white world to himself. He had liked the sense of solitude, the feeling there were no interruptions to his thoughts or his work, save the birds who would come and sit on his balcony and wait for him to throw them crumbs from his breakfast tray.

But this morning someone was awake as early as himself. Idly he watched. The skater moved across the ice; the balcony obscured his view, then he saw her again. She skated well, he thought; and then, as she came again within his sight, something made him rise from his chair.

"Here, wait a minute, my lord. You can't do that alone," Smith said, and came hurrying across the room to his side.

Hugo let the man help him on to the balcony and there he stood looking down on to the rink below. There was nothing to obscure his view now and he saw at once that he had not been mistaken.

He could not see the small, pointed face of the skater clearly; but now no red hood hid the pale gold curls, which seemed to dance with every movement of her body, and he was sure he had not been mistaken.

The opening of the door behind him and the clatter of plates and cutlery told him that the waiter was arriving with his breakfast.

"Come here!" he said to the man.

"*Oui, Monsieur.*"

"Do you know who that is skating down there?" he enquired.

"*Oui, Monsieur.* That is the pupil of Ernst Zippert."

"The skating instructor?"

"*Oui, Monsieur.* That is Ernst there."

The waiter pointed, and now Hugo saw there was an elderly man standing at the side of the rink watching every movement of the girl who was skating on the ice.

"And what is the girl's name?"

The waiter put his hands to his forehead.

"I am afraid I have forgotten, Monsieur, or perhaps

20

Ernst has kept it a secret. He thinks to win the International Championships with this pupil of his. Competitors are coming from all over the world to compete, but Ernst has been boasting in the bar that a Swiss girl will be the winner this year."

"Indeed!"

Hugo watched the girl below for some moments in silence. She was good, there was no doubt of that. She was spinning now, a tiny spiral of blue and pale gold. Then she sped across the ice with a grace and swiftness that reminded Hugo of a bird in flight. He turned to the waiter.

"Go down to the rink," he said; "convey my compliments to Ernst Zippert and say I should very much like to see him again. Tell him I should be honoured if he and his pupil would have breakfast with me when their practice is finished."

"I will convey Monsieur's message immediately," the waiter said.

He went from the room. Hugo still stood in the window.

"She is good, my lord," Smith said suddenly. "If you ask me, it is worth a small bet on her being in the first three."

"Good gracious, Smith, do they gamble on the Championships?" Hugo exclaimed.

"Of course they do, my lord. Now I come to think of it, I heard the odds last night. They were offering two to one against the German and English girls, but the Swede was odds on."

"Well, here's your chance to back an outsider," Hugo said. "Now, suppose you give me some clothes. If Mademoiselle Switzerland is going to honour me with her company, I had better look respectable."

There was no reason to hurry. Hugo was dressed and had waited nearly an hour in the sitting-room opening out of his bedroom before Smith ushered in his guests.

He had not been mistaken in guessing the identity of the girl who had been skating on the rink below—it was Utta. Her eyes were shining and her lips smiling as she held out her hand to greet him.

"You are better?" she said. "I am so glad."

He had remembered that she was pretty; but now in the clear morning light she had a radiance that was almost indescribable. She had changed from her short, tightly fitting skating costume into the skiing clothes she had worn the night she rescued him. But the hood was thrown back from her shining head and her cheeks were flushed from exercise.

Hugo thought as he looked at her that he had never seen anyone so alive or so vital. He turned to greet Ernst Zippert.

"It is a great pleasure to see you again, my lord," the grey-haired Swiss said, shaking his hand heartily. "I was hoping that you would come out this year. I did not know you had arrived."

"I got here three days ago," Hugo replied, "and I was, of course, coming to see you, but I had an accident. Didn't your pupil tell you about it?"

Ernst Zippert looked down at Hugo's bandaged foot and then glanced at Utta. Then he clasped his hands together.

"So it was my lord you rescued?" he said.

"I did not know his name," Utta replied.

"And you only told me that your name was Utta," Hugo added. "Yesterday I wanted to write and thank you for your kindness to me, but when I enquired at the hotel if anybody knew someone called Utta, they told me there were dozens of girls in St. Moritz with the same name."

"You do not know her then?" Ernst Zippert asked. "When I tell you who she is, my lord, you will be very interested."

"Well, who is she?" Hugo enquired with a smile.

"She is the grand-daughter of Nicolaus Kindschi."

For a moment Hugo looked puzzled, then his expression cleared.

"Nicolaus Kindschi—the famous guide about whom the book was written?"

"The very same," Ernst Zippert said proudly.

"Then I am very delighted to meet you," Hugo said to Utta. "And I must congratulate you on having such a distinguished grandfather. The book about him was a bestseller in England for years."

"You must not think me rude," Utta replied, "if I tell you that my grandfather was not at all pleased about that book and does not like to speak of it. He said that he only did his duty. He did not wish to be made out a hero. When the author sent him a copy of the book, he burnt it."

"Good Lord!" Hugo exclaimed. "But come and sit down. I have ordered breakfast—it should be here at any moment."

Even as he spoke, the waiter who had carried the message to the rink came hurrying into the room with covered dishes, steaming coffee, golden pats of butter, and the scented flower honey which is indispensable on every St. Moritz breakfast table.

Utta sat down at the table with her back to the window. The sunlight played on her hair, making it seem almost as if a golden halo encircled her tiny head.

"Now, tell me what you are up to, Ernst," Hugo said.

The Swiss instructor settled himself comfortably in his chair and the waiter whisked away the cover from a plate laden with sausages and eggs.

"You have been hearing things about me?" Ernst Zippert enquired.

"About you and a pupil who is, I am told, 'a dark horse' for the Championships," Hugo replied.

Ernst Zippert made a gesture with his hands.

"You see," he said to Utta, "we can keep nothing to ourselves, nothing. That is why we practise so early; and yet, even so, someone is peeping from behind the shutters."

"But I must practise," Utta replied.

"Of course, of course," Ernst Zippert agreed, "but if too many people see you, there will no longer be a secret."

"You really think she is likely to win?" Hugo enquired.

Ernst Zippert looked at him.

"Do you remember Huldi?" he asked.

23

"Of course I do," Hugo answered. "She was a world champion for two, or was it three years?"

"Three," Ernst Zippert answered. "Well, Utta is better; you can believe me. I know what I am talking about —Utta is better than Huldi."

Hugo raised his eyebrows and smiled across the table at Utta.

"You must be very good," he said; but there was a little twist on his lips as if he was teasing her.

She looked at him without any trace of selfconsciousness.

"Perhaps Ernst is wrong," she said. "I cannot judge. I have never skated in any competitions, so how can I tell if I am good or bad."

"You can only know what Ernst has told you," Hugo said.

"Yes, that is true." Her eyes seemed to light up as if sudden hope illuminated her from within. "I want to believe that Ernst is right," she added simply. "We shall know in three days' time for certain—when I try for the Swiss Championship."

"That comes first?"

"Of course," Ernst Zippert replied. "It is like this, my lord. This year the Swiss Amateur Championship is being held here. Every important town in Switzerland will send a competitor and the choice of a girl to represent St. Moritz has been left to me. The winner of the Championship will automatically be our country's representative in the International Championships which begin two days later. Those are also taking place here— which makes it very easy for Utta and—for me."

"How long have you been working?"

"For a year," Ernst answered. "Utta likes best to ski, but last year I saw her skating. As I watched her move across the ice I knew—I knew for certain she had the makings of a Champion."

"Your grandfather must be very pleased," Hugo said.

To Hugo's surprise, Utta put up her hands in horror.

"Hush, do not say such things," she begged. "Grandpapa does not know. He would be angry, very angry, with me, with Ernst, with Grandmama because she has let me do it. You understand, he does not like to be in the public eye. We just live quietly. He disapproves very much of . . . of . . . what is the word?" she asked of Ernst Zippert.

"Publicity," he supplied.

"Yes, that's right," Utta said. "Publicity! Grandpapa thinks it is wrong . . . degrading. A man should only be in the papers when he is born and when he dies."

"What is he going to say if you win the Championships?" Hugo asked.

"I do not know," Utta answered. "I cannot bear to think of it, but Ernst says it will be all right—if I win. Personally, I think Grandpapa will be very angry indeed."

"It will be too late then for him to interfere," Ernst said, reaching out his hand towards the coffee-pot.

Utta sighed.

"I worry about it very much," she said. "Sometimes I think I was wrong to agree to it being kept a secret. If we had asked Grandpapa to begin with, he might have said yes."

"Much more likely to have said no!" Ernst replied.

"It all sounds very Victorian to me," Hugo said, his eyes on Utta, watching the way the expressions would come and go across her face.

Everything about her was exquisite, he thought. Not only her looks, but the delicacy of her hands; the way her head was set on her shoulders; the neatness of her ankles; the way she moved so that every action was as rhythmic and graceful as a poem. No wonder Ernst Zippert wanted to make her a champion! No wonder he was afraid that someone might interfere and prevent him from training his discovery.

Hugo bent forward.

"And do you always, in other things as well, do exactly what your grandfather wishes?" he asked. "Is your training with Ernst the only time you have broken bounds, or do you sometimes get away and have a little fun?"

He was teasing again, but Utta answered him quite seriously.

"Ernst has made me very naughty," she replied. "Usually I am good, very good. I love my grandpapa very much; I am very happy with him and my grandmama. Because I love them, I want to do what they want me to do."

"How admirable!"

Again there was laughter behind Hugo's words.

As if she guessed that he was mocking her, Utta looked up at him a little uncertainly. She was very young, he thought suddenly. Too young for him to treat as if she was a girl of his own class, living in his own world.

Yet, somehow, he found himself doubting what he had heard and what Utta and Ernst wished him to think. She was too pretty for him to believe that she was as innocent as she appeared.

Living in St. Moritz, the playground of all nations, she must have come in contact with dozens of men. She would have learned from them that she was both pretty and desirable, if she had learned nothing else!

Utta had finished her breakfast. She had eaten very little, but now she held a steaming bowl of coffee in her hands and glanced at him over the rim of the cup.

There was something in her eyes, which he saw were gentian blue fringed with dark lashes, that made him feel almost ashamed of the thoughts he had about her . . . and then he told himself, he was merely being a gullible fool.

Women were women, wherever one might find them; they would lie and pretend anything to achieve their own ends, to create an impression which would make them more desirable and hard to get.

"I wish you every success," Hugo said, but somehow his voice lacked warmth.

As if his tone woke Utta to her responsibilities, she glanced at the clock on the mantelpiece.

"It is half-past seven, Ernst!" she said. "I must go. If I am late getting home Grandpapa will ask many questions as to where I have been."

"Where are you supposed to have been?" Hugo enquired.

"Skiing," she answered. "I ski every morning for an hour before breakfast, but I am supposed to go to the north where there is seldom anyone about."

"That sounds very unsociable," Hugo smiled.

"It is best, I think," Utta answered solemnly. "We have nothing in common with people who come to St. Moritz. They are visitors—we live here all the year round."

"Well, as a visitor, I am very grateful to you!" Hugo said. "If you hadn't come to my rescue the other night, I hate to think what might have happened to me."

"You would have been frozen!" Utta answered.

"You would indeed!" Ernst Zippert disposed. "You know that run isn't much used now; there has been too little snow for it to be really safe. Most people prefer to come down by Wegerhaitte."

"I should have made enquiries before I started," Hugo agreed. "It is entirely my own fault and I have no one to blame but myself that I have to hobble about like an old crock."

"I am sorry about that," Utta said.

"It won't prevent me coming to see the Championships though," Hugo answered.

"I should like to say 'Don't come'," she said quickly. "I should like no one to be there—that is what frightens me—not the skating, but the crowds of people watching. Ernst says I shall forget all about them; but when I think of them I am afraid."

It was almost as if she shivered at the thought, and Hugo had an absurd desire to put his arms round her and tell her not to worry. There was something small and pathetic about her in that moment, and once again he challenged himself for being a fool.

"I must go!" Utta said hurriedly. "Thank you very much for my good breakfast."

She held out her hand and Hugo took it in his. Her fingers were soft and yet he sensed the strength of them; no one could be weak and fragile and a good skater. Once again he felt himself disbelieving this insistence on secrecy, the atmosphere she created of being obedient to the strictures of her grandparents.

27

"Listen!" he said. "We must drink to your success. Will you dine with me tonight?"

Utta shook her head.

"I am sorry," she replied, "but that is quite impossible."

"If not tonight, what about tomorrow?" he insisted.

"You do not understand!" she answered. "My grandfather does not know that I have been here skating with Ernst. He would be very angry if he knew I had come to Suvretta House. If I have not met you, how can I dine with you? Besides, I am never asked out to dinner."

"Am I dreaming or is this the twentieth century?" Hugo enquired.

She laughed at that and he noticed, for the first time, there were two tiny dimples in her cheeks.

"You are English!" she said. "You do not understand."

"Ernst is Swiss, but he can take a girl out to dinner," Hugo answered. "What is all this about, Ernst?"

The instructor looked at Utta and shook his head.

"Nicolaus Kindschi is a strange man!" he said. "I have known him for a great many years—in fact since I was a boy—but I cannot say that he is a friend of mine. Nicolaus has very few friends. He arranges his household as he sees fit and Utta is his grandchild."

"And yet you have managed to climb over the garden wall, you old fox!" Hugo exclaimed. "Or maybe Utta has jumped over to you. Am I going to admit failure where you have succeeded?" He laughed and turned again to Utta. "Next time I invite you to dinner, Mademoiselle, I have a feeling that you will say yes!"

"I would love it!" she said quickly. "But it is impossible."

She turned towards the door and Ernst Zippert followed her. She looked back for a moment and smiled at Hugo, the same smile she had given him two nights ago when she left him alone at the little hut on the edge of the mountain and went to fetch help.

He had thought then that she was like a sprite—an immortal. Now he knew that she was unmistakably human—but different, in some way that he could not describe, from anyone he had ever met before.

Utta and Ernst went from the room and almost immediately after they had gone the telephone on the table began to ring. Hugo knew instinctively who it was and for a moment he contemplated leaving it alone unanswered; and then, because its shrill, insistent tone annoyed him, he dragged himself within reach of the receiver.

"Hello!"

"Darling! I knew you would be awake. I was bored; I thought I would like to talk to you."

"Good morning, Carole! I thought nothing roused you before ten o'clock."

"It must be the air . . . or could it be excitement?"

"Excitement! About what?"

"Being here in Switzerland with you, of course."

"There are two other people with us as well, or have you forgotten?"

"Darling! Do they count?"

"It depends what you mean by that."

"Oh, Hugo!" Carole began to laugh.

"Why are you laughing?"

"At you, of course! You are always being so English, so cautious, so afraid of giving anything away."

Hugo found himself unreasonably annoyed by the implication, even though he knew it was justified.

"It is too early for an abuse of nationalities," he said stiffly.

"Darling! As though I would abuse you! What I really wanted to know was what you are going to do today."

"I don't know exactly. Aren't you going skiing?"

"No, of course not! I am going to stay with you. Shall we take a sleigh ride with one of those fascinating horses covered in bells to draw us? Do let's! They are so romantic."

"Actually, I thought of watching the skating," Hugo said.

"What, here or at the Palace?"

"I don't know. Let us find out where they are likely to be practising for the Championships."

"At the Palace, I expect."

"We might drive down there and have luncheon."

"Can I come and have breakfast with you and talk about it?"

"I have had my breakfast."

"Yes, of course, I forgot! You have it so early. Shall I come along and talk to you all the same, or would you be shocked to see me in my dressing-gown?"

"I haven't finished reading my mail!"

"What, yesterday's! Well, that can wait until tomorrow. Let me come and make plans. There are so many things I want to do and I want to do them with you."

"All right, come if you wish!"

"That doesn't sound very eager, but I will forgive you. Good-bye for the moment!"

He heard the click as she replaced the receiver. He replaced his own and hobbled back to the chair by the breakfast table; then, as he reached it, he realised that Carole would ask questions if the table was there when she arrived. "Whom had he been breakfasting with? Why?"

He could hear her voice inquisitive and a little shrill. He had deliberately refrained from telling her who had found him on the mountainside and who had come to his rescue. He had excused himself by averring that Carole was too curious, avoiding the real explanation that she was jealous.

Hugo rang the bell for the waiter impatiently. He did not know why, but he suddenly felt annoyed and irritated. He had a sensation of being cornered. It was a sensation that he disliked and which was calculated to make him more angry than anything else.

He was free . . . of course he was free. Yes, free, and master of himself.

3

Carole chose from her wardrobe a dress which had been the success of the Dior Winter Collection. It was of blood-red lace sprinkled with diamanté, and she knew it would accentuate the darkness of her hair and the whiteness of her skin.

She wanted, above all things, to look lovely tonight because she was dining with Hugo. With considerable cleverness she had managed to persuade the two other members of their party, Mary and Jimmy Baker, to go out to dinner at the Palace and leave them alone.

The Bakers were one of those bright, pleasant couples who always seemed to be found in the *entourage* of rich people. They had no money, and little to recommend them except their charm and their ability for keeping their heads financially above water.

They managed always to be in the right place at the right time and to have friends of every nationality who were able to entertain them on the world's playgrounds. They paid for their keep by being amusing, entertaining and, without being in the least subservient, useful.

Carole could quite easily have told them that she wished to be alone with Hugo and they would have understood and made themselves scarce with discretion and diplomacy. But somehow she was not prepared to admit, even to people she knew as well as she knew Mary and Jimmy, that she was pursuing Hugo. And yet it was the truth, the truth that she must admit to herself however much she might disguise it from other people.

"I love him," she whispered the words to herself as she stared at her reflection in the looking-glass.

She was attractive, there was no doubt about that, and she was clever enough to make the very most of her looks.

Masseurs, beauty specialists, doctors of endocrinology, cures and treatments at fashionable spas, had all

31

contributed to the finished picture that was Carole Munton.

Yet, when her photograph appeared in the glossy social weekly papers of England, which Hugo called laughingly 'the Snob Press', or in *Life* and *Harper's Bazaar* of America—to the envy of all the other young matrons who had been excluded from that particular issue—Carole would look at herself critically and question the captions which proclaimed her one of America's greatest beauties.

Always in her mind's eye she could see herself trudging from studio to studio; always at the back of her mind she could hear the same refrain: "Nothing today! We'll let you know if we want you."

How often she had heard that phrase! To feel the hope ebbing away from her heart; to feel despondency and despair creeping into her very bones.

It was funny now to remember how bitterly she had wept at her failure to get into the Films; wept because she had learned, in the hardest and harshest manner of all, that she was not as attractive or as pretty as she believed.

"Mrs. Carole Munton, one of New York's leading hostesses, whose beauty has been acclaimed both in America and Europe."

The magazine which had printed that was lying beside her bed at this very moment; and yet, as Carole looked in the mirror over her dressing-table, she saw instead of her calm, beautiful face, the puckered grimace of a young girl shedding tears of exasperation and anger.

"What's wrong with me, Momma? Do I stink or something? I'm as pretty as the other girls who get jobs —even prettier. But it's 'No! No! No!' all the time. Tell me why."

She could feel her foot stamping on the kitchen floor and hear her mother's calming voice:

"It's just luck, honey, that's all it is. You'll hit the jackpot one of these fine days. Now, if you are doing nothing, pop upstairs with that cup of coffee for Miss Macey in the third front."

Carole could remember the resentment in her heart as she trudged up the stairs with the coffee. She wanted to be a film star, but instead she was nothing more or less than an unpaid waitress in the boarding house which her mother ran with the minimum amount of profit and the maximum amount of hard work.

She had taken in the coffee to Miss Macey—a boarder who paid regularly and was therefore entitled to special consideration—was told sharply that she had slopped the coffee into the saucer and would she kindly remember to shut the door quietly when she went out.

"I'll show her one day, the old cat! I'll show them all, damn them!" Carole muttered aloud as she ran downstairs.

"I'll show them! I'll show them!"

The refrain was constantly running in her mind when nobody seemed to want her and there was nothing for her to do but to hang around the film studios.

"I'll show them!" It became a kind of theme song to everything she did and thought and planned.

Los Angeles was enjoying a boom period; but even though the film studios were said to be employing thousands more people then they had ever employed before, Carole did not get a job.

At last, in desperation, she got employment as a manicurist at one of the hairdressing establishments which catered for both men and women.

She would not have demeaned herself to take a job so very far short of her aspirations if the alternative had not been to help her mother at home.

The boarding house was doing badly. The lodgers paid irregularly or else left without paying at all. There was no chance of employing outside help for it could not be afforded, and Carole realised that she must either contribute something to the household expenses or take on the permanent job of housemaid and waitress.

She disliked work of all kinds, but being a manicurist was not too arduous once she had got used to the long hours in the hot, scented atmosphere and the way her back ached from bending over her clients' hands.

Anyway, it introduced her to Dave Munton. He had

come in for a shave and a haircut and asked for a mani-cure.

He was not particularly sober at the time, otherwise perhaps the play she made with her eyelashes, the soft pressure of her fingers on his hands, might have gone unnoticed.

He asked her out to dinner. She waited for him in trepidation lest he should have forgotten he had given her the invitation, but he turned up.

For Carole it was the greatest opportunity for which she had been waiting. She made the most of it. She did not know at the time, of course, exactly how rich Dave Munton was. She knew him to be a member of the Munton family; she had seen his picture often enough in the social magazines, which were then her only reading material.

"Dave Munton, Jr. on the polo field"; "Dave Munton, Jr. at the wheel of his new sports car"; "Dave Munton, Jr. with friends at Palm Beach."

She knew who he was all right, but she wouldn't have recognised him if the barber had not been so impressed by him.

She had prayed when she left the salon that evening —a prayer which had made her shake with the very intensity of her plea.

"Oh, God, let him be there! Oh, God, let him be there!"

Her prayer was answered. Dave turned up, ten minutes late. Ten minutes which had seemed to pass like ten centuries and during which Carole had died a thousand deaths.

"Sorry I'm late!"

He was drunk, very drunk, but Carole didn't care. He had kept his appointment with her and that was all that mattered.

He sobered up during the evening, and then she had to listen while he told her how much he loved another woman.

Lucille Lunt was then at the top of her fame. She was about ten years older than Dave and was living with the

34

man who had directed her last film. He didn't care, he loved her.

"She's lovely!" he told Carole. "I want to marry her, but she won't listen to me."

He talked about Lucille Lunt until the early hours of the morning, and when he drove Carole home he put his arm around her shoulders and hugged her.

"You're a sport!" he said.

"Shall I see you again?"

The softness of Carole's question hid the terror which lay behind her fear that this was the end.

"Of course! Lunch with me tomorrow."

He wouldn't have thought of it if she hadn't prompted him. It was the same with a dozen meetings they had after that. It was always she who suggested that they should see each other.

She gave up her job. She spent all the money she had and all that she could wheedle out of her mother in buying herself some new clothes.

She concentrated fiercely and exclusively on what she wanted so that, when her mother or anyone else spoke to her in the house, they would often have to ask her the same question three or four times before she heard what they said or even knew that they were near her.

She was only eighteen, but she had grown up in a hard school which had made her immeasurably older than her actual years. She had seen her mother change from a pretty, attractive woman to a middle-aged drudge. Her father had been clever when it came to learning, but as far as everything else was concerned he was a fool. He could speak eloquently on world economics, but he was incapable of earning even the smallest salary that would keep them from starvation.

When he died from pneumonia, through sitting up one cold winter's evening to watch an eclipse of the moon, Carole had thought callously it would be one less mouth for her mother to feed.

"I won't live like this when I'm grown up!"

She had made the vow one day to herself when she was only a child. She had repeated it all through the years of her adolescence until it had become an obsession with her.

She had got to have money. It was the lack of money which kept one cooking and scrubbing in the backbreaking kitchen, or washing up at an old-fashioned sink, or scrubbing floors and doorsteps. It was lack of money which made one look old and haggard with lines under tired eyes; which made what had once been a smiling mouth turn down at the corners.

Money . . . money . . . money . . . that was what Carole wanted.

It had taken time to make Dave Munton grow dependent on her and time was the thing of which Carole was afraid.

There was nothing to keep him in Los Angeles now that Lucille Lunt was bored with him. He had friends and relations all over America who would welcome him with open arms should he decide to go away from the sun-baked, white-roofed town which, as he told Carole so often, had no longer any attraction for him.

And still he stayed.

She was clever enough not to leave him alone for a moment longer than was absolutely necessary. If she made a date with him for lunch, she stayed until dinner and then again until the early hours of the morning.

He began to be bored with his own misery about Lucille; he wanted to be gay. He wanted parties and dancing, midnight bathing, music and laughter.

He had a habit of asking everyone with whom he had the slightest acquaintance, to dine and there were hundreds of people in Los Angeles only too eager to be entertained so long as it was free and there was plenty of drink.

Carole was more frightened now than she had ever been before. Every woman to whom Dave spoke seemed to be more beautiful than the last. "It is only a question of time," she kept thinking, only a question of time.

It was then that she learned that her body was made of steel and that her mind was a driving force of power and energy. She managed never to be tired, never to relax her grip. She forced Dave to notice her and she made him, by sheer determination, conscious of her as a woman.

Then one evening, drunk but coherent, he said the words she wanted to hear:

"Don't know what I should do without you, sweetie-pie. We'd better get tied up for keeps."

She married him over the border that night and then, almost before he realised what had happened to him, she made him take her to New York.

She never saw her mother again. She told her in-laws she was an orphan.

The Muntons were only too pleased to hear that she had no appendages. They were horrified and distressed by Dave's marriage. They had imagined fondly in their own minds that he was only sowing his wild oats; and if he wanted to play around with film stars, it was the same type of behaviour which they had tolerated in his father's generation, who had played around with chorus girls.

But while their first reaction was one of horror, when they saw Carole they decided that things might have been much worse and they must make the best of her.

Accordingly, the Muntons as a body took it upon themselves to groom Dave's wife into stardom. Clothes, jewels, furs, a magnificent apartment and two cars were but a small part of what she received from them. What was more important was the poise, distinction and social education they gave her. They created a background which was as glamorous and interesting as anything Carole might have invented for herself.

"Member of a well-known Southern family"—that was how she was written up in the gossip columns. All the best families were of Southern extraction and if there were people who were prepared to say they had never heard of Carole's family—well, America was a big place.

Carole had woken up one morning to find she was one of the most acclaimed and sought-after young women in New York.

One of the disadvantages of her new position was

Dave himself, who was bored with the society he had known all his life. He found the presence of his relations remarkably dull entertainment.

"Let's go to a night club," he would say impatiently to Carole when she told him they were dining with the Vanderbilts.

When she persisted that she had accepted the invitation and they could not get out of it, he complained angrily:

"Oh, stuff! You used to be much more fun than you are now."

How long she would have been able to hold Dave on a tight leash was very problematic. Carole would not have bet on it herself; and when he was killed in a motor accident, coming home drunk from a party on Long Island, she was secretly relieved.

She inherited an enormous amount of money. She had been cute enough to see that he made a Will in her favour, and she found, after Dave's death, that his fortune was even greater than she had anticipated.

Enormous sums had been left to him in trust by his grandparents. Although his family tried to argue that she was not entitled to this money, the law upheld her claim and she found herself, as one of her critics put it very aptly, "a very Merry Widow indeed."

It was then that Carole began really to enjoy herself.

She travelled. She came to Europe and found that her wealth and beauty laid down the red carpet for her wherever she went.

She returned to America and went the whole length and breadth of the continent, finding that her name and her money could open all doors—and then she discovered England.

There was some snobbery in her which made her decide that she wanted a title. Perhaps it was a throwback to her father's ancestors, who actually had been English.

She had heard titles sneered at and laughed at in her own country; she had heard people in Europe say they were out of date—and yet she wanted one. She thought of it like a tiara set upon her dark hair.

She also had a sudden desire to forget that she had ever been Dave's wife. She had never told anyone that there had been ugly scenes before finally he was killed. He had accused her of trapping him.

He said he had never meant to marry her . . . that she had held him to something he had said when he was too drunk and incapable to know what he was talking about. He had seen through her, he told her.

He had only been kind to her because she had attached herself to him like a stray dog.

Somehow those words had seared their way into Carole's consciousness. She had never forgotten them. They were there always to haunt her . . . to make her feel inferior and a failure even when people were fawning upon her and flattering her.

"No, nothing today!" "Attaching yourself to me like a stray dog!"

Those two sentences encroached upon her enjoyment, spoilt her pleasure in everything.

"I am pretty, I am!"

Carole did not realise that she had spoken the words aloud until her maid came hurrying to her side from the other side of the room.

"Did you speak, madam?"

"No, it is nothing, Adèle. I was only thinking aloud."

"Madam looks lovely tonight! Can I put another star in your hair?"

"Yes, please, Adèle. One on each side. I will wear my small diamond necklace as well."

Adèle carried to her side the heavy leather jewel case which had been brought upstairs from the hotel safe a little while earlier.

As she opened the trays Carole stared at the jewels. Diamonds, rubies, emeralds. There was a great fortune in the velvet trays, all sparkling brilliantly as she looked at them.

But suddenly she knew they did not mean what another woman's jewels would have meant—gifts of love. She had bought them for herself or they had belonged to Dave's mother. The Munton necklaces; the brooches and clips bought with Munton money—and not one of them given to Carole because she was loved.

She knew then, as she clasped a bracelet round her wrist, what she wanted and what she intended to have. She had known it the first time she had seen him—so tall, so handsome in that easy, unobtrusive way which made an Englishman so outstandingly distinguished.

He had been brought to one of the enormous parties she had given in London.

"You know each other, of course?" the Duchess of Melchester had asked, as, accompanied by a tall man, she came up the stairs to where Carole was receiving.

"No, I don't think we have met," Carole replied.

"Not met Hugo! But how ridiculous! Of course you must know each other!" the Duchess exclaimed. "This is Lord Roxburton—the biggest rake in London. We all love him, so don't lose your heart, because it is quite useless. And, Hugo, this is Carole Munton. She is divine, isn't she?"

"Divine!" Hugo answered, with a faintly mocking smile.

Carole had looked up at him and known, in that moment, something strange had happened to her heart. She had never felt like this about any man. There was something in those quizzical, twinkling eyes, in those firm, slightly smiling lips, which made her feel suddenly weak and yet, at the same time, wildly elated.

"Come and dance with me and we will try to get to know each other," Hugo suggested.

"Dare I?" Carole enquired. "What about my guests who are late?"

"If they are later than we are, then it is their own fault," Hugo replied.

Masterfully he put his arm around her and took her on the dance floor. She surrendered herself happily to his arms. And then, as they moved slowly into the crowd, he said in that faintly mocking voice which she found almost unbearably attractive:

"You are not the least bit what I expected."

"What did you expect?"

"Something hard, brazen and much, much older."

"I am twenty-five—and very hard boiled."

"I doubt it! Shall we try and find out how soft and sweet you are?"

She felt herself tremble with excitement.

"You make me feel shy."

"I am glad about that. I like women who are shy, it makes them so much more feminine."

She had never forgotten he had said that, and yet it was so hard to keep up the pretence of being shy, when he was so elusive.

He flirted with her all that evening. She had waited all the next day and the day after that in the hope that he would ring her up or come to call at the Ritz, where she was staying.

Finally, she had been reduced to telephoning to the Duchess and suggesting that she and "that charming young man to whom you introduced me" should come and dine.

"Where have you been?" she asked Hugo, when he came to dinner.

"In the country, shooting," he answered. "Haven't they told you that Englishmen find nothing so attractive in November as pheasants?"

He knew quite well that she had been longing to see him; and before the evening was out she realised that she was employing her old tactics of trying to make herself indispensable. Yet with Hugo it was far more difficult than it had ever been with Dave.

For one thing, he seldom seemed to be in London. Finally, after a great deal of manoeuvring, he asked her to Rox; and when she got there she saw so little of him that she wondered, at times, if he was deliberately avoiding her.

The men shot all day; on Sundays they played golf and in the evenings there were so many more distinguished guests than herself who had the privilege of sitting at their host's side that she was far away down the table.

She had also made many enquiries about Hugo, and what she heard depressed her more than ever.

His love affairs were innumerable. Half the great ladies in Society had lost their hearts to him, and yet he had an unpredictable way of falling in love with someone quite obscure, of making them, for the moment, the talk of the town and then dropping them again into obscurity.

"Hugo Roxburton!" one man exclaimed, when Carole asked about him. "He's living in the wrong century; he's a roué and they went out with hansom cabs! You'd better keep away from him. The girls tell me he's dynamite."

"Why doesn't he marry?" Carole asked.

"Marry! He's too wily an old fox for that," was the reply. "Every match-making mamma has been hunting him for years. If you ask my opinion, he will live and die a bachelor."

Comments of this sort only strengthened Carole's resolve to make Hugo fall in love with her. She was frank enough to admit to herself that she was already desperately in love with him.

When she heard that he was coming out to Switzerland she made a wild gamble on an outside chance that came off.

"Please let us join up," she said. "I am going out to Suvretta House with Mary and Jimmy Baker and I hear you are going too. It's so miserable being two women to one man. Do let's make it a foursome."

She was so astonished when Hugo accepted that for the moment she could hardly believe her own ears. And when it was once arranged, she had hurriedly got in touch with Mary and Jimmy Baker.

Carole had half-guessed then that Hugo was making up his mind to marry her, but she felt she could be sure of nothing until he actually said the words.

Yet there was nothing in his manner to raise her hopes unduly. He was charming; he teased her; he flirted with her; she had felt, however, that she was of no more importance to him than Mary or any other woman with whom he was acquainted at Suvretta House.

Tonight she would be alone with him. She would have the chance to make him concentrate on her.

She stood up and looked at herself in the long mirror.

She looked what she was: the product of every artifice of modern civilisation—her hair, like her jewels, shining in the electric light. Her figure was perfect and her dress accentuated the lovely lines of her body and the smooth purity of her skin.

She looked at herself closely. For the first time in her life she could feel her heart beating because she desired a man.

"I have never, until now, had any time for love," Carole thought to herself. There had been men who made passes at her, but she hated them because they in no way furthered her ambitions. They had wanted her, but she had not wanted them.

Now, she desired a man not only for what he could give her, but for himself. She thought of Hugo and her breath came quickly; and taking her sable wrap from her maid's arms, she went slowly downstairs.

They dined in the big dining-room where a band softly played. Hugo chose the dinner with his accustomed skill and taste, but Carole felt as though she could eat nothing.

"Aren't you hungry?" he asked.

She sipped the champagne the waiter poured into her glass and smiled at him.

"Not particularly. And you?"

"How can I be hungry when I have had no exercise? Curse this leg!"

"What does the doctor say?"

"He thinks I shall be able to use it in a few days. I tried to make him promise that I can skate even if I can't ski."

"I am glad in a way," Carole said softly.

Hugo raised his eyebrows.

"How can I see anything of you," she said, answering his unspoken question, "if you are always at the top of a mountain? I think the gods have been kind in tying you to my side."

"You flatter me," he answered.

They finished dinner and then, at Carole's suggestion, drove to a small, amusing little night club down in the town.

It was low-ceilinged and there were convenient little alcoves set round the very small dance floor. The piano played, with lowered lights, tunes of the past; and as they drank more champagne and followed it with liqueurs, Carole could feel that Hugo was getting more mellow and perhaps a little sentimental.

"What are you thinking about?" she asked at length, realising that his eyes were resting on her face.

"I was thinking of you," he said. "Tell me about yourself."

"What do you want to know?"

"What you really think and feel," he answered. "Do you realise that we have known each other for a long time and I have never heard you speak of your people?"

"Perhaps it's not very interesting," she answered.

"I always thought all Americans wanted to talk about their old-fashioned mammas," he replied.

Carole had a sudden vision of her mother, bending over the wash-tub in the kitchen of the boarding house. Once or twice she had sent her money—dollars in a plain envelope without anything to show where they had come from. "I will send her some more tomorrow," she thought suddenly.

"I am an orphan," she said aloud.

"You don't sound very sad about it."

"Don't I? It wasn't a very happy thing to be when I was a child."

Hugo was looking at her.

"I don't think I understand you," he said at length.

"Do you want to?"

"Perhaps."

He smiled at her and then unexpectedly called for the bill.

"Let's go back to the hotel," he said. "It's hot and stuffy here and my leg is hurting."

She wondered if it was an excuse, but she rose obediently and led the way to where a car was waiting for them. It was bitterly cold outside, but the stars bejewelled the sky, the moon revealed the silent peaks and the beauty of the night was unbearable.

They drove back to Suvretta House in silence. As

44

they went upstairs in the lift, Carole had a sudden feeling of fear lest he should send her to bed and she would see no more of him.

"I would love another drink," she said. "Will you order one in your sitting-room?"

"Of course," he replied.

They went into his room. The rose damask curtains were pulled over the windows—a shaded light on the writing-table was the only illumination.

"This is nice and cosy," Carole said, settling herself on the sofa.

Hugo rang for the waiter.

"Would you like some more champagne?" he said. "Or a liqueur?"

"A yellow chartreuse, please," Carole answered, "and some sandwiches as well. After eating nothing at dinner I feel rather hungry."

Hugo gave the order. When they came, Carole only picked at the sandwiches although she drank the liqueur.

Hugo settled himself in the big armchair beside the sofa. His leg was stuck out a little stiffly in front of him, but in his evening clothes Carole thought how attractive and, at the same time, athletic he looked. No one could mistake him for anything but a man of action, a man who enjoyed outdoor life and who was unmistakably an English gentleman.

She thought then of his title. To be Lady Roxburton —that was what she wanted above all things. It seemed to offer her a sense of security, an impregnable position. If she had it, she could forget the film studios who had refused to take her, and Dave who had died hating her.

Impulsively she put down her glass and rose from the sofa.

"Hugo!" she said, standing in front of him. "Tell me something honestly. What do you think about me?"

"You really want me to answer that question?" he asked.

"I want you to answer it truthfully," she said. "I don't want you just to say that I am pretty or pay me any of those silly compliments, which come so easily to your lips and which you say to every attractive woman you meet. I want to know the truth . . . the real truth."

He smiled a little at that—sure of himself in a manner which made Carole tremble because she was so unsure, so uncertain.

"To tell the truth," he said at length, "I don't know what to say. I want to know so much more about you. I want you to tell me about yourself—to teach me what you are really like."

With a sudden swift movement she knelt beside his chair.

"Do you really want to know what I am like?" she asked softly, and the breath came quickly between her parted lips.

For a moment Hugo did not move. And then, as she waited, her face very near to his, her eyes half-closed, her mouth raised invitingly towards him, his hands came out to clasp the nakedness of her shoulders.

"What are you suggesting?" he asked, and his voice was low and deep.

"That I should show you what I am like," Carole whispered, and then she was close in his arms and his mouth was on hers.

4

"Is that you, Utta?"

The sweet voice came from the sitting-room as Utta came into the little hall, her feet making a clatter on the polished boards.

"Oui, Grand'mère," she answered in French and a moment later pushed open the door of the sitting-room and went in.

Her grandmother was watering the many plants which filled the bottoms of the three windows and scented the air with a delicate fragrance. As she turned to greet Utta, the sunlight on her face, the likeness between them was remarkable. There was no need to

46

wonder where Utta had inherited her delicate bones and tiny, petite body.

Madame Kindschi looked like one of the lovely French marquises whom Fragonard delighted to portray in his pictures. Although she was dressed very simply, there was something about her presence and the elegant way in which her white hair was piled high on her head which made one feel that here in this unpretentious Swiss chalet was a *grande dame*.

It was, in fact, the truth. Madame Kindschi was the daughter of a noble French family; and even if one had been blind, her exquisite Parisian French would have betrayed her birth and breeding.

"You are late, *ma petite*," she said to Utta. And then with a hint of mischief in her twinkling eyes, she asked: "It went well?"

"Very well, *Grand'mère*. Ernst was pleased with me."

"Good! I have a surprise for you upstairs."

"What is it?"

"Your dress has arrived from Paris."

"Oh, *Grand'mère!*" Utta clasped her hands together with a look of ecstasy—and then in a very different tone she added: "I am afraid!"

"Afraid, *ma chérie?*"

"Yes, afraid, *Grand'mère*. Suppose I am not as good as Ernst thinks! Suppose I fail! What then shall we say to Grandfather?"

Madame Kindschi put her hands up to her face.

"Do not think of it," she said. "It is always bad luck to think of the worst. You must believe in the best, in yourself, and then you will win the Championships and Grandfather will be so proud that he will forgive you. You see if I am not right."

"I hope you are," Utta said, and then with a pretty gesture she put her arms around her grandmother and kissed her on the cheek.

"Thank you for the dress," she said. "Is it lovely?"

"Lovely! It has been designed by the great Dior himself."

"*Grand'mère!* It must have cost a fortune."

47

"A fortune more or less," her grandmother agreed. "But what does it matter? To look right is always half the battle, whatever one is doing."

Utta nodded.

"Yes," she said. "I am sure that is the truth. And sometimes, *Grand'mère,* I long for lovely clothes like the women wear who stay at the Palace or Suvretta House."

Her grandmother looked at her quickly.

"How do you know they wear wonderful clothes?" she enquired.

"I have heard, I have read the papers and, of course, sometimes I have seen. I would love above all things to go out to dinner in evening dress like those the women wear in the magazines you bring home from France."

Madame Kindschi gave a little sigh.

"My dear, you are still very young."

"I am eighteen," Utta said. "Eighteen, *Grand'mère!* And I have never been anywhere or seen anything."

Madame Kindschi sighed again.

"Yes, you are growing up," she said. "Perhaps it is wrong of us to keep you here, living alone with us so quietly. It is, of course, dull for a young person."

"You know it isn't that," Utta said impulsively. "Don't think I am not happy, *Grand'mère.* Don't think I do not love both you and Grandfather with all my heart. It is just that sometimes I feel I would like to go out to see what other girls see, to do what they do."

"Yes, yes, I understand," Madame Kindschi said, watching her grandchild's face and the emotions flitting across it. "But you know what your grandfather is like. Sometimes *ma petite,* he seems very strict, but I assure you he has good reasons for everything—and yet, I understand! I was young once, and when one is young and pretty one wants gaiety and beautiful clothes and the company of those of one's own age."

"How well you understand!" Utta sighed.

There was a little pause. She walked across the room to stand in the sunlight, looking down at the freshly watered flowers. After a moment she said in a very low voice:

48

"Something happened this morning."

"What was it?" Madame Kindschi asked.

"I met again," Utta answered, "the man whom I rescued the other night."

"He was up so early?" Madame Kindschi enquired. "I thought no one at Suvretta House roused themselves until nearly noon."

"No, he was not down on the rink," Utta answered. "He saw Ernst and me from his window and . . . and, *Grand'mère,* he asked us to breakfast!"

Madame Kindschi clasped her hands together.

"Oh, darling! And you went? Pray Heaven your grandfather never finds out!"

"Ernst knew the gentleman well . . ." Utta began, and then suddenly she made a gesture of impatience and turned round to face her grandmother. "Why should Grandfather mind? Why should I never speak to anyone or go anywhere? He asked me to dinner, *Grand'mère,* and Ernst and I tried to explain why it was impossible for me to go. He didn't believe me—I could see it in his face and in the smile on his lips. He thought I was pretending, playing some absurd sort of game . . . and yet I wanted to go."

Utta's voice throbbed across the room and Madame Kindschi suddenly sat down in the high-backed armchair.

"My poor little one!" she said in a voice that suddenly seemed broken.

At the very first word Utta, turning to see her grandmother's face, sped across the room to fall on her knees beside her.

"Don't look like that, *Grand'mère,*" she cried. "I have upset and distressed you. It is wicked of me. I will say no more and you must forget what I have already said. I love you, you know that. It is unkind and ungrateful of me to want more than you and Grandfather have given me already. Forget what I have said and forgive me . . . please forgive me, *Grand'mère!*"

She laid her young cheek against her grandmother's soft and wrinkled face.

Madame Kindschi put up one hand to touch the

springing gold curls, and her smile was very sweet as she answered quietly:

"There is nothing to forgive you for, my darling. What you want is only what you should have. You are young; you cannot remain cooped up here with us forever. I will talk to your grandfather. I will make him see reason."

"No! no! *Grand'mère,* not now," Utta said in a sudden panic. "Not just before the Championships—after, perhaps. He will be angry anyway when he hears that I have entered. Someone will be sure to tell him—you can be certain of that. I could not bear him to be cross with me at this moment. Besides, he might forbid me to enter, and how could we disappoint Ernst?"

"No, that is true," Madame Kindschi said. "But when the Championships are over, we must make your grandfather see reason. He has been spoiled all his life—that is what is wrong with him."

"And who has spoiled him, I would like to know?" Utta asked, sitting back on her heels and laughing up into her grandmother's face.

"Yes, it is my fault," Madame Kindschi answered. "But I have always loved him so very much . . ."

"And he has loved you, too," Utta said softly.

"Yes, that is true," her grandmother replied. "We have been very, very happy—Nicolaus and I."

"You have never regretted running away with him?" Utta asked, knowing the answer only too well.

"Never, never!" Madame Kindschi replied. "When I go back to France, when I see my sisters with their dull, pompous husbands, when I hear from my friends how they have to close their eyes to liaisons with other women, when I hear of divorces and separations—not only among the young, but even among people of my own age—then I thank God on my knees that Nicolaus and I had the courage to run away together . . . to cherish this great love of ours all through the years."

"Oh, *Grand'mère!* I wish something so romantic would happen to me," Utta said.

"But it will, my dear," Madame Kindschi answered, "one . . . day."

There was a pause between the last two words.

Utta, getting to her feet, walked across the room a little restlessly.

"You were eighteen when you got married, *Grand'-mère*," she said at last. "That is the same age as I am now."

Madame Kindschi felt her heart turn over at the note of yearning in Utta's voice. She had expected this for a long time, she told herself. That was why, over a year ago, she had agreed that Ernst Zippert should coach Utta in ice skating. It had kept the child's mind occupied—given her something to think about.

Nicolaus, much as she loved him, did not understand. He could be extremely obstinate when he wanted to, this man she had married. He had the solid, imperturbable calm of his peasant ancestors, which could remain unruffled even when she raged at him, often a-fire with impatience at the slowness of his methods.

When they were young, they had fought and quarrelled like two puppies snarling and fighting with each other. It was very funny to remember it now, for in their old age they seldom disagreed except on one subject—that of Utta.

Nicolaus was getting old. He did not understand that Utta was growing older, too. She was no longer a child, no longer a pretty little girl he would dangle on his knee and make happy with a bonbon or a toy that he had brought her from the village.

"She is getting restless and bored, living here along with us," his wife told him, not once but a dozen times.

"She is happy! What more can she want?" Nicolaus would reply with a shake of his grey head.

"Do you think that I would have been content with a life like this when I was Utta's age?" Madame Kindschi enquired.

"You had everything you wanted," he replied in his slow, even voice, "but you were not happy."

That was true enough and she had to admit it. She had not been happy when she met Nicolaus quite by chance, during a holiday in Switzerland. He had been

51

employed as a guide by her eldest brother, who was keen on mountaineering.

Marguerite Duvais, as she was then, came down the stairs of the *schloss* which her father had rented for their visit and saw Nicolaus Kindschi waiting in the hall.

She had never been able to forget her first sight of him. Tall and broad shouldered, he seemed to her, for the moment, almost gigantic. And then he turned his face up to hers and she saw the fine lines of his face, his square jaw, the deep blue eyes set in his brown, sun-burnt face.

She had fallen in love with him at that moment.

"You are taking my brother up the mountain?"

She talked for the sake of talking.

"Yes, Mademoiselle, but we will not go far. Monsieur is not yet very experienced."

"Do you like climbing?"

"It is my life!" Nicolaus answered.

"How I wish I could come with you!"

He had laughed at that and she thought, as his lips parted in a smile, that he was, without exception, the most handsome man she had ever seen in her life. He was like some Greek god such as she had studied in the Louvre—only there the statues were white and cold while Nicolaus was glowing with health, strength and a virility which she sensed even in her innocence.

That had been the beginning. Snatched meetings, seconds when they could talk together, moments when they were alone in the hall, on the steps or in the yard where the skis and sledges were kept.

As the days went by, Marguerite realised that her whole life centred round the few minutes in the morning or evening when she could talk to Nicolaus.

She grew astute at being on the stairs when he arrived in the morning, or at returning in the evening from some expedition at the same time as he and her brother. And then at last the moment came when the fire which was burning fiercely within two hearts could no longer be suppressed.

Marguerite returned later than usual from a skiing expedition with her sisters and their governess. It was cold and they kicked off their skis impatiently and hurried into the house. Marguerite was left behind; she was slow deliberately because she had seen that Nicolaus was in the little room off the yard, waxing her brother's skis.

As the others passed him going to the house, he came to her assistance. He knelt down to undo the straps and she saw that his hands were trembling.

He lifted the skis from her feet; then, still kneeling, he looked up at her and their eyes met.

"Nicolaus!" she hardly breathed his name above a whisper and yet he heard her.

"I must go away!" He spoke dully and yet his eyes seemed alight with his desire.

"Why?"

She asked the question almost unconsciously. He rose to his feet to stand towering above her.

"You know why!"

His voice was deep and hoarse with emotion.

It was growing dark now. The shadows seemed to be closing in upon them and yet she could still see his face, still feel the fire within his eyes searing its way into her heart . . . drawing her . . . holding her.

"I love you!"

The words seemed to burst from between his lips, and then there was no reason for him to say any more. . . . She was in his arms . . . her lips were seeking his . . . everything was forgotten save that her whole body trembled with a joy and a rapture such as she had never believed possible. . . .

For a week they had both been tortured with the thought that they must be parted. Marguerite was well aware that her father was already talking of her becoming betrothed to the son of an old friend. The young man in question was the heir to great estates and an honoured title. As his wife her position would be assured as one of the most distinguished women in France.

She knew, as Nicolaus knew, that for her to suggest that she should marry an ordinary Swiss guide would be to bring down an avalanche of paternal fury and to ensure only that they should be separated without delay.

The holiday was growing to a close. Soon they would pack up, leave the *schloss* and return to Paris. Marguerite felt that each minute that passed was like a dagger stabbing her to the very heart.

"I can't leave you, I can't, Nicolaus," she sobbed one evening when she had crept out to meet him while her sisters had gone up to dress for dinner.

"Stay with me!"

It was the first time he had suggested such a thing, yet it seemed to her it was a command rather than a plea.

"How?"

She hardly dared breathe the question.

"We would be married at once. I am making money—good money. I can keep you. Not with richness and the luxury you have known in your home, but comfortably.

"But Papa; he would come and take me away. He would never allow it."

"We will hide until we can find a priest to marry us," Nicolaus said. "Once you are my wife no man can take you from me."

"You are sure of that?"

"Quite sure."

Marguerite hid her face against his shoulder.

"I am afraid," she whispered.

"Of leaving home?"

"Of you."

He hardly heard the whispered words, but when he did he took his arms from her and, kneeling down at her feet, raised the hem of her dress to his lips.

"Listen!" he said. "I love you. I know I have no right even to raise my eyes to you. Nevertheless I love you—and I believe that you love me. If you will honour me by becoming my wife, I swear to you here and now, before God, that I will never let you know anything but happiness. My whole life shall be devoted to serving you."

She had felt the tears come into her eyes at the sincerity of his voice and the solemnness of his vow. Then, as she reached out her arms towards him, he rose to his feet. But he did not touch her.

"Unless you are very sure that our love is enough, Marguerite," he said, "I want you at this moment to walk away from me and return to your family. I am a man—I know what I am doing and I know in loving you I am fulfilling the very purpose for which God made me strong, for which he made me a man.

"For you it may be different. You are young; you have not seen very much of the world, and there may be other men who could mean more in your life than I. If that is true, leave me now. I shall not try to stop you and I shall have . . . my memories."

Marguerite was trembling and again she held out her arms.

"Nicolaus! Nicolaus!" she cried.

But he stepped away from her.

"It is your last chance," he said. "If I take you now, it will be for ever. Once you are mine, I will never let you go."

"Take me . . . please take me, Nicolaus."

She flung herself against him—her heart pounding against his, her little face raised to his, her arms reaching out towards his neck.

And then, as he clutched her to him, as his mouth found hers, the world seemed to fade away beneath his kisses and she knew that nothing mattered except this. This was why she had been created a woman . . . to love, and be loved by Nicolaus.

They were married and went to live in a tiny house at the foot of the Matterhorn. As Nicolaus had promised, he hid her until she became his wife, and after they were married they were no longer afraid of being found.

After the first interchange of reproach and bitterness, Marguerite's family cut her out of their lives and she had no further communications with them for nearly twenty years. It was only when her mother was dying that they sent for her and she became reconciled with her father.

She went home after that at regular intervals—not always liking to leave Nicolaus, but feeling that she had a certain duty towards her father, who was growing old and whose memory was beginning to fail. At times he forgot that she had even married and he talked of arranging that she should be betrothed to the son of his old friend.

When she was at home, she never spoke of Nicolaus; and when she was with Nicolaus, she seldom spoke of her family.

She had never regretted the life of luxury and importance that she had given up. As Nicolaus promised, he kept her in comparative comfort, and she loved the little wooden houses she owned, first beneath the Matterhorn and lastly here at St. Moritz.

Nicolaus was still handsome—still magnificent to look at even in his old age. His hair was white now, but his eyes were still steady and blue in a sunburnt face.

He had retired for some years, but men still came to him for advice; and the book which had been written about him after he had rescued a party who were lost on a glacier had made him famous.

He was just as simple as he had been when Marguerite first married him. He said what he thought; he was direct and upright in everything he did or undertook. Only at times did his obstinacy clash with the flashing impetuosity of his more volatile wife.

Marguerite had inherited money when her mother died and again when her father's estate was settled. She was, in actual fact, a very well-off woman; but she was content not to alter her life and to let it continue as it had always been—simple and unassuming, although at times rather lonely.

As Nicolaus grew older he wished to withdraw more and more from the company of his neighbours. He had always liked the white loneliness of the mountains; and now, so long as Marguerite was beside him, he asked for nothing else but the glory of the peaks and the companionship of the birds, for which he had a strange fascination.

The house, with its small garden, seemed to attract every bird in the vicinity. They would sit twittering on the window ledges or in the bushes in the garden until

Nicolaus appeared, and then they would fly towards him, perching themselves on his shoulders or on his hands—eating the breadcrumbs he offered them, but seemingly more content with him than with what he provided.

"I think the birds talk to Grandfather," Utta had said when she was a very little girl, and her grandmother had agreed, feeling there was some strange affinity between Nicolaus and his feathered friends which enabled them to communicate with each other.

A whistle from outside now told both Utta and her grandmother that Nicolaus was calling his birds.

Madame Kindschi held up her hand.

"You must see your dress," she said, "and then we must give your grandfather his breakfast."

They went upstairs side by side.

The house, built of wood, was warm and heated by great porcelain stoves which stood in every room. There was the fragrance of cedar and the perfume of the plants which stood in every corner and which even ornamented the landing.

From Madame Kindschi's bedroom windows Nicolaus had always declared there was the finest view in Switzerland. High on the mountainside, the house looked over the valley with its lakes and had a perfect view of all the mountain peaks of the Engadine.

" 'I will lift up mine eyes unto the hills from whence cometh my strength'," Marguerite Kindschi had once quoted softly as she stood in the window, and her husband had answered her in all seriousness:

"The mountains do bring strength and peace to those who love them."

But neither Utta nor her grandmother had eyes for the view this morning. On the bed with its pale peach satin cover, which Madame Kindschi had brought with her from Paris on her last visit, lay a dress box.

Utta ran towards it as her grandmother shut the door. Then the lid was opened and the soft tissue paper pulled back. Utta stood for a moment looking down at what lay revealed to her, and then she gave a little cry of sheer delight.

"Oh, *Grand'mère,* it's lovely! I never imagined anything could be so beautiful."

Of soft, turquoise blue satin, the bodice was embroidered with sequins of the same colour, and then below the satin frothed out the minute skirt—frill upon frill of turquoise blue tulle.

Utta picked it up in her hands and taking it from the box ran to the gilt mirror ornamented with cupids which hung on the wall between the windows. She held the dress up to her face; the colour made her skin glow like a pearl.

"It's lovely!" she exclaimed. "Lovelier than anything I ever imagined. Oh, thank you, *Grand'mère.*"

"I am glad you are pleased, *ma petite,* and if you skate as well as you look then the Championship will be yours."

Utta kissed her and then put the dress reverently back into the box.

"Shall I leave it here?" she asked, "or take it to my own room and hide it?"

"Perhaps that would be best," Madame Kindschi replied. "Your grandfather is often very curious. If he saw it, I am afraid he would not believe me if I told him it was mine!"

Utta gave a little gurgle of laughter.

"No, I do not think even Grandfather would believe that," she said. "But . . . darling *Grand'mère,* I wish you could come to the Championships. I should feel happier if you were there."

Madame Kindschi shook her head.

"I shall stay here and keep your grandfather from becoming too inquisitive as to what you are doing. Are you practising again tomorrow morning?"

"Yes, of course! Every second I can practice is of importance now."

"And will you be breakfasting again with this gentleman who entertained you this morning?"

Madame Kindschi's question was spoken gently, almost tentatively, as if she invited Utta's confidence and yet was half afraid to force it.

A little shadow passed over Utta's expressive face.

"He asked me to dinner; but, as I told you, of course I had to refuse," she said.

Madame Kindschi was silent. Utta had no idea how regretful her voice sounded. She looked down at the box she held in her hands. She did not see the French label on the white cardboard, but instead two eyes looking quizzically into hers and a mouth that twisted a little at the corners.

She had not imagined that a man could look so distinguished and yet, at the same time, be so provocatively attractive. She remembered how his arm had rested around her shoulders as they travelled laboriously down the hill to the log hut. "He was strong," she thought, "and yet his hands could be gentle."

She thought of his sitting-room with its bowl of hothouse flowers, the gleaming breakfast table and the richness of the furniture, curtains and carpets.

She had always wanted to go inside one of the big St. Moritz hotels, but even in her imagination she had not realised how rich and over-ornamented they were.

He had been sitting in an armchair by the window when they entered and, as he looked up, she thought, as she had done at the first moment when he turned towards her in the snow, that he was very English and very different from any other man she had met before. She had felt shy and a little afraid of him as she sat down at the table.

There was so much she wanted to say, yet the words would not come to her lips. She had thought of him so much since that night when Hans and Ludwig had turned into the drive which led to the door of Suvretta House and she had sped away into the darkness alone.

Her grandfather had questioned her as to why she was late home and she had made some excuse about a broken strap to her ski. Grandfather would not have understood that she must go back with Hans and Ludwig to make quite certain that they found the hut.

She knew that it was unnecessary even when she escorted them up the mountainside and they told her, not once but a dozen times, that there was no need for her to exert herself.

They knew the hut as well as she did; but she insisted on going with them—and when she saw the Englishman's face in the light of the lantern, she was glad she had done so.

He had been cold and miserable and in pain—and yet he had managed to smile at her. She liked that sort of courage; it was the sort of thing she understood and expected from a man.

"And yet what do I know of men?" she asked herself now.

There were a few of her grandfather's friends who came to the house for a glass of wine or an occasional meal. There had been callers who had come from France and Germany and England after they had read the book which had made her grandfather appear as a hero and a man whom everyone must admire.

But these people had been given short shrift and been sent away—often with only a few curt words to compensate them for their journey.

Apart from these people and their ordinary neighbours in St. Moritz, such as the doctor, the parson and the shopkeepers, Utta saw no one.

She had gone to school at the Convent in the village of Gamasee until she was sixteen. After that she had had special classes with individual teachers. French, German, English—her languages were perfect. Madame Kindschi had seen to that.

It was the one thing she had been most insistent upon. History and mathematics were taught by an old retired schoolmaster—a man nearly as old as her grandfather—who came plodding up the mountain twice a week to give her two hours' tuition.

She was well educated, Utta was aware of that. And yet she felt that she was gauche and inexperienced when it came to meeting anyone socially. She had felt afraid as she had walked through the big, pillared hall of Suvretta House and entered, with Ernst, the lift which carried them up to the second floor. The corridors, with their red carpets and gilt mirrors, had filled her with awe.

"What do people do and think and say who live in places like this?" she wondered.

She had felt tongue-tied and stupid as they were ushered into the sunlit sitting-room where Lord Roxburton was waiting for them.

"I want to see him again!"

The words seemed almost to have been spoken aloud in Utta's ear. For a moment she wondered if she had, indeed, spoken them herself, and then she realised that the room was silent and that she was standing staring at the box which contained her skating dress.

She felt then a little pang of dismay at her disloyalty towards her grandfather. Impulsively she put down the box and moved across to her grandmother's side. They were the same height, and very gently Utta laid her cheek against the older woman's and held her close.

"Dear, dear *Grand'mère*, you are so kind to me," she said. "I am thrilled with my dress, but happier still because you understand . . . because I can tell you things I could never, never tell anyone else."

"And what have you got to tell me, my darling?" Madame Kindschi asked, putting up her hand to touch Utta's little pointed chin.

It was as if her question was too searching, too enquiring for Utta to meet it.

"Nothing . . . nothing in particular," she stammered. "It is only that . . . if there was something . . . something secret and wonderful that no one else must know . . . I should still tell it to you."

"*Merci, ma petite!* That is indeed the best present you could have given me," Madame Kindschi answered. "And now run along and change your clothes. It is half-past eight and your grandfather will be getting hungry."

Utta turned towards the door—then, as she reached it, her grandmother's voice arrested her.

"One moment, darling!" she said. "There is something I do want to ask you. What is the name of this gentleman with whom you had breakfast and whom you rescued the other night?"

Utta looked back and smiled.

"Didn't I tell you?" she asked. "How stupid of me!

But of course, I didn't know it myself until Ernst told me who he is. He is a very important Englishman, I think, and his name is Lord Roxburton."

She spoke lightly and was just about to leave the room when she stood, transfixed by the expression on her grandmother's face.

For a moment the older woman stood, the blood receding from her face, an expression almost of horror in her eyes; and then, before Utta could move or ask what was the matter, Madame Kindschi put up her hands to her face.

"No . . . no! Not that . . . not that . . ." she whispered brokenly.

5

The big dining-room at the Palace Hotel was crowded.

There was the usual incongruous mixture of mink coats and serviceable skiing clothes. The invariable collection of fragile women, whose pale complexions and exquisitely coiffeured hair made it obvious that they never ventured out of doors, were being stared at contemptuously by sunburnt, hearty Amazons, while men of all nationalities, creeds and colours were linked together by a common desire to conquer the snow.

Hugo and Carole sat at one of the coveted tables in front of the huge, high glass windows overlooking the ice rink. The sunshine poured in, warm and golden, and women at other tables were already asking that the silk curtains should be drawn to save their complexions.

Hugo sipped the glass of sherry which the waiter had set before him and then smiled across the table at Carole.

"Like a cat, I want to purr in the sunshine," he said.

She lifted one of her hands, with its long, crimson nails, to shield her face.

"The weather in England has certainly been abominable."

"Yet it is 'my own, my native land'," he quoted, "and I wouldn't change it for anywhere else in the world."

"How insular you are!" she teased.

"Aren't we all?" he enquired.

Carole shook her head.

"I am heterogeneous or cosmopolitan, whichever word you prefer," she said. "Actually I would rather live in Europe than in my own country."

There was a meaning in her words which he could not fail to understand. But to her chagrin his face betrayed nothing but a polite interest—and then the waiter interrupted them to bring an enormous menu from which they could choose their meal.

"I am not hungry," Carole told him, "so order me something very light."

"Is that the truth or are you thinking of your figure?" Hugo enquired. "I, personally, am ravenous, so, if you don't want to be bored, you had better keep me company."

"I won't be bored," Carole answered softly.

Hugo took some time choosing what he would have. He appreciated good food as he appreciated everything else in life that was the best of its kind. When finally the waiter had left them and the wine had been chosen, he said to Carole:

"What did you think of the competitors this morning?"

She shrugged her shoulders a little petulantly.

"Ice skating is always invariably the same," she said. "To me there is little or nothing to choose between the experts."

"I thought the Danish girl was exceptionally good," Hugo remarked, "though I think the Swede will beat her."

"Why the sudden interest?" Carole enquired.

"I do not know that there is anything sudden about it," Hugo replied, a note of irritation in his voice.

He was well aware that Carole was resenting the attention he had paid to the competitors for the Championships instead of devoting himself to her.

"I am beginning to wish that we were back in the fog and rain of London," Carole said suddenly.

She raised her dark eyes with their long lashes to him as she spoke and, against his will, she forced him to remember the closeness of their intimacy.

During the first weeks after they had met Hugo had been at a loose end. He had, in actual fact, just finished a love affair, which had lasted for nearly a year, with an exquisite young Jugo-Slavian film star who had found him as gay and as inconsequential as she was herself.

He had gone everywhere with her, to the annoyance of his friends, who found him strangely elusive—because when Matita was working on a film they were obliged to keep the most unconventional hours.

Then, just before the inevitable anti-climax had overtaken them, Matita had the offer to go to Hollywood. They had said good-bye with violent protestations of affection, which both knew would be forgotten as quickly as the flowers with which Hugo had decorated her cabin on the *Queen Elizabeth* withered and died.

He had liked Matita because she had never been anything but a joyful interlude in his life—never demanding more of him than he wished to give. She had been a healthy, attractive, greedy young animal who had made him laugh at life and at himself, and who had left, most surprisingly, a wake of memories behind her.

It was her laughter he found himself missing—the way she had of transforming the most prosaic and dull actions into a symphony of gaiety and joy. She had been a creature of a thousand moods—and all of them entrancing.

He had thought how heavy and prosaic his countrywomen seemed in contrast with Matita, and Carole had come into his life at exactly the right moment to stifle the last little aching want in his fickle heart.

For the first week or so he had imagined himself madly in love with her—and then he had found that her beauty grew unsensational with familiarity and her conversation had a way of being exactly what one expected.

And yet she was intelligent, and he told himself, as he had done so often before, that he expected too much.

Women were women—what more did he want? What was it he was looking for?

He had no answer to any of these questions; he only knew that every time his heart beat a little faster he expected something different from what he got. He could not even put into words that elusive something for which he searched—not knowing what it would be like when he found it. It was out of reach . . . round the corner . . . out of sight . . . intangible . . . untouchable—and yet he could not prevent himself yearning for it.

Carole, as his sister Pamela had said, was undoubtedly the person he must marry. She was lovely; she was amusing; she had an excellent social sense and, what was more, she was very rich. What more could he ask? What more had he the right to expect? It was as if he was travelling swiftly towards the inevitable.

He looked across the table now and thought how easily Carole surpassed, in appearance, every other woman in the room. She was always exquisitely dressed and everything about her had an elegance which he well knew denoted unceasing effort and immense expense.

Today she wore a dress of deep, ruby red wool and over it a coat of the same colour, trimmed with sable. It was simple, yet faultless, just as her jewels of rubies set in platinum were deceptively simple in design.

"A penny for your thoughts!" Carole asked.

"I was thinking of you," he said.

"Were you really? I sometimes think that I engage far too little of your attention."

"If you expect me to flatter you by giving you the correct reply to that remark you are going to be disappointed," Hugo said.

"I do not expect anything," she answered. "As I told you this morning, you are so very English."

"And you are so very American."

"Meaning that I am fêted and spoiled?" Carole questioned. "Perhaps you are right. But you are not in a position to throw stones, my dear Hugo."

"Very well then, we start on equal terms," he said; "but unlike you I dislike flattery."

"Nonsense!" Carole laughed. "You love it—what man doesn't?"

Hugo was about to reply when they were interrupted. Someone came up to the table. Carole looked up and then, for a moment, her whole face seemed to freeze.

A small man with a swarthy complexion which proclaimed his South American origin stood beside her. He conveyed the impression of being grossly overdressed. There was a diamond ring on the hand that he held out towards her.

"It is indeed exciting to see you again, Carole," he smiled. "You have not forgotten me, I hope?"

For a moment Carole hesitated and it seemed as if she might have denied this newcomer's acquaintance. Then, with a little effort, she put her hand in his.

"It is a surprise, Carlos," she said. "I did not expect to see you in Switzerland."

"I have come for the Championships," he said. "I saw you watching the competitors this morning. I thought to myself, 'There is Carole—more beautiful than ever.'"

He raised her hand to his lips and then, almost too swiftly, Carole took it away.

As the newcomer straightened himself, he looked at Hugo and it was obvious that he was waiting for an introduction. With a bad grace Carole said a little sulkily:

"I don't think you know each other. Hugo, may I introduce Don Carlos Jacára? . . . Lord Roxburton."

"I am delighted to make your acquaintance," Don Carlos said with a bow. "I have heard of you, of course. But, as Carole may have told you, I have heard of everyone—it is my job."

"Indeed?" Hugo queried.

"Yes! I am what Hollywood calls a 'talent scout'. I am here in Switzerland to find a leading lady for a new film we are making—a romance of the ice."

"Then I should think the Swedish girl we saw this morning is what you are looking for," Carole said. "She skates well and she is good-looking."

Don Carlos shrugged his shoulders.

"She is all that," he said, "but she lacks some-

66

thing—shall I call it 'the star quality'? You should know, Carole, you have always been a star in your own particular circle."

He smiled as he spoke, but she met his eyes with an air of defiance.

"Go away, Carlos, and let us finish our lunch in peace," she said. "I do not believe for one moment, any of the nice things you say about me—although, of course, I am delighted to hear them."

There was a slight edge on her voice, and once again Don Carlos raised her hand to his lips.

"We will meet again," he said. "You are staying at Suvretta House, I understand; so am I."

He bowed to Hugo and walked away with a slight swagger. Carole watched him go. It was as if a little shudder shook her before she turned again to Hugo. He did not notice her expression. He was looking at the excellent *entrecôte* which the waiter had just set down before him.

"Who is your friend?" he asked a little later.

"He is no friend, only an acquaintance," Carole replied sharply.

"If that was all, he seemed a trifle familiar," Hugo remarked.

"You know what those people are," Carole said almost petulantly. "I have met him at cocktail parties with all sorts of people. If someone like that sees you continually, they magnify a few chance encounters into a close friendship."

"I can't say he looks very prepossessing," Hugo criticised.

"He isn't," Carole answered. "He's slimy and beastly —the type of man one wouldn't trust out of one's sight."

She spoke vehemently. Hugo looked at her and laughed.

"It sounds as though he has got under your skin."

"I hate his type," Carole pouted. "Let's talk of something else."

"Not ourselves," Hugo said quickly.

"Why not?" she enquired.

"It is too heavy a subject for lunch! Tell me the scandal and the gossip of everyone we see around us. There's Letty Montellier over there—what has she been doing lately?"

Hugo was asking to be entertained, Carole knew that. And yet she found it hard to force the laughter to her lips—the light, witty remarks to her tongue.

Why had Don Carlos forced himself upon her? she wondered. What had he meant when he said he would see her again? It was sheer bad luck that he should have turned up in St. Moritz at the same time as she was there.

She remembered the last time she had seen him. It was just after she had married and she had bumped into him at a cocktail party in New York. She had been terrified lest he should say anything—be indiscreet in front of her husband's relations, several of whom were in the room. But he had been discretion itself.

"Congratulations, Carole!" he had murmured as his thick lips brushed her hand.

She pushed back her coffee cup now with a petulant gesture.

"Let us get out of here," she said. "It's hot and the chatter of so many voices speaking far too many languages gives me a headache."

"I thought you liked this sort of thing," Hugo protested.

"I do—in moderation," Carole replied. "But today I feel stifled. Let us go for a drive."

Alone in the sunshine with the beauty of the mountains around, surely Hugo would say what she had been waiting so long to hear?

"Yes, we will go for a drive," he agreed. "Do you mind if I smoke?"

He drew out his cigar-case from his pocket.

"No, of course not," Carole answered. "But ask for the bill. They always take such a long time to bring it."

She felt as though every nerve in her body was tingling with the desire to get away. Somewhere in the crowded room Carlos might be watching her. The very thought of it was unbearable—although, she told herself, she had nothing really to fear. There was nothing now that he could do to hurt her.

But as soon as Hugo had paid the bill, she rose to her feet, wending her way between the tables towards the door while he must follow more slowly on two sticks.

When they reached the lounge she told him to order the sleigh while she went to the ladies' room. There she stood for a moment looking at herself in the mirrors which reflected and re-reflected from every wall. The sight was somehow assuring.

"Why should I be afraid?" she asked herself. She was Carole Munton, one of the richest women in America. She was young, she was beautiful and at any moment she would become the wife of an Englishman. There was nothing for her to fear from Don Carlos; if there had been, she would have known of it many years ago.

She powdered her nose, put lipstick on her already crimson mouth and, with a last look in the mirror, felt calm and even vaguely amused at her own panic. Don Carlos belonged to the past. It was the future of which she would think . . . the future, and Hugo! She smiled, walked slowly back through the lounge and into the hall, where she guessed Hugo would be waiting for her near the front door.

The sleigh was comfortable, with red cushions and a thick fur rug which was tucked securely round them. The horse wore crimson plumes on his head; his harness was ornamented with dozens of silver bells.

"This is heaven," Carole exclaimed, snuggling a little closer to Hugo and looking up at him in a way which she knew made her eyes seem even larger than they were naturally.

"I don't know about heaven," he replied, "but after such a good luncheon I feel at peace with the world."

"We do have fun together, don't we?" Carole asked.

She could not help making the conversation personal, even while she was experienced and sophisticated enough to realise that Hugo was restless. Like all men he was jibbing at the thought of losing his freedom, and if she were wise, she would give him his head.

But while her brain told her one thing, her body rebelled at such sane commonsense. She wanted him . . . wanted the security of knowing that she bore his name, that he could not escape her even if he should wish to do so.

She wondered now if she had been crazy to surrender herself to him the night before—and yet she could no more have stopped herself at that moment than have stopped a flood tide flowing in over the shore.

She was a woman—and a woman who had known passion. She had no control over her desire once Hugo's arms were around her. She had felt the leaping flame flicker within her body; her lips were warm and hungry for his, and her heart had throbbed agonisingly against her breast as her arms went round his neck.

"I love you."

She could hear her voice saying it over and over again; but only now did she remember, with a sudden cold dismay, that he had made no response in words.

This morning they had met as if nothing had ever happened. He had been polite, charming, and complimentary, as he was invariably not only to her, Carole thought bitterly, but to any woman if she was attractive. She had deliberately waited for him to make some reference to what had happened the night before. But in vain.

Carole had been cool and calculating enough when they were in London to keep him at arm's length. She had heard of his reputation long before she had met him. She had been told by innumerable people that Hugo Roxburton was dangerous where women were concerned.

"You be careful of that young man!" one of her older friends advised her. "He is the sort that kisses them and rides away."

Carole had vowed then and there it should not happen to her. She attracted Hugo, she was well aware of that, and he had made no bones about it those weeks when they had seemed to lunch and dine together day after day, night after night.

He had taken her down to Rox for the week-end to

meet his sister. He insisted on introducing her to his grandmother, and that, Carole had guessed, was the most fundamental step of all. And yet he had never asked her in so many words to marry him.

"I love you! I love you!"

She could hear her own voice saying it over and over again, wildly, passionately, exultingly . . . and then very softly as finally she said good-night.

"I . . . love . . . you."

Three such simple words and yet he had never said them in return—but that was, of course, only because he was British and inarticulate. He loved her, she was sure of it. She was sure, too, of him, however much he might seem reluctant to take the last fatal step which would mean the surrender of his bachelorhood.

With a little gentle movement Carole slipped her arm through Hugo's.

"Haven't you anything nice to say to me today?" she asked in a soft, inviting voice.

He took his cigar from his lips and turned to smile at her.

"You are a witch, Carole," he said. "I think you be-witched us both last night. Do you really want me to say thank you? Such dull, prosaic words for a moment of enchantment."

She felt as if the sunlight was more golden than it had ever been before. There was nothing she could reply except to murmur his name and press her cheek against the sleeve of his coat.

"I want to give you a present," Hugo said. "Shall we stop in the village and try to find something or will you wait until I can choose something really adequate in Paris or in London?"

"I would like something now," Carole answered a little breathlessly.

She would choose a ring, she thought to herself, no matter how inexpensive. A ring had a meaning which no one could ignore.

But when they arrived at the jeweller's, she found that Hugo had very definite ideas on what he wished to give her. When he had inspected the large pieces of jewellery in which the salesman tried to interest him and waved aside the rings which Carole was trying on, he chose a bracelet hung with tiny charms. They were all in diamonds and the bracelet itself was of platinum and pearls. It was a costly trifle and lovely because the charms were so exquisitely fashioned.

Hugo clasped it round Carole's wrist.

"I like this," he said. "Will you wear it to remind you of me?"

There was a mocking twist to his lips as he asked the question.

"Will I need to be reminded?" Carole enquired.

"I hope not," he replied, and she had to be content with that.

She rose to her feet, feeling unreasonably disappointed that she had not achieved what she intended. And yet, she told herself, Hugo was not the type of man to give expensive presents unless he was really interested in the woman. That was a consoling thought, but a poor exchange for an engagement ring. It was hopeless to hurry Hugo, Carole thought—he would do things in his own way, in his own good time, and nothing she could do would change him.

"He loves me," she repeated the words to herself as she got back in the sleigh. And then, as she looked at the little bracelet round her wrist, she felt her fears were quite groundless.

There were two hearts amongst the other charms—one pierced with an arrow, the other surmounted by two little love-birds. Hugo would have noticed those, she thought. Perhaps, after all, the bracelet was more symbolic than she thought. There was a bell, too, in platinum and diamonds. Was it, she wondered, a wedding bell?

She was smiling and her eyes were shining as Hugo came from the shop. As the salesman opened the door, she saw him hand Hugo a little package which he slipped into his pocket.

"He has bought me another present," she thought.

Hugo came hobbling back to the sleigh, the rug was tucked round him again and then they were off.

"We are going to drive along the bottom route by Silvaplaner See," he told her. "It is a nice drive."

Carole didn't mind where they went as long as they were alone.

"Thank you for my lovely present," she said sweetly. "I shall always treasure it—you know that."

"I am glad you like it," Hugo smiled. "You are a nice person to give presents to, Carole. You are not spoilt like so many women."

"I am glad you think that," she answered in a low voice. "You see, I have not always had money and lovely things, so perhaps I appreciate them more than many people."

"It's absurd, but I know really very little about you," Hugo said. "I am aware, of course, that you married young Munton and that your family came from the aristocratic South! Tell me about them."

"My father had a big cotton plantation . . ." Carole began.

It was a story she had told many times since her marriage. She had almost begun to believe in that long white house with its big portico, which had seen better days. She could hear herself sobbing bitterly when her father died; feel again the misery and horror of her family when they found that their only inheritance was debts. Debts of kindness, Carole always added.

"My father was the most generous man alive to those who turned to him for help."

It was a most convincing story related in Carole's soft voice. One could almost see the devoted negroes and the fields of white cotton, smell the delicious meals cooked by an old black mammy, and her Carole running through the big, lofty beautifully furnished rooms! She had, of course, been adored by the servants, who called her "the little missy."

Most of the details Carole had cribbed from *Uncle Tom's Cabin;* but her listeners were seldom critical and sometimes Carole herself felt like weeping at the pathos of it all, especially at the end of the story—how, to support her mother, failing in health, and pay back the last of her father's debts she had tried to seek work.

There was always an audible sob in her voice when she told of "little missy" struggling for existence, ignorant of the cold, hard world into which she had been thrust through no fault of her own.

"Where did you say your home was?" Hugo enquired.

"In Virginia."

"Virginia is a big place."

"I don't suppose you would be much wiser if I told you its exact location," Carole said. "We were very isolated. I suppose, as a child, I missed the companionship of other children, but I was too happy to realise it."

"What happened to your mother?"

"She died. Even now I can't bear to think of how few comforts I could give her—how little I could do for her at the end."

"You weren't married then?"

"No . . . no . . . it was just before I met Dave."

"Poor Carole!" Hugo spoke kindly.

"I try not to think about it," Carole said bravely. "But I suppose I shall never be able to forget."

"Poor dear!" Hugo commiserated, and then changed the subject. "There is the Silvaplaner See. Pretty, isn't it?"

Carole looked towards the frozen lake they were approaching.

"Lovely," she said automatically.

"There is quite a crowd of people watching the skating," Hugo said.

"Perhaps they are holding their own village championship," Carole suggested. "Shall we stop and watch?"

She was intuitive enough to realise that Hugo was no longer interested in her confidences. Perhaps she had spun them out a bit long; it was hard not to get carried away by her own imagination. When she talked of those entirely fictitious days of her childhood and made them seem so real, she often wondered whether, in fact, she had the gift of writing.

They were approaching the shore of the lake. As Hugo had said, quite a crowd of people were standing watching those who were skating on the ice. Then, as they drew nearer still, Hugo saw it was only one person who was being watched.

She was wearing the plain blue costume that he had seen that morning from his balcony. As they approached, she ran across the ice and sprang into the air. It was as beautiful and effortless as a ballet dancer, and then, with arms outstretched, she moved towards them like a swallow in flight.

"She must be the village champion," Carole remarked.

"A little more advanced than that," Hugo replied drily.

He called out to the driver of the sleigh to stop. The horse came to a standstill a little to the side of the crowd, so they could see very clearly.

"She is good . . . very good," Hugo said, almost to himself.

"Do you know who she is?" Carole enquired.

He nodded his head.

"The pupil of Ernst Zippert."

"Is she? Why, Ernst taught me to skate last year. Is he here?"

"Yes. There he is over there."

"Do let's speak to him."

Hugo called a boy who was standing on the outskirts of the crowd, pointed out to him where Ernst was standing and told him to go and attract his attention.

The boy ran off. Ernst turned when the small messenger reached his side, saw who was in the sleigh and waved his hand. A few moments later he called Utta off the ice. While she stopped to take off her skates, Ernst came towards the sleigh.

"Good afternoon, Ernst," Hugo said. "Here's an old pupil of yours who wishes to congratulate you."

Carole held out her hand.

"How are you, Ernst?" she asked. "And, as Lord Roxburton says, I want to congratulate you. She is very good."

"Thank you, Mrs. Munton. That is what I think," Ernst replied.

"You are certainly keeping her hard at it," Hugo remarked.

"We have only got two more days, my lord," Ernst said. "You know it is not always easy for us to practise. Nicolaus Kindschi has gone to Pontresina this afternoon and so Utta came to tell me she was free. We cannot go to the Palace or the Suvretta rinks and so we come here. No one who matters is likely to see us—but the village turn out, as you can see."

"Are you surprised?" Hugo asked. "They don't usually get such excellent entertainment free."

As he spoke he saw that Utta was coming towards them. She had slipped a coat over her skating dress and put on ordinary shoes and she carried in her hand her white boots with their shining silver skates attached.

She had not realised, as she changed, to whom Ernst was speaking. She had only seen the sleigh draw up and seen him walk off towards it when her practise was finished. Now, when she looked at her watch, she saw it was late and realised they must not be too long in returning home.

Ernst had brought her down in his car and as she walked towards him now she decided to tell him that she would wait in the car until he finished talking to his friends. Then, as she approached the sleigh, she saw who was in it. For a moment her eyes widened and then a faint blush stole over her cheeks.

She had been thinking of Lord Roxburton so much since she had seen him that morning, that now it seemed almost a coincidence that he should be here talking to Ernst. Then she saw Carole and for a moment there was a strange feeling in her breast such as she had never known before.

Ernst turned to smile at her as she approached.

"His lordship has been congratulating me," he said, "and Mrs. Munton."

"How do you do?" Carole said, holding out her hand. "I have just been telling Ernst that I am quite certain you will win the Championship. Lord Roxburton and I were watching the competitors this morning and they didn't seem to me half as good as you are."

76

Carole was only being conventionally charming. It was a charm that she could turn on and off like a tap, but Utta was not to know this and thought Carole the most lovely person she had ever seen in her life. She had never imagined that anyone could be so beautiful.

Her furs, her face, her sparkling ear-rings which seemed to match her crimson lips, made a picture at which Utta could only stare—feeling suddenly very gauche and unimportant.

"Thank you very much," she stammered at length, the colour coming and going in her cheeks in a way that made her look little more than a child.

"Will you both have breakfast with me tomorrow morning?" Hugo asked.

He did not know why he asked the question. He had not planned to issue the invitation and yet it seemed to come almost spontaneously from his lips without his conscious volition.

"I do not know, my lord," Ernst replied as Utta looked at him. "I shall need every second of the time Utta can spare me tomorrow morning."

"I will try to come a little earlier," Utta said, "and then, if we hurried . . ."

She made no pretence about wanting to accept Hugo's invitation. He suddenly felt absurdly pleased that she would come.

"I shall expect you soon after seven," he said.

"Thank you," Utta answered.

She looked up at him, her eyes vividly blue against the whiteness of her skin.

"We mustn't let the child get cold," Carole said sharply.

"No, of course not. Until tomorrow morning, Ernst," Hugo said. "Good-bye, Utta."

Their driver whipped up his horse; Hugo waved his hand, and in a few moments they were out of sight.

"You didn't tell me that you had met this girl before," Carole remarked accusingly.

"Why should I?" Hugo enquired.

"She is very pretty."

"Do you think so?"

77

"Don't you?"

"Yes, very pretty—and a good skater. I hope she wins the Championship for Ernst's sake."

He spoke deliberately with a cold indifference, and then hated himself because he was pretending to Carole —hiding from her jealousy the fact that he was definitely interested in Utta.

6

Carole was in a bad temper. She walked listlessly around her sitting-room, picking up a book only to slam it down again and chewing at the end of her cigarette-holder until finally, in exasperation, she flung it into an ash-tray.

The day had gone wrong from its very beginning. Hugo had left her room in the very early hours of the morning. After he had gone, she had lain awake for a long time, torturing herself with the thought that he had not yet asked her to marry him.

Once again the old question reiterated itself. Had she been foolish? Surrendered herself too easily, giving him what he wanted before she had a wedding-ring on her finger?

She could not believe that she had shocked Hugo. After all, it was an accepted fact in America that, while American women married their lovers, English women slept with any man they thought desirable.

Besides, Hugo was a man of the world. Yet, the thought came to her like the clutching of a cold hand, it was not as a man of the world that she wanted him, but as a husband.

It was dawn before Carole had fallen asleep and noon before she awoke.

She realised that she had overslept as soon as she saw the face of the pink quartz and diamond clock which always stood beside her bed. She was aware by this time that, however late Hugo was in bed, he had breakfast at six-thirty; and before Carole had even rung for her maid to pull the curtains she reached out her hand to the telephone.

Smith answered from Hugo's room.

"His lordship has gone out, madam."

"Where to?"

"I am afraid I don't know, madam."

Carole slammed down the telephone. With fingers that trembled she dialled the Bakers' room. They were not there. She was wide awake by this time and sitting up in bed she rang first for her maid and then for her secretary.

Carole always travelled with a retinue. She had learnt, as soon as she was widowed, to copy other rich American women who went to Europe with a whole staff to minister to their needs and requirements.

Carole's secretary had been recommended by her lawyer's office in New York. She was neat, precise, extremely efficient and maddeningly inhuman.

"Where are Mr. and Mrs. Baker?" Carole snapped at her when she came into the room and stood waiting for orders.

As if Miss Withers had anticipated the question, she had the answer ready:

"They are down on the skating rink, Mrs. Munton. They left a message with me to say that was where they would be should you want them."

"Is Lord Roxburton with them?"

"No."

"How do you know?"

"I went down there about a quarter of an hour ago to give Mrs. Baker a cable that had come for her. They were sitting alone and Lord Roxburton was not with them."

"Where is he then?"

"I will try to find out, Mrs. Munton."

"It is no use asking Smith because he doesn't know. Enquire at the desk. Find out who has seen him. I want to know where he has gone and who was with him."

"Very good, Mrs. Munton."

Miss Withers went from the room, her face calm and

expressionless as if to be sent hunting an elusive lord was a commonplace occurrence.

Carole got out of bed. Slipping into a négligé of white satin trimmed with platina mink which her maid held out for her, she walked restlessly backwards and forwards across the sunlit room.

"Where can he have gone?" she said aloud. "Why can't he have left a message for me?"

"I expect there is one at the desk, madam," her maid said soothingly.

Adèle had been with Carole for five years now. She knew these moods only too well and was better able to deal with them than anyone else of Carole's acquaintance.

"Yes, perhaps you are right, Adèle."

"Miss Withers will bring it up if it is there. Sit down in a chair while I bring your breakfast," Adèle went on. "You will give yourself lines on the forehead if you are not careful. Worry is death to anyone's looks, as I always used to say to Mrs. Vanderbilt."

Adèle never let Carole forget for a moment who had been her last employer. At times, when she was really incensed, Carole would forget her soft air of good breeding and shout at Adèle:

"Shut your mouth! I'm sick to death of the Vanderbilts and all the other stuck-up snobs in the Social Register. Think about me. I'm the person who pays you."

Adèle was the one person with whom Carole could relax. It was impossible for her to keep up permanently and for twenty-four hours of the day the act of being a gracious and well-bred Society woman who had been born in that charming, white-pillared house in Virginia.

Not that she would ever admit to Adèle, or anyone else, the truth about her birth; but she must, for her own sake, relax in the presence of someone—and it had best be her maid, who after all, as she put it so bluntly, was paid to serve and not to ask questions.

Adèle brought her breakfast now. Orange juice, toast and coffee—no butter, no honey. Carole had always to think of her figure.

"He might have gone out to the Corvelia Club,"

Carole said after a moment, as she sipped her orange juice.

"He will have left a message for you, don't you worry, madam," Adèle replied.

She tidied the room and slipped out of the door with the dress that Carole had worn last night over her arm. Coming down the passage she saw Miss Withers.

"Have you got a message for her?" she enquired.

Miss Withers shook her head.

"I'm afraid not."

"The Lord help us!" Adèle exclaimed. "I don't envy you breaking the news."

She went on down the passage, humming a little tune beneath her breath. It didn't worry Adèle very much what Carole was feeling. She was finding St. Moritz very much to her liking. The second *concierge,* who was unmarried and good-looking, had already asked her to go dancing on her evening out, and one of the floor waiters was equally attentive.

"I am afraid there is no message from Lord Roxburton," Miss Withers was saying in her calm, impersonal voice.

Carole put her empty glass down with a clatter on the breakfast tray.

"Then where is he?"

"He went off in a car, one of the porters told me. Someone called to see him and caught him just as he was going down to the ice rink. They talked for some time in the lounge and then Lord Roxburton drove away with the gentleman."

"It was a man then?" Carole said quickly.

"Yes, a man, Mrs. Munton."

Carole felt some of the tension she had been feeling leave her body. She did not know what she feared and yet at the back of her mind there was a vision of a little, pointed face with gentian blue eyes looking up at them as they sat in the sleigh.

She had been cross for the rest of the day.

She snapped at the Bakers during lunch and when they suggested going skiing in the afternoon she had refused to accompany them.

"I've got a headache," she admitted grudgingly to Mary's enquiries; but she had made herself so disagreeable that she knew they were relieved that they could leave her at the hotel and hurry off alone into the sunshine.

"He has no right to treat me like this, none at all," she stormed to herself, and was not even pacified when two o'clock brought a message dictated over the telephone:

"Lord Roxburton is sorry but he has been delayed and will not be back for luncheon. He will look forward to seeing Mrs. Munton at dinner."

"I ought to have received this before lunch," Carole said accusingly, tapping the piece of paper with one of her long nails.

"I don't think it was the hotel's fault, Mrs. Munton," Miss Withers answered. "Perhaps there was some delay in sending it from Lord Roxburton's end."

"It doesn't help me whose fault it is," Carole retorted. "That's all, Miss Withers."

Alone in her sitting-room again, she read and re-read the message and finally threw it into the waste-paperbasket. There was nothing for her to do but to wait for Hugo's return and in the meantime to worry because he could leave her for the whole day without, apparently, any regrets.

The hours passed slowly while Carole sat and smoked and walked about the room, resenting her own enforced solitude, yet finding it impossible to make up her mind to do anything else.

There was laughter and music from the ice rink below. The nursery slopes around the hotel were filled with inexperienced ski-ers and children enjoying themselves in the sunshine.

Carole sat in the super-heated atmosphere and hated everybody, including herself. She felt as though the ache of her body for Hugo was something that was slowly poisoning her mind. She wanted him . . . she wanted to capture him as she had captured so many other things in her life. What hadn't she achieved since she had first taken Dave's hand in hers and looked down at his thick, square-cut nails?

She remembered the antagonism of Dave's family. She had conquered them. She had surmounted, too, the difficulties in getting herself accepted by the more exclusive New York Society. She had gone to England and forced an entrance into the best and most formal houses.

She had made Hugo notice her when everyone had told her that he was the most difficult man to get in the whole of England.

He was her lover. She thought of his lips on hers . . . of his arms holding her . . . of those moments of wild, ecstatic passion which seemed to burn their very personalities away from them and leave them primitive and, at times, almost savage in their love-making.

Carole closed her eyes. Yes, she held him by chains stronger than steel, she was sure of that. He wanted her—he could not escape his own desire even as she could not escape hers.

Then, as her lips parted in the ecstasy of remembering, there came a knock at the outer door. She turned round quickly. A sudden light in her eyes, a softening of her whole expression.

She heard Adèle come from the bedroom and open the door. There was the sound of voices—a man's voice —and then slowly Carole's elation ebbed away. It was not Hugo.

Adèle came into the room, closing the door behind her.

"There is a gentleman to see you, madam."

"Who is it?" Carole enquired.

Adèle held out a visiting card. Carole glanced at it and her whole body seemed to stiffen.

"I can't see him," she said quickly. "Say I am indisposed . . . in bed . . . anything you like. But get rid of him!"

"Very good, madam."

Adèle turned towards the door, but she was too late. It opened softly and Don Carlos stood there, his thick lips parted in a smile.

"You are alone, Carole?" he said. "That is what I hoped."

"It is not really convenient for me to see you now," Carole said coldly. "I am just going to change and go down to tea. My friends will be back soon; they have gone skiing."

"There is still a little time before the sun will sink in the heavens and it will grow cold," Don Carlos said. "I want to talk to you."

"Suppose I don't want to talk to you."

"Are you being wise in taking up that attitude?"

He settled himself as he spoke in one of the armchairs and crossed his legs. Linking his fingers together in his lap, he looked up at her with an undisguised expression of amusement.

"What do you mean?" Carole asked.

"Exactly what I said," Don Carlos replied. "Are you wise to turn an old friend into an enemy?"

Carole walked across the room quickly to see if Adèle had shut the door. She turned towards the man in the chair and said in a low voice which seemed to shake with sudden emotion:

"What do you want of me?"

"I want to talk to you," Don Carlos replied. "I want to hear how you have been getting on."

"Why should it interest you?"

"Why not? I have always taken an interest in the little girl who I remember wanted a job in the films."

"You called yourself Charlie Jackobi in those days."

"What of it? What's in a name? I was born in the slums of Chicago, for your information. We have much in common, my dear Carole."

"We have nothing," she answered with an almost savage intensity. "Why must you come here to hound me, to dig up the past which I have forgotten a long time ago?"

"I doubt that," Don Carlos said. "None of us ever really forgets our past or what happened when we were young."

"Well, I want to forget mine," Carole said. "You are

the only person who has ever recognised me. Why can't you leave me alone?"

"My dear Carole, is that fair? I have never interfered in your life. I have, indeed, watched your climb to fame with interest and, shall we say, at times with amusement. I keep some of the newspaper cuttings in which you describe your life on your father's estates in Virginia."

"How do you know that wasn't true?" Carole asked furiously. "I said that when he died we lost all our money. I came to Los Angeles to look for work for . . ."

"I know . . . I know," Don Carlos interrupted. "To support your poor old widowed mother who died soon afterwards. I like that part about your not being able to give her the comforts that she needed. As a matter of fact, for a long-interred corpse your mother is looking extremely well."

"You have seen her?"

"Yes, about six months ago. I happened to be at a loose end. I thought it would be amusing to see the mother of the wealthy Mrs. Dave Munton."

Carole was silent for a moment. Almost heavily she sat down in the chair opposite Don Carlos.

"You say she was well?" she said after a moment in a low voice.

"Well indeed. She has married again, did you know?"

"No, I had no idea. Whom?"

"A nice man—your mother introduced us. He keeps a drug store. She explained to me that she always liked them to be learned."

Carole put her hands up to her face. She could see all too clearly the type of man her mother would marry. She remembered the drug stores in the sordid neighbourhood around their house. She had eaten at one often enough.

The sandwiches and sundaes slapped on the counter; the high stools jostled by youths whose boisterousness made their pushing and teasing often more painful than amusing; the girls, like herself, giggling together or talking rather loudly to attract attention.

"The man from the drug store." They used to laugh

at him and try to cheat when he wasn't looking. She looked up suddenly.

"Why are you telling me this? Is it blackmail?"

"My dear Carole, you always were dramatic," Don Carlos replied. "I ought to have given you a part in the films when you wanted it. I believe you would have made good. You have certainly put on the best act I have ever seen and it is a part that has lasted a long time."

"What has it got to do with you?" Carole enquired. "I have worked hard for what I have wanted, just as you have. It hasn't been all roses and blue ribbons by any means. Dave drank. When he was drunk, he was a beast."

"You didn't have to put up with him for long," Don Carlos said suavely, "and now you are planning to be married again."

"Who told you that?"

Don Carlos shrugged his shoulders.

"My dear, has one ever been able to stop people gossiping? I heard from someone in London what a success you were with the rich and handsome Lord Roxburton. "Carole Munton, looking fabulous, was with him at the film première," she wrote, "and the betting is three to one against her pulling it off this time."

"Three to one against," Carole whispered, then she threw back her head. "I don't want to hear what your vulgar friends wrote or said about me. Get out of here and leave me alone. I don't want to see you again. It makes me feel uncomfortable to know you are there, sniggering and believing you have got some power over me because you know the truth about where I come from."

"And haven't I?" Don Carlos asked.

Carole's eyes met his and she was very still.

"I have asked you before what you want."

"Nothing, as it happens," Don Carlos replied. "You are too suspicious; you should learn to trust people. One day I may want money and then I know, of course, it would be quite easy for you to give it to me. A hundred thousand dollars here or there—what would it mean to you? But at the moment I am prosperous and, in my own world, quite a success. I have made some fine discoveries in the last few years—but you wouldn't be interested in that. I didn't discover you and that, I acknowledge now, was a mistake. Still, you might not have been such a success if you had not been acting entirely from the point of view of self-interest."

"I think I hate you," Carole said. "You come here to gloat over me; to make me feel uncomfortable. You hope I will be afraid of you and of what you might do. You fancy yourself as a snake playing with a rabbit, but let me tell you I don't intend that you shall blackmail me. When the time comes and you ask me for a lot of money to keep your mouth shut, I shall say, 'Tell the truth and see who believes you.'

"The Muntons are stronger than you are. They have given out that I am from Virginia, a member of a respected Southern family. They won't go back on that whatever you or any other gutter-snipe from Chicago may like to say to the contrary."

"Very fine and very heroic," Don Carlos approved. He drew out his cigarette-case as he spoke. "Do you mind if I smoke?"

Carole didn't answer. He put a cigarette in his mouth and lit it from a gold lighter that had his initials on it in diamonds. Then, as he blew the smoke softly from his mouth, he said:

"As you say, the Muntons will support your lies because it suits them to do so. But what about this handsome young lord you have in tow? Englishmen are snobs, my dear."

"You can leave him out of it," Carole said brusquely.

"But why? I am very fond of the English. Sometimes I think that in my old age I will settle in London. It is quiet, peaceful and serene after the hurly-burly of New York, the bustle of Chicago. I have a respect for their old-fashioned traditions, for the reverence that the English have for good breeding—whether it concerns horses or women."

"You are trying to frighten me," Carole said swiftly. "You know perfectly well that you have no intention of going to Hugo Roxburton and telling him what you know about me. You have nothing to gain from it."

"Can you be sure of that?" Don Carlos replied. "He might be grateful."

"No one is ever grateful to the messenger who brings bad news," Carole said scathingly. "Besides, he would not listen to you."

Her eyes flickered as she spoke and Don Carlos laughed.

"He might . . . that is what you are afraid of, my dear . . . he might."

Carole stamped her foot.

"Leave me alone," she stormed. "What have I ever done to you that you should treat me like this?"

"That's better," Don Carlos said. "Now you are more human. There was a genuine emotion in your voice then. I have hopes of you yet."

"Hopes! What do you mean?"

"That one day you might become human—might even have a little genuine feeling for anyone except Carole."

"Are you turning revivalist?" Carole said with a sneer. "At any moment you will be quoting the Ten Commandments."

"I might do worse. You might try remembering the Fifth," Don Carlos said.

"The Fifth?" Carole wrinkled her brow.

" 'Honour thy father and thy mother . . .' "

"Oh, I remember. So it's my mother who is sticking in your gullet. Well, I sent her money—what else could I do? Besides, if I had sent too much, you know as well as I do that the neighbours would have talked. She wouldn't have been able to keep it to herself. 'My daughter is so kind to me. My daughter is so generous.' Then they would begin asking questions as to who her daughter was and what had happened to her."

"Do you think she doesn't know?" Don Carlos asked.

Carole's eyes opened wide.

"Does she? Has anyone told her? Have you told her?"

He shook his head.

"No, I haven't said a word. I am just watching and waiting to see what happens." He smoked for a moment and then added: "You know, being in the films, Carole, gives one a sense of drama. I suppose I have begun to look upon everything and everybody as part of a story. I want to see what happens to yours. Perhaps one day, when I am old, I shall write it down—become another O. Henry. Who knows? Stranger things have happened."

"If you do, I will buy up every copy of your book and have them burnt, if it costs me every dollar I possess."

Don Carlos laughed again.

"So you are as frightened as that," he exclaimed. "Well, we will wait and see. Where have we got to now, I wonder? About chapter five or six. There may be a dozen to go."

"I said I hated you just now," Carole cried. "It was an understatement. I loathe you. If my dislike of you could kill, you would be a dead man."

"And that would dispense with the Sixth Commandment," Don Carlos said imperturbably.

Carole stamped her foot.

"Oh, you . . . you make me sick!"

Don Carlos got slowly to his feet.

"Well, I will leave you," he said. "This has been a very amusing interview. I shan't forget it; neither, I think, will you. We shall see each other at the Championships. When all else fails, Carole, I might be able to offer you a job on the films."

"I wouldn't take a job from you if I was dying of starvation," Carole said.

"No? That's what you think now, but wait until the time comes," Don Carlos replied. "And in the meantime, there are many other charming little ladies who are only too anxious to attract my attention."

Carole's expression suddenly altered.

"You are looking for someone who can skate?" she said. "I will give you a tip—which is generous of me considering the way you have behaved. It is a girl no one knows about and who will appear for the first time tomorrow. She has been taught by Ernst Zippert—you remember him? He is a skating instructor here now, but he won the International himself many years ago."

"Yes, I know Zippert," Don Carlos said. "Go on!"

"Her name is Utta and I have seen her on the ice. She skates well—she is pretty, too."

"Your interest in her is entirely impersonal, of course?" Don Carlos said.

"What do you mean?"

"Why are you telling me this? My dear Carole, you would not throw me a lifeline if you knew I was drowning. You have a reason for recommending this girl. Can it be her looks which are disturbing you?"

Carole gave a scream of sheer anger.

"Get out of here!" she yelled. "Get out before I kill you!"

She picked up a small ash-tray that was on the table near her hand and flung it at Don Carlos. It missed him and shattered into a thousand pieces against the leg of his chair.

"Excellent, my dear Carole," he said. "Excellent. If you go on like this you will become a real person, not just a dressed-up tailor's dummy. But I am insulting you. Dummies can't scheme and you have always been a schemer, haven't you?"

He laughed again as Carole threw a book at him; and then, still laughing, he went from the room.

He left the door open and she heard him chuckling as he went down the passage. It was then that she beat her clenched fists against the back of the chair and there were tears of rage in her eyes. She stamped her foot at the same time.

The fury in her heart was almost suffocating—she wanted to strike Don Carlos, knock him down and stamp on him and laugh as he lay writhing at her feet. If she had had a gun in her hand, she would have shot him; but what was the use? She was impotent, helpless. She could only writhe beneath his sarcasm and his laughter.

"God, how I hate him!" she said the words out loud —and suddenly saw a reflection of herself in one of the mirrors on the wall. She looked almost demented, with a white face, eyes which seemed at the moment to be sunk deep in her head, and her hair falling untidily about her cheeks where she had shaken it in her agitation.

And then quite suddenly she stood still, for she realised that she looked not only angry, but old. With trembling hands Carole pushed back her hair and sat down in the chair trying to breathe normally and stop the tumultuous hammering of her heart.

She had had these rages before—bouts of anger when she had yelled and screamed at Dave and hit him, too. Times when she had raged at other men because they would not give her what she wanted, or at women because she was jealous of them.

For the first time Carole was frightened of herself; and then, with an effort which had something heroic in it, she tried to dismiss Don Carlos from her mind.

Hugo was coming back soon. When Hugo was with her she would forget the horrors Don Carlos had conjured up—her mother married to the keeper of the drug store; people knowing who she was, pointing and sniggering about her.

She must marry Hugo at once. Marry him and go away to England where no one knew anything about her save that she was rich and American.

She knew now that she had always been frightened of being exposed; but then, as the years passed, she had almost come to believe the story she had invented so skilfully of her antecedents and her life on the cotton plantation in Virginia.

And yet deep down in her consciousness there had always been that nagging fear.

She had a picture of her mother which somehow, whatever she did or whatever she thought, would never be erased. A picture of her bending over the sink, a coarse apron round her thickening waist, her hands red and chapped from being continuously in water, and her hair, unkempt and unbrushed, straggling against her neck.

At times she couldn't even remember her mother's face—only that back view of her, her shoes down at heel, seeming a part of the untidy, none too clean floors.

"Let me forget . . . oh, let me forget," Carole whispered now.

She jumped to her feet and went into the bedroom. She rang the bells by her bed. One had been specially installed which went to Miss Withers' room, another for Adèle and one for the floor waiter. They were all with her in a matter of a few seconds.

"Where have you been?" she demanded angrily of Miss Withers. "I have been alone all the afternoon. I should have thought you would have brought me the newspapers or the letters."

"I don't think they have come yet, Mrs. Munton," Miss Withers answered, "but I will go and ask at the desk."

She turned away before Carole could think of anything else to say to her.

"Bring me a whisky-and-soda," she ordered the waiter, and then turned to Adèle.

"I want to change my dress. Get me another."

"Would you like the new purple silk from Balmain?" Adèle enquired. "Or would you like the green chartreuse which was delivered last week?"

"I don't care. Bring me anything you like," Carole answered, "but get rid of this dress—the one I have got on. Throw it away . . . burn it . . . do anything you like with it, but never let me see it again."

"Of course, madam," Adèle said gently, but there was a little smile at the corner of her lips.

This was good news indeed. A lady in the hotel was asking only last night if there was any chance of buying Mrs. Munton's clothes when she was tired of them. She would get a good price for this one, which had only been worn a few times. Carole was tearing it as she dragged it from her shoulders, but it could be mended.

"You are tired, madam," she said. "When you have had a drink, you will feel better. Wear the Balmain gown; you always look so wonderful in that colour."

"I shall look like hell in anything today," Carole retorted, peering at her reflection in the mirror.

"No! no! How can madam think anything so silly? One of the head waiters said to me last night that you were the loveliest person he has ever seen in the hotel! And all the beauties of Europe have been here at one time or another."

Carole gave a little smile.

"Did he really say that? We must remember to tip him when we leave."

"Madam would be surprised if she heard all the compliments that are said about her."

"Tell the hairdresser to come up before dinner tonight," Carole said, "and find me a really lovely dress— one I haven't worn before."

"Madam shall look like a princess," Adèle promised.

Carole sipped her whisky-and-soda as Adèle buttoned her into her dress. When she was ready she felt better and, as if the easing of her tension was rewarded, the telephone rang just as the last jewel had been clipped into place and Adèle was fetching the shoes that matched the dress.

Carole snatched up the receiver.

"Hello!" Then, with a little cry: "Is that you, Hugo? So you are back; I am so glad. I want to see you . . . I have missed you so much. Yes, terribly. I have had a beastly day. Everything has gone wrong . . . everyone has been so tiresome. . . . No, I am just alone here. Come and have a drink; I am just having one myself, as a matter of fact. . . . You will meet me downstairs for tea? Very well. Are you sure you won't come and pick me up? . . . Yes, please. I would like you to. . . . Yes, you know why."

Her voice was very soft, her eyes were shining as she put down the telephone. Hugo would be along in a few minutes—all her worries were forgotten.

She went back into the sitting-room. The broken pieces of ash-tray had already been cleared away, but the smell of cigarette smoke lingered there.

She felt for a moment as if Don Carlos still watched her, with a sarcastic smile, in the shadows. Impulsively she threw open the windows. The cold air came rushing in. The sky was brilliant with colour—breath-taking in its beauty. But Carole was concerned only with the erasing of the last traces of Don Carlos.

When the room grew too cold to be bearable, she shut the window again and fetched her scent spray from the bedroom. It was a scent which cost an exorbitant amount in Paris, but she sprayed it liberally over the room until, scented and fragrant, she felt that the last trace of Don Carlos had been erased.

It seemed to her a long time before Hugo arrived. When at last he stood in the doorway, Carole ran across to him and reached up her arms to draw down his head to hers.

"Darling, I have missed you so much."

"Have you?"

He kissed her with an easy familiarity and then, disentangling himself from her arms, walked to the chair and settled himself comfortably.

"What will you drink?" Carole asked.

"I don't want anything," he answered, "except some tea. It seems only a short time ago I had lunch."

"Where have you been?" Carole enquired. "Do you realise that I didn't know until two o'clock what had happened to you?"

"You didn't anticipate anything drastic, did you?" Hugo asked. "I meant to leave a message before I left that I wouldn't be back to lunch, in case any of you waited for me, but I forgot until we reached Ian Mayfield's villa at Samadan."

"Is that where you have been?" Carole asked.

"Yes. I hadn't seen Ian for years. He lives out here because his wife's got T.B. We were at Eton together and were in the same regiment. I'm his trustee, among other things, so when he heard I was here he came over to see me and persuaded me to go back to lunch with him."

"You might have taken me with you," Carole pouted.

"I never thought of it," Hugo answered. "I expect they would have bored you, they are very simple people."

"Your friends would never bore me," Carole answered. Suddenly she walked over towards his chair and

94

put her hand in his. "Don't you understand?" she said softly. "I want to share everything with you—your friends, your interests, your life. Oh, Hugo! you can be very dense at times."

Automatically he lifted her hand to his lips.

"Now I'm here don't keep reproaching me about when I wasn't," he said. "You're as bad as the parsons who always complain to the people who are in church about those who aren't."

There was an edge on his voice which Carole could not ignore.

"Darling, I'm terribly pleased to see you," she said. "Tell me how you enjoyed your breakfast."

"My breakfast?" Hugo queried.

"Yes, of course. With Ernst and his little pupil. You didn't forget that you had invited them, I hope?"

"No, I hadn't forgotten," Hugo replied, "but they sent a message to say they couldn't come."

7

Utta stood watching one of the competitors, Leni Prokosch from Davos, finish her exhibition. The applause from the spectators broke out as she ended with a double loop, then sped into the middle of the rink to take her bow.

Utta gave a little shiver and looked up at Ernst.

"She is good," she said. "Better . . . much better than I am."

"Are you crazy?" Ernst asked. "She should never have attempted those jumps. She will not even be in the first three when the judges have finished their marking."

"Nor will I," Utta whispered.

He looked at her in mock severity.

"Are you suggesting that I am no judge of skating?" he asked. "I, who was World Champion for five years and have produced no less than three Champions since I retired. Are you seriously suggesting that I am a liar?"

Utta gave a little laugh that was half a sob and reached out to clasp his arm.

"No! no! Ernst. Of course not. I believe in you implicitly. It's only that my knees are wobbling and there is a funny sinking feeling in my tummy."

"Was there ever an artiste who didn't feel like that?" he enquired. "My dear, forget the crowd, forget the judges. Skate as if we were alone early in the morning with only the birds to witness your mistakes. You will win easily!"

"I will try to do as you say," Utta said softly.

"Think how lucky we have been," Ernst went on. "Your grandfather away, and I half-afraid that we should start the day with an argument. Even to be cross can upset the best and most experienced skaters."

"Yes, we have been lucky," Utta agreed.

"You are talking about luck," a voice said behind them, "and that is what I am here to wish you."

She turned round quickly, one hand still on Ernst's arm. Standing behind them was Hugo. For a moment his face swam before her eyes and then she saw that he was smiling and that today he was using only one stick instead of two.

"Why have you been avoiding me?" he asked before she could speak. "I have been watching for you every morning from my window, but the rink has remained depressingly empty."

Utta's eyes dropped before his. She could not explain to him the reason why she had cancelled her and Ernst's engagement to have breakfast with him the morning before last. Indeed, she did not know the reason herself. When she had returned home and told her grandmother that she was to see Lord Roxburton again, Madame Kindschi had begged her to refuse the invitation.

"I cannot explain why, *ma chérie*," she said. "You have just got to trust me. You must believe that what I am asking is the best for you."

"Do you know anything against Lord Roxburton?" Utta asked.

She had been puzzled by her grandmother's behaviour when she first told her the name of the man she had rescued from the mountainside and with whom she had had breakfast at Suvretta House.

As she said "Lord Roxburton", her grandmother's hands had gone up to her face and she had cried out with what seemed to Utta a sound almost of pain.

"What is the matter, *Grand'mère?*" she had asked. "What has upset you?"

But her grandmother had passed it off lightly.

"It is nothing, darling. Something I suddenly thought of . . . something I remembered. It is nothing."

To all Utta's enquiries she had refused to give any other explanation, but now she was speaking openly—making her feelings very clear.

"I have never asked you to do anything for me, my little one," she said. "The necessity has not arisen till now. But now I ask something of you; something which is of the utmost importance."

"Tell me why, *Grand'mère*. What has he done? What have you heard about him?" Utta insisted.

"What is this man to you?" Madame Kindschi retorted. "You have seen him three times in your life—three short encounters. Can he be so important as all that? Besides, you told me he had a lady with him. Perhaps she is his wife or his *fiancée.*"

"No, he is not married," Utta replied. "He may be engaged—I do not know."

She felt some of the happiness and excitement she had felt on coming home from the lake slowly ebbing away from her. She had been so thrilled as she watched the sleigh drive away, because she knew she would see him on the morrow.

Even Ernst's praise of her performance as he spoke the words she had hoped to hear from him vanished into insignificance beside the fact that she was to see the Englishman again. She wanted to listen to his voice; to see the smile on his lips, the twinkle in his eyes as he alternately complimented or teased her.

"Why, *Grand'mère?* Why can't I go?" she asked.

Madame Kindschi pressed her lips together.

"I have nothing more to say, Utta. If you care for me

97

so little that this stranger means more than I do, then of course you must do what you wish."

The cold tone of disapproval, the sudden steel in her grandmother's eyes, brought Utta to her knees beside her.

"No, *Grand'mère*. No, of course I don't mean that. If you don't want me to go, I will, of course, obey you. It was only that he . . . he seemed different from anyone I have ever met before. He was so interesting and . . . well . . . I can't explain. It's just that I meet so few men."

Madame Kindschi put her arms around Utta and held her close.

"I understand, my dearest. I understand only too well. But I promise you it is for your own good that I ask you not to see him any more."

"Very well, *Grand'mère*." Utta's voice was very low. "I promise."

But this was different, she thought, as she faced Hugo now. She had not been to breakfast with Lord Roxburton. She had made Ernst send a message to say that neither of them could come. They had not gone to Suvretta House again to skate. But it was one thing not to accept his hospitality and to keep her promise to her grandmother, and quite another to avoid speaking to him when he came up unexpectedly. Not without being offensive and unnecessarily rude could she do anything but reply.

Yet what could she say to his question? There was no explanation she could make—nothing concrete that she could put into words to explain exactly why she had been avoiding him. Womanlike she took the easiest course.

"We have been very busy, Ernst and I," she said. "And now the great moment has arrived and I am frightened—far too frightened, I think, even to move."

"Nonsense!" Hugo laughed at her. "You can beat all these people hollow and you know it, and when the first hurdle is over we shall see you waltz away with the International Championships."

"You are all far too optimistic," Utta replied. "I

don't want to think about the International—today is enough to worry about."

"Don't worry! Just skate as you skated that first morning I saw you," Hugo said. "You were like a little blue bird on the ice; that is why I brought you this charm to bring you luck."

He took a little box from his pocket as he spoke—a jeweller's box in pink leather.

"For me?" Utta asked. "How exciting!"

She forgot for a moment everything save the thrill of receiving a present. She opened the box eagerly. Inside, lying on white satin, was a tiny charm—a blue bird made in different coloured sapphires, resting on a twig fashioned of baguette diamonds.

It was an expensive trifle, but Utta, for the moment, had no thought for the value of it in money or of the fact that she should not accept jewels from a man. She was only aware that someone in friendliness had offered her something lovely, and in friendliness she wished to accept it.

"Oh, thank you! Thank you!" she said. "I am sure it will bring me luck. It is just like some of the little birds that come when Grandfather calls them."

At the mention of her grandfather she started and looked up at Ernst.

"We have been lucky already," she smiled, "and now this."

"The third thing must be the trophy," he answered.

She gave a little laugh at that.

"You are so confident," she said. "I wish I felt the same."

"What was your first bit of luck?" Hugo asked curiously.

"Grandfather has gone away for a week," she replied. "I could hardly believe my ears when he told me yesterday morning that he had had a letter from his sister in Davos asking him to go and see her at once. She is ill, so I ought to be sorry, although I never cared much for my Aunt Lisette."

"It makes things very easy, my lord," Ernst interposed. "I have been afraid all along that something would happen to prevent Utta from entering for this competition, and that something had every likelihood of being Nicolaus. I am afraid of him—I have never pretended that I am not."

"There is really no reason to be," Utta told him. "Grandfather is strict, but he is very kind and very gentle. I have never known him lose his temper. Still, of course, he gets his own way. Even *Grand'mère* can't stand up to him once he makes up his mind."

"Nor can you," Ernst answered. "It has given me sleepless nights, I don't mind telling you, wondering whether you would say at the last moment, 'I am sorry, Ernst, but after all I cannot enter for the competition!' Then I should have lost my reputation for ever. St. Moritz would never have forgiven me."

"Oh, Ernst! I never thought it would have done you harm; how terrible of me!" Utta exclaimed. "But I see now that it would have been a terrible let-down for you. People might have thought that, after all, your pupil was no good."

Utta looked so stricken that Ernst bent forward to pat her hand reassuringly.

"Don't worry," he said. "You are here; your grandfather is in Davos and you are going to show them that once again Ernst Zippert is the finest instructor in the whole of Switzerland."

"I think you mean in the whole world, don't you?" Hugo interrupted.

"If she wins the International . . . yes," Ernst agreed.

"My little blue bird will make sure of it," Hugo said to Utta.

"I will pin it to my dress," she smiled, "just inside the bodice, where no one can see it, for Ernst does not approve of competitors wearing jewellery."

She undid the front of the heavy tweed coat she wore and Hugo had a glimpse of turquoise blue satin with sequins sparkling in the sunshine.

He watched her as, finding a safety-pin, she pinned the little charm to the front of her bodice, where it would lie in the soft white valley between her breasts. Then Utta raised her eyes to his . . .

"Thank you," she said very softly.

He had a wild impulse to bend forward and kiss her red lips. He almost did so, thinking she was little more than a child and that she might accept the kiss in the manner in which it was given.

Then he remembered all the talk there had been of her grandfather's strictness and it stopped him. Perhaps, after all, there was something in this extraordinary Victorian atmosphere which she and Ernst managed to create between them. Could he really credit the severity of autocratic relatives who prevented her behaving with the untrammelled freedom of her contemporaries? Her untouched beauty and air of virginity was the answer he sought.

"I know it will bring you the very best of luck," he said, speaking of the charm and finding his voice was unexpectedly sincere.

Looking down into Utta's eyes as he spoke, he had a strange sensation that he looked into something deep and mysterious—something he had not expected to find in so young a girl. It was as if he saw there the soul of someone who was capable of deep emotion, of exhilarating joy and, perhaps, of great suffering.

Then Utta turned her head and he knew he must have been imagining things, for she was only a child—exquisitely feminine and provocatively beautiful, but still a child.

There was another burst of applause from the spectators and now Utta glanced at Ernst apprehensively.

"You have plenty of time," he said reassuringly. "There are two more in front of you."

As he spoke a competitor came from the rink. Another who had been waiting disdainfully with a heavy mink coat draped over her shoulders, now cast it aside and swept on with an assurance and self-possession which Utta envied.

"That is Eugénie Velhelm," Ernst explained, "from Lausanne."

"She is good!" Hugo said.

"Very!" Ernst commented. "And she expects to win this year. She was second in last year's competition."

"So that's your most dangerous rival," Hugo said to Utta.

She turned her back on the rink.

"I am not going to look," she answered. "Let's talk about other things—about my little blue bird for instance."

"Excuse me a moment," Ernst interrupted. "I must just have a word with a man over there."

He moved away, leaving Utta and Hugo alone.

"I will tell you a secret," Utta said. "I have another mascot which I am going to wear at the last moment, but Ernst does not know. He is very insistent that no pupil of his shall wear jewellery; he thinks it looks ostentatious and detracts from their movements. But I have a ring which belonged to my mother. It was actually her engagement ring and whenever I wear it I feel protected—as if she is watching over me, keeping me safe from whatever makes me afraid."

"Then you must certainly wear it today," Hugo told her.

He liked the expression of gravity in her face when she spoke of her mother, the softness in her voice, the way her lips drooped a little wistfully as if she longed, above everything else, for the comfort of her mother's arms. How right he was in thinking she was only a child who should be protected and looked after!

"I shall slip it on when I take my coat off," Utta went on. "You won't tell Ernst, will you?"

"No, of course not! Your secret is safe enough with me—in fact any secret you might want to tell me."

"I don't think I have any others."

"I can't believe that," Hugo said. "Why, you are full of secrets. Secrets about your grandparents; secrets about where you skate and at what time. You are Ernst's secret competitor for this competition—and you are my secret, too."

"Yours?" Utta asked.

"Yes, mine," he replied. "You are my secret rescuer from the mountain. I have never told any of my friends that you came to my aid. You see, when you disappeared that night I thought that perhaps you weren't

102

real—just a sprite or perhaps one of the fairies who live in the peaks where no mortal foot may tread. So I didn't tell anyone about you because they might have laughed at me and told me that you had never happened."

Utta gave a little cry of delight.

"What a lovely story! I only wish it were true! Really we ought not to have met again and then you would always have thought that perhaps I never had existed."

"In this case I am delighted my story wasn't true," Hugo replied.

"Why?"

It was the artless question of someone who had never learned the art of flirtation.

"Do you really want me to answer that question?" he enquired.

She understood then and saw the answer in his eyes. She blushed and turned a little away from him.

"Where's Ernst?" she asked.

"He will be coming in a moment," Hugo answered. "Do we really want him to make a trio of our conversation?"

"Yes, of course I want him," Utta replied quickly, but her words somehow lacked conviction.

Hugo laughed a little softly.

"You are so young," he said. "I had forgotten that women still exist who would blush. When I watch the colour coming into your face, I can hardly believe it is natural."

Utta put her hands up to her cheeks as if to hide the telltale crimson which flooded there at his words.

"You are talking nonsense," she said.

"Nonsense?" he queried. "When I tell you how lovely you are . . . the loveliest person I have seen for a very long time . . ."

She was suddenly very still. For a moment her eyes were held by his—and then she looked away again.

"I don't think you ought to say such things to me," she said very softly, hardly above a whisper.

"Why not?"

"Grandfather would not . . ."

"Oh, bother your grandparents," Hugo interposed.

"Haven't you a thought or any feeling apart from them? Forget them for a moment or two. Remember that you have a life of your own. They are old; you are young and very shortly the world will be at your feet. I have a feeling—I may be wrong—that I am the first man who has ever told you that you are beautiful. So listen to me, because in a year's time you will get tired of hearing it, but today it will seem new and perhaps a little exciting."

He put out his hand as he spoke to touch her fingers. They were trembling he found, almost as a bird might flutter and tremble beneath the hand of its captor.

"You are lovely, Utta."

There was a sudden deep note in his voice which seemed to throb through the air between them. Her fingers clung to his; her breath came quickly from between her parted lips; her breasts beneath the tight satin bodice moved a little—and then she lifted her face towards him and the glory in her eyes was almost dazzling.

They stood spellbound, looking at one another, forgetting the world around them, the noise of the crowd. They might have been alone on top of one of the mountains. For a moment it seemed as if even their heartbeats were stilled—before the spell was broken.

"You are next, Utta."

It was Ernst who spoke. They had not heard or seen him approach. Now, two faces were turned towards him.

"Are you all right?"

There was a sudden consternation in his voice, for it seemed to him that Utta looked strange. She released Hugo's hand.

"I am going to win," she said.

As she spoke she took off her coat and laid it in Ernst's arms. Then, without a backward glance at Hugo or Ernst, she stepped on to the ice and moved forward to where, as a competitor, she must make her entrance.

The two men stood in silence, watching her. There were cries and cheers for the girl from Zurich; then the orchestra struck up the music which Ernst had chosen for Utta's performance.

104

It was something very different from what had been played before. Soft, rippling notes like the trickling of a stream over the mountain rocks in spring preluded the beginning of a melody which instinctively made one think of the forests and the birds who lived in them.

And then on to the ice came a little figure in turquoise blue—arms outstretched, moving effortlessly and yet with a grace and rhythm which made the crowd, a little bored by now with so many competitors, straighten themselves and instinctively take notice.

It was almost possible to hear the hush come over the spectators. When she leapt in the air, there was a sudden outburst of clapping. But almost immediately it died away into that intent, almost breathless silence which comes when a crowd of people is concentrating on one particular object.

It seemed to Hugo, watching, as though her programme was incredibly short. All the time he had the feeling that she had not got skates on her feet, but wings. She seemed to move almost above the ice instead of on it and, as he thought before, when she sprang in the air she was like a bird in flight.

The music rose to a crescendo as, combining spins and double jumps in quick succession, Utta finished as she had begun, slipping gracefully from the ice so that one could hardly believe that her performance was over.

There was a sudden gasp and then the applause burst out—a thousand hands being clapped and voices from all sides of the rink shouting and cheering.

"Bravo! Bravo!"

It was the noise of this which seemed to wake Ernst from his reverie. Hastily he rushed to where Utta was standing, an expression of surprise on her face as though she had suddenly become aware that the people were applauding her.

"Take a bow," he commanded.

For a moment he wondered if she had heard and then she went on to the ice, for the first time looking shy; for the first time moving without that inspired beauty which had so captured the audience. She bowed and then came hurrying back to Ernst.

"Was I all right? Was I?"

"You were perfect."

She seemed pale for a moment, as if she had been afraid of his verdict. Then, as he wrapped her coat over her shoulders, she looked to where Hugo was waiting. The colour came back into her face as a moment later he stood beside her.

"You were wonderful!" he said. "I told you you would be."

She gave a little laugh of enchanted happiness.

"Now we will all go and have a drink," he went on.

They found some comfortable seats on the terrace of the hotel from which they could still watch the competitors, while a waiter hurried to ask Hugo's requirements.

"We must have a bottle of champagne," he said to Ernst. "This is a great moment."

"Great indeed, my lord," Ernst replied. "I was not afraid. I was sure of my own judgment. At the same time, one never knows in competitions, and the first time in front of an audience is an ordeal for anyone, especially someone like Utta."

"Why me especially?" she enquired.

"Because you are very sensitive. You are an artiste, my dear, and all artistes have their moods; they feel things more intensely than other people. But just now I knew that you were more than an artiste, you are a genius—for it is genius that people recognise not with applause but with silence."

"Oh, Ernst, don't talk like that, you make me want to cry," Utta whispered, and Hugo saw there were, indeed, tears in her eyes, making them look like gentians soaked in the rain.

Impulsively he put out his hand and laid it over hers.

"There must be no tears today," he commanded.

"No, of course not," she answered. "But happy tears don't count, do they?"

"Not when they make you look so adorable," he answered.

She flushed at that and slipped her hand away from him. The waiter brought the champagne at that moment

106

and by the time Hugo was able to look at her again the tears had gone.

He raised his glass.

"To Utta, the new Swiss Champion—and in a few days Champion of the World."

"You are asking too much," Utta said. "Besides, we haven't heard the result."

"Do we really have to have it in writing?" Ernst enquired, making a gesture with his hand towards the rink where a new competitor had slipped and fallen while doing an intricate spin.

"If they don't declare you the winner, I shall make a public announcement to the Press," Hugo said, laughing.

Utta gave a little exclamation.

"If I am declared the winner, Grandfather will read it in Davos tomorrow."

"What if he does?" Ernst asked. "It is too late now. I had thought of that and I knew that it would not matter. If you are the Swiss Champion, even Nicolaus Kindschi is not strong enough to defy public opinion and make you withdraw from the International Championships."

"I am not sure. Grandfather is very determined."

"And you must be determined too," Ernst said. "Listen, Utta. I have not spoken of this before for fear of upsetting you. But you are eighteen; most girls of your age are out earning their own living. Your grandfather cannot prevent you from entering the competition if you want to. He has brought you up and you love him; but this is a modern world and children no longer obey their parents, or their grandparents, as they used to do. If he is difficult, which somehow I feel he won't be, you must be brave, my dear, and tell him that you intend to lead your own life."

"I don't think I want to do that," Utta answered. "Oh, Ernst, you know how much I love Grandfather and *Grand'mère*. They are both very wonderful people; I would not wish to hurt them."

"I know your feelings; I know what a good child you have been—but that is not the point," Ernst replied. "You have a duty not to hide your talents, not to keep them from the world, which has need, always, of the best."

"That is true," Hugo added. "If you were a mediocre performer, then it would not matter whether you remained in seclusion or struggled to work your way to the top. But you are at the top. It is only right that you should not be selfish and keep such a gift to yourself."

Utta looked from one to the other with a tremulous smile.

"It all sounds wonderful when you say it, but when I get home—what then? *Grand'mère* will understand, but Grandfather . . ."

"I think I had better talk to your grandfather," Hugo said. "Perhaps he would listen to me."

"No, no! You can't do that," Utta cried impulsively.

"Why not?"

"Because I promised *Grand'mère* . . ." She stopped suddenly.

"Well, go on," Hugo prompted.

"I promised *Grand'mère* that I wouldn't meet you again," Utta said. "There, I didn't mean to tell you—it sort of came out."

"Why did you promise that?" Hugo enquired.

"I do not know. She didn't tell me why, but that was why Ernst and I couldn't come to breakfast. *Grand'-mère* was very insistent."

"I wonder what has upset her?" Hugo said reflectively. "Do you think, Ernst, my reputation has preceded me?"

Ernst shrugged his shoulders.

"I cannot understand, my lord," he replied. "Madame Kindschi is usually very understanding. Perhaps she does not wish Utta to meet people outside their own world. After all, they have never mixed with their neighbours and they have no contact whatsoever with visitors."

"But Utta is young; they cannot keep her shut up as though she were a nun in a convent."

Ernst Zippert made a gesture with his hands.

"You must talk to Nicolaus Kindschi," he said, "not to me. I am on your side."

"It is fantastic!" Hugo ejaculated. "And you, Utta. Don't you want to go out and meet people and go to dances—do all the things girls of your age do?"

"I don't know," Utta answered. "I have been very happy. I have had my lessons; I have been able to ski. In the summer I go for long walks in the woods. I haven't wanted anything else—except to skate. *Grand'-mère* knew about that, even though we kept it a secret from Grandfather."

"And yet she disapproves of me," Hugo said.

"She didn't say she disapproved," Utta corrected. "She only said that I was not to see you again . . . that she had a reason for asking this of me."

"I am afraid it must be my reputation," Hugo sighed. "You see, Utta, I have always enjoyed life; and if people enjoy themselves, there are always a lot of busy-bodies who make it their business to look down their noses and say how disgraceful it all is."

"Yes, I can understand that," Utta answered. "Even in villages there are those who disapprove of everything that other people do. They peep behind curtains and whisper to their friends. I expect it is just the same wherever one goes."

"Exactly," Hugo said. "And now I have got a good idea. I shall come and call on your grandmother. She will see me and she will see how harmless I am, and then we can be friends—not only in secret but openly."

"That would be wonderful," Utta replied. "But perhaps *Grand'mère* will be annoyed if you come to call."

"I don't think so," Hugo answered. "And now that it is settled let me give you some more champagne."

As he filled up the glasses, Ernst asked:

"Where is Mrs. Munton today? She sounded very enthusiastic about the competition. I expected her to be here."

"I think she had made other arrangements," Hugo replied a little evasively.

He was not prepared to explain to Ernst and to Utta that he had taken the precaution of telling Carole the night before that he was going over to see his friends again.

"I hope to be back fairly early," he said, "but don't wait any meals for me. Why don't you three go up and lunch at the Corvelia Club? It's wonderful up there in the sunshine."

His suggestion had been hailed by the Bakers with enthusiasm, and somewhat reluctantly Carole had allowed herself to be persuaded into going too. She forgot that it was the Swiss Championships, as Hugo had intended. He knew that she was thinking of the International ones two days later; and so she had gone off with the Bakers while Hugo, annoyed at having to prevaricate and lie, had gone down to the Palace to look for Utta.

He had felt resentful because he could not be open about it, but now he was glad that he had taken so much trouble. The child was entrancing, and he thought as he watched her that her youth was like a spring flower coming into bloom after the barren desolateness of the winter.

Suddenly Ernst jumped to his feet.

"Fool that I am!" he said. "I have thought of something."

He turned and almost ran from the terrace down on to the rink.

"What is the matter?" Utta asked.

"I have no idea," Hugo replied.

They watched him wend his way through the crowd, almost pushing people out of his way, to where a man sat at the table checking the competitors. They saw Ernst talking to him and then they turned to each other with a smile.

"It can't be anything so very serious," Hugo said. "But he sprang up as if he had been stung."

"Dear Ernst—he has been so very kind to me," Utta smiled. "He has given me so much happiness this year."

"He was a great skater," Hugo told her. "I remember watching him and thinking, as I thought about you, that he was better than anyone I had ever seen before."

"You are so kind," she answered. "I think really it must have been your little charm that brought me such good luck."

110

She touched the front of her bodice as she spoke.

"Is it quite safe?" Hugo asked.

"Absolutely," she answered.

She pressed her left hand against her breast in reassurance. It was then he saw that she wore on her little finger a small, gold signet ring.

"Is that the lucky ring?" he asked.

She looked down.

"Oh, I forgot to take it off!" she exclaimed. "What a good thing Ernst didn't notice."

"He was so excited at your performance that he wouldn't have noticed if you had worn a tiara and several ropes of pearls," Hugo answered.

She laughed at that but drew the ring carefully from her finger.

"Let me look at your mascot," Hugo asked. "Is it a signet ring?"

"It is," she answered. "It was my mother's; it was given to her by my father. It was the only engagement ring she had, because they were married secretly."

"Let me look."

She put the ring into his hand and Hugo looked down at it. Then from what had been a casual, amused glance, he stared at it intently, lifting up the ring to hold it closer to his eyes.

"Where did you get this?" he asked.

"I have just told you," Utta replied. "It was my mother's."

"You say it was given her by your father?"

"Yes. I have just told you, he . . ."

They were interrupted by Ernst returning, his face wreathed in smiles.

"Everything is perfect," he announced as he sat down at the table. "I thought I had made a mistake, but no—everything is settled. You need not worry any more."

"What do you mean?" Utta asked.

"You have been worrying about your grandfather seeing the papers. Fools that we were! I had forgotten for a moment that I had entered you under only one name. I wished to keep everything secret, so when they first asked me who you were I just said my entry was called 'Utta'. Then I forgot all about it, and when the secretary asked me today if the entry was to stand as it had been, I said 'yes', forgetting that it was only 'Utta' I put down.

"But now, you understand, it is providential. I have told him that under no circumstances is anyone, including the Press, to know your other name. When you win, they will announce that 'Miss Utta of St. Moritz is the winner'. Your grandfather is not interested in ice skating; he will not scan the photographs of the competitors very closely. If he reads the names of those who have won, 'Utta' will mean nothing to him. We are safe, little one—safe for another week until he returns!"

"Oh, Ernst, how wonderful! And the Press—won't they be curious?"

"We will tell them that your name is 'Utta'. It is the truth. Lots of skaters have only one name—what about Belita? No one ever asks for any more; Belita is enough."

"And Utta will be enough too!" Utta exclaimed. "Oh, Ernst, you are clever."

"That is what I think," Ernst said complacently.

Hugo was still staring at the ring. He had taken no part in the conversation and had not even looked up at Ernst's arrival.

Utta turned towards him a little uneasily.

"May I have my ring, please?" she asked.

He did not give it to her. Instead he said:

"Do you know the crest engraved here?"

"Yes, of course. It was my father's."

"Will you tell me your father's name?"

Utta looked down for a moment.

"I am sorry," she said, "but that is rather an awkward question. You see, everyone here calls me Kindschi because that is the name of my grandfather and grandmother. Many years ago, when I was only a little girl, they told me about my father. They said that as long as I lived with them it would be easier for everyone if I used their name. It is not exactly secret, but no one has ever asked me for it before."

"I am asking you now."

112

"When I went to school I was called Utta Kindschi; my teachers spoke of me in the same way and so do the people in the village."

"And your real name?"

"Are you really so interested?" Utta asked.

"Very!"

She knit her forehead together.

"Because of the ring?"

"Yes, if you like, because of the ring."

"I think perhaps you have guessed," Utta said, "that my father was an Englishman."

"English?" It was Ernst who interrupted now. "I always thought you were Swiss."

"Yes, of course, because I live with my grandparents and I was born in Switzerland. But actually my father was English."

"What was your father's name?" Hugo enquired.

"Andrew Graye," Utta answered.

Hugo looked down at the ring and back at Utta.

"Andrew Graye was my cousin," he said coldly, "and as far as we know he was never married."

8

There was a long silence.

The blood receded from Utta's face, leaving her strangely pale. Then Hugo put the ring down on the table in front of her and said:

"That was my cousin's ring. The crest is the same as mine. I should like to meet your grandfather and grandmother."

"No, no! You can't do that."

The words came impulsively.

Hugo did not look at her.

"I am afraid I must insist on making their acquaintance," he said a little stiffly.

For a moment Utta did not reply and then, with a dignity that he had not expected, she answered:

"Very well. I am afraid my grandfather is away. My grandmother is at home; shall I take you to her?"

"What's all this about?" Ernst suddenly interposed, looking bewildered. "You can't go away, Utta. Look here, my lord, she has to be present at the finals."

Hugo looked down at the programme which was lying on the table.

"There are a great many more entrants," he said briefly. "You won't hear the results until later in the afternoon; we will be back by then."

"Yes, of course, I promise," Utta said. She put out her hand and laid it on Ernst's arm. "I am sorry, Ernst; but it is right he should see *Grand'mère.*"

There was something in her face which stilled Ernst's objections. He stood to watch them walk away from him. Utta, with her small head held high, walked swiftly from the rink while Hugo followed, limping because of his bad leg, yet managing with the aid of a stick to keep up with her.

Hugo hired a taxi, Utta gave the man the address and they sat side by side on the back seat. The taxi-man tucked a rug round their knees and they were off.

For some minutes they drove in silence and then Hugo said, a little wryly:

"You must forgive me if I have hurt your feelings."

"It doesn't matter what I feel," Utta replied quietly; "but if, indeed, my father was your cousin, then it is right for you to see my grandmother. She will explain to you anything you wish to know."

"But you must have known he was my cousin," Hugo said.

She turned towards him then, and he saw the astonishment and surprise in her eyes.

"But how should I know?" she asked.

"The name," he answered. "Graye is, of course, the name of my family; Roxburton is only the title."

"I am afraid I don't understand," she said. "I thought you were called Roxburton; I had no idea you had any other name."

Her voice was so sincere that despite the ugly suspicions which would not be entirely dispersed, Hugo found himself believing her.

"What is the game?" he wondered. He could not help remembering how he had found it hard to credit Utta's stories of her grandfather's strictness, her apparent innocence and lack of experience where men and for that matter other people were concerned. He had thought at the time that no girl in the twentieth century could live so divorced from reality, and now his doubts came back a thousandfold.

What was behind all this? Andrew's ring worn by a girl who said she was his daughter and yet whose whole background pointed to her being Swiss.

They had driven on for some way before Hugo spoke again; then he said:

"How old are you?"

"I am eighteen."

"And, of course, you cannot remember your father?"

"No."

The monosyllable was repressive and he realised that she had no intention of being communicative. He respected the pride which made her hold herself stiffly.

She turned her face away from him to look out of the window, so that he could see her profile—the exquisite delicacy of her features, the tiny straight nose, the fullness of her soft lips, the little pointed chin above the rounded white column of her throat.

She was lovely, and yet it was hard to trace any resemblance to Andrew. It was true he had been fair. Bigboned and by no means classically handsome, he had an attraction for everyone who knew him. He was so gay, wild and uninhibited. But that this should be his daughter seemed not only incredible, but extremely unlikely.

"There is some mistake," Hugo told himself, and instantly the hard suspicions which he could not dismiss came rushing back into his mind.

Andrew had been only twenty-two when he was killed. That he should have had a wife and kept it secret so that no one should have learned about it all these years was not feasible.

115

The taxi turned up a twisting, slippery road and was having difficulty climbing the hill.

"I think perhaps we had better walk," Utta remarked, "otherwise he will get stuck."

Hugo bent forward and tapped on the dividing glass.

"We will get out here," he said.

The taxi-man was only too pleased to bring his car to a standstill. Hugo opened the door and climbed down on to the slippery road. He put out his hand to help Utta, but she avoided it and slipped past him.

Slowly, side by side, they walked perhaps fifty yards and came to a wrought-iron gateway. A stone path rising in a series of steps led the way to the house, which stood high above the road.

It was a pretty house, Hugo noted, but there was nothing either pretentious or prosperous about it. It was the type of Swiss chalet that one saw everywhere in Switzerland.

Utta opened the door and walked into the small hall.

"Grand'mère!" she called.

There was a note of urgency in her voice.

"I am here, *ma chérie*," came an answering cry, and Utta opened a door which led into the sitting-room.

"Will you come in?" she said to Hugo, and for the first time since they left the ice rink she looked him straight in the eyes.

He saw then that she was hating him. Her eyes seemed very dark; there was something deep and smouldering in them which made him feel suddenly ashamed and apologetic.

Impulsively he wanted to tell her that his suspicions were untrue; whatever he thought or imagined, he knew that she, at any rate, was not mixed up in it; but there was no time to say anything. She had moved into the sitting-room and he was obliged to follow her.

For a moment he had only an impression of sunlight and flowers, then he saw that sitting in an armchair was a white-haired old lady. It was possible to see at a glance Utta's likeness to her grandmother, but Hugo saw other things as well.

The nobility of her face bespoke not only good

116

breeding but fineness of character. The sweetness of her smile suggested a charming personality.

And then, as Madame Kindschi saw who was with her grandchild, her expression changed from one of loving affection to what appeared to be tragedy. She looked at Hugo and then back again to Utta before she put out her hands towards her grandchild.

"Lord Roxburton wanted to see you, *Grand'mère*," Utta said. "I had to bring him."

"Yes, dear," Madame Kindschi replied.

She put out her hand towards Hugo, who took it and, surprising even himself, raised it to his lips.

"Utta has spoken about you," Madame Kindschi said quietly. "You wished to see me?"

He nodded.

"Yes, please—alone."

"But I want to stay," Utta expostulated. "Please, *Grand'mère,* it is only right that I . . ."

"I think, darling, it would be better if I saw Lord Roxburton alone," Madame Kindschi said firmly. "But first tell me, were you successful?"

"I think so, *Grand'mère;* Ernst was pleased."

"She has undoubtedly won the Swiss Championship," Hugo said.

"I do not know whether to be glad or sorry," Madame Kindschi replied. "Go now, Utta. There is some milk waiting for you in the dining-room."

"Very well, *Grand'mère.*"

Hugo could not help but admire the obedient way she went from the room, closing the door softly behind her. He watched her go and then turned to look at Madame Kindschi.

"Won't you sit down?"

She indicated a chair opposite hers, with a gesture that was as graceful as one of Utta's on the rink.

"Thank you." He settled himself. "I expect you know why I have come."

"Would you like to explain?" she parried.

"Utta is wearing a ring today which she told me had belonged to her father."

"So that was how you found out!" Madame Kindschi remarked.

"I think you owe me an explanation," Hugo said. "You know, of course, I am now the head of the family?"

"Yes, I knew," Madame Kindschi replied. "When I heard that Utta had met you I knew that fate had been too strong for me. I suppose, if I had done the right thing, I should have come to see you and told you the truth—a truth which ought to have been told many years ago. But I hoped, stupidly I suppose, that it was just a chance encounter—that you would go away and that Utta would obey my instructions not to see you again."

"And why did you give such instructions?" Hugo enquired.

"Because," Madame Kindschi replied, "I prayed that my husband would be dead before I must reveal to the Graye family the existence of Andrew's daughter."

Hugo hesitated for a moment and then he said the same words he had said to Utta.

"As far as we know Andrew never married."

Madame Kindschi gave him a little sad smile.

"I thought that might be your attitude," she said.

She rose from her chair and crossed the room to a bureau which stood in the light from the window. From a small drawer she drew out a paper and taking it across the room handed it to Hugo. He read it carefully.

"I see," he said at length, "that Andrew married your daughter on the 6th January, 1936."

"Yes, that is so," Madame Kindschi replied.

"Three weeks before he was killed," Hugo remarked.

Madame Kindschi nodded, then she gave a little sigh that was half a sob.

"I had better tell you the story from the beginning. I ran away to marry my husband. We have been happy, happier than perhaps I deserved to be. Never for one moment have I regretted it. My husband, too, has been happier, I think, than any man of his acquaintance—and yet men are funny creatures. Because he found his own happiness in such a manner, he was determined that his daughter should never go through the anxiety and terrors which we thought were well worth while.

"He brought her up very strictly. She was called Marguerite, after me, and she had a little, perhaps, of my fire and my adventurous spirit. Sometimes I have accused my husband of being too strict, but always he has been master in his own house; and though I can often influence him, I can never oppose him in anything about which he makes up his mind.

"How Marguerite met Andrew Graye I do not know, but I imagine it was on the mountainside, skiing, or perhaps in a party with other young people. For Andrew loved Switzerland, as I expect you know. He came out for two or three years before his death."

"Yes, I remember that," Hugo interposed.

"He, of course, spent most of his time mountaineering," Madame Kindschi went on, "and we all used to laugh about the mad young Englishman who wanted to attempt peaks that no one else had ever climbed, or take routes which were judged too dangerous to be passable.

"Marguerite brought him to the house because he was anxious to meet my husband. We were living then, I must explain, at the foot of the Matterhorn, and Andrew had bought a little chalet not far away. He wanted to own a piece of Switzerland, he told us. He loved this country. I think it was his genuine love for the mountains which made my husband fond of him.

"We saw a lot of him, one way or another. Then, of course, his holiday would come to an end and he would disappear for six months at a time. He never wrote, there was no reason why he should, but he would turn up smiling and be as impetuous and daring as ever before and take up our friendship just where he left it off.

"I must have been very blind or very stupid, but I never realised that Marguerite was falling in love with him. I suppose, rather like my husband, I thought of her as such a child that I did not realise she had a woman's heart and a woman's feelings.

"The last year that he came I was only there for perhaps a week after his arrival. My mother, whom I had not seen since I married, became desperately ill, and my father sank his pride and asked me to come home because she was dying. I went to Paris expecting to stay a few weeks—but in actual fact I was away for nearly seven months.

"My mother lingered on and we all expected every day to be her last. The doctors had given up; there was nothing they could do except relieve the pain she was suffering—and yet she did not die.

"I was torn between my love for a mother whose company I had missed more than I had ever dared admit myself and my love for my husband and my child.

"My husband told me not to hurry back; he understood, and in one of his letters he told me that Andrew Graye had been killed. He had insisted on climbing against the advice of all the more experienced guides. He had gone out in impossible weather, under impossible conditions, and he had not come back.

"My husband is not a very fulsome correspondent; his letters are full of brief statements and nothing more.

"In my anxiety and sorrow over my mother's suffering and subsequent death I must admit I forgot Andrew Graye.

"When I came back home after the funeral, it was summer. I remember feeling ecstatically excited at the thought of seeing my husband and my daughter again. I arrived late in the evening.

"My husband met me at the station and then, when we got back to the house and he went to put away the car, I expected to see Marguerite on the doorstep—instead she was in the sitting-room. It was not very light in there. I hurried in, kissed her and then I said:

" 'Let me look at you. It seems so long that I have been away that I have forgotten what you look like. Are you well? Are you happy? Oh, darling, have you missed me?' "

"I held her at arm's length; and then I saw what seemed to me a strange expression on her face.

" 'What is the matter, darling?' I asked. 'You don't look well.'

" 'It is nothing, Mother, I will tell you later,' she said.

"I went to my room to take off my travelling things. I had dined on the train, but Marguerite disappeared to the kitchen to make me some coffee and a few sandwiches. She came back with them and then, as I looked at her in the light, I saw that something was really wrong.

She had always been small, beautifully made and very slender. She had a figure like mine. Now she was changed. It was then that a terrible suspicion laid hold of me. I could hardly believe it, hardly credit my own thoughts. I stood staring at her, and then the blood flared up in her face and she turned towards me.

" 'Mother . . .' she began.

"Then in my terror I lost my temper. I raged at her. I asked her what she had been doing, what had been happening while I was away. I told her to tell me who had done this thing to her and swore that I would kill the man if I ever laid hands on him.

"She said nothing. Her shame and her confusion seemed to me to proclaim her guilt without words. Finally I said:

" 'Get out of my sight! In the morning we will decide what is to be done about this. Now I only know that you have killed my love and everything I ever felt about you.' "

Madame Kindschi's voice faltered and for a moment she put her hands up to her face.

Hugo bent forward.

"Please don't distress yourself," he said.

"It is a long time ago," Madame Kindschi answered.

She took a little white handkerchief from her pocket and wiped her eyes.

"It has worried me, those things that I said in my horror and indignation. I was so stupid, so untrusting. I can never forgive myself—never."

"But it was all right," Hugo said. "She had married Andrew."

"Yes, she had married Andrew," Madame Kindschi agreed. "But I did not know it at the time, and those words of bitterness and injustice were the last I ever spoke to Marguerite."

"The last?"

"Yes, the last. When morning came, she was gone. There was a little note pinned on her pillow; it said, 'I am going away, Mummy. I am sorry to have upset you so much. I cannot speak of him yet.' "

"Was that all?" Hugo enquired.

"That was all," Madame Kindschi said. "It did little to make me feel happier or kinder. I told my husband and he was as horrified as I was, only at first he did not believe me. Being a man, he had not noticed that Marguerite had altered. She did not seem very well, he thought, and stayed much more in the house than usual.

"But he had been busy, out all day, often spending three or four nights on the mountain. At that time he was not only the most popular guide on the Matterhorn, but chief of all the guides who worked from the village.

"I shall never forget how miserable and upset we were those long, empty summer evenings when the house seemed strangely quiet without our only child.

After a week, when we were beginning to get anxious as to what had happened to her, I had a letter from Marguerite's old nurse, who lived near Lausanne. Marguerite was with her, she said. She had arrived not feeling very well, but the change seemed to be doing her good and we were not to worry.

" 'We must go down and fetch her back,' my husband said. But I delayed, dreading the moment when I must see Marguerite again, when I must ask her for an explanation, when I must demand that she tell me the name of the man who had done this terrible thing to her.

"Neither of us for one moment suspected Andrew. I do not know why. Perhaps, like my parents, we were foolishly blind, or perhaps, because he had always seemed such a boy, we had never connected him with anything so responsible as marriage or a family.

"Three weeks went by and then finally I made up my

mind. 'I will go tomorrow,' I told my husband. But tomorrow was too late!" Madame Kindschi raised her handkerchief to her eyes. "The telegram came," she went on, "when I was actually packing. Marguerite had died, but the child, born prematurely, was alive.

"I went down to Lausanne. It was too late for me to tell my daughter that I loved her, that nothing she could do could ever really destroy the love and trust I had in her.

"I wanted to hate the baby which had been the cause of all this suffering, but when I saw it I knew it was my own daughter come back to me again. It was tiny, but it was big enough to fill a little of my empty, aching heart."

Madame Kindschi gave a little smile.

"It was almost like having another baby of my own after so many years when I had longed for children and not been able to have them. They had not expected the child to live, but Marguerite's old Nanny told me that it had fought for life, despite the fact that the doctor had christened it, thinking it would die. He had called it Utta, the first name that came into his head, and Utta she remained, for I would not have it changed, thinking it might be unlucky.

"I buried my little Marguerite; then my husband and I went back to our home, taking with us Nanny and the baby. The child seemed to make all the difference to the emptiness and silence which I had dreaded, knowing that Marguerite's voice would never be heard again singing in the kitchen, or her light, eager footsteps running up and down the stairs. Utta came to take her place and Utta, too, took her place in our hearts.

"She must have been six months old and the light and delight of our lives before, blind that we were, we learned the truth. We had never spoken since Marguerite's death of the man who we imagined had betrayed and deserted her. I never discussed it with my husband, but I knew the bitterness of it had eaten deep into his soul.

"But then one day, when Nanny was bathing little Utta and I was sitting watching her, she said:

123

" 'She is going to have nice strong legs. Marguerite said that if it was a boy he must be strong and tall like his father.'

"I was silent for a moment, from sheer surprise that Nanny should know what I had never known, and then I said:

" 'Did Marguerite tell you the name of Utta's father?'

"Nanny looked up in surprise.

" 'Yes, of course,' she said. 'She talked of him all the time, poor, sweet child. She had bottled it up inside herself for so long that it burst out like the ice breaking in the spring. If you had been at home, it would have been different; but she had always been a little afraid of the master and so she had bottled up her grief for so long that it was beginning to poison her.'

" 'Her grief?' I repeated stupidly. 'Because he had left her?'

" 'Aye, because he had left her,' Nanny replied, misunderstanding my words. 'But, as I said to her, "those whom the gods love die young." He will be happy, child, wherever he has gone, and he will be looking after you and your baby, you can be sure of that.'

" 'He is dead then?' I said. 'I had not realised that.'

"Nanny lifted Utta out of her bath and sat her on her knee, and then she looked at me over the child's head.

" 'Are you trying to tell me, ma'am,' she asked, 'that you don't know the name of Marguerite's husband?'

" 'Husband?' I cried. 'If he had married her, I shouldn't be asking the question.'

" 'God in his Heaven have mercy on you!' Nanny exclaimed. 'I had no idea that you didn't know. She told me that she had not said anything to her father and that you were angry with her and that was why she had gone away. She didn't tell me what wicked things you were thinking, things that no woman should believe of a child as sweet and true as Marguerite.'

"I burst into tears at that and then Nanny told me the truth.

"Marguerite had been married secretly to Andrew Graye. She had had, she said, a kind of premonition

124

that he might be killed. They were wildly and passionately in love with each other and he had wanted to go at once to her father and tell him the truth.

"Marguerite knew that my husband would never listen to any talk of marriage or consent to an engagement until she was of age. Because I had been so young when I ran away with him, he had said that all women should wait until they knew their own minds.

" 'We have been lucky,' he would say in his quiet solemn way. 'Things might have been very different. You might have been unhappy and then you would have thrown over everything for a man who was unworthy of you.'

"Marguerite knew that she had no hope of getting her own way where her father was concerned, and I was in Paris. It would have been Andrew, of course, who had persuaded her into a secret marriage. It was the sort of thing he would have most enjoyed—the danger and excitement of it would have made it seem all the more attractive."

"That's true," Hugo agreed. "It would have been just like Andrew to want to do something that was forbidden."

"He was, of course, according to Swiss law, domiciled in this country," Madame Kindschi continued. "The only difficulty they had to encounter was the fact that Marguerite was not of age and therefore the permission of her parents or guardians would have to be obtained.

"Even that was not an insurmountable difficulty where Andrew was concerned." She gave a little smile. "In my desk I have another document—Marguerite's birth certificate, on which the date has been changed very skilfully and quite deceptively if you look at it. They were married at Berne, as you see, on the 6th of January. It was only a few hours' journey and then they came home as though nothing had happened.

"I suppose they must have met at Andrew's house. Perhaps, when Nicolaus was away, he came to ours. I do not know. I can only guess that they found great happiness together in those stolen hours, when love must have been very sweet because they had fought so hard for what they both wanted.

"And then Andrew was killed. I can't guess even now to what dark depths of despair my daughter sank when she heard the news. My husband was not at home at the time. When he returned, she was, to all intents and purposes, quite composed, although he felt that she was upset. I can only imagine the hell she went through, to be unable to speak of her misery, knowing she was widowed and then finding that she was about to bear his child.

"It was all these things which made her run away when, in my unthinking cruelty, I condemned her for a crime she had never committed. Even now I cannot bear to think of what I said."

"You must not reproach yourself," Hugo said. "It is perhaps because we know so much of the world that we find it easier to believe the worst than the best."

Madame Kindschi looked up at him at that.

"You, too?" she said.

"Yes! I thought that when I saw Andrew's ring and Utta told me it belonged to her father."

"It is what most people would think, I am afraid," she said.

"But that still does not explain," Hugo went on, "why you never let Andrew's family know. He was a very rich man, do you realise that?"

"It didn't matter what he was," Madame Kindschi answered. "Even when my husband knew the truth, he was not prepared to forgive Andrew for the secrecy and the underhanded way in which he had behaved. It was as if he had always been afraid that something like this must happen; and when it did, he blamed not Marguerite, but himself, for not having taken greater care of her. And just as he had been strict to the point of real severity with his own daughter, so he is just the same with Utta."

"She is still Andrew's child," Hugo said gently.

"Yes, I know. I knew that it was right that we should let Andrew's relations know, but having not known the truth for six months I took another six to think about it.

In 1938 came the Munich crisis—I told myself that there might be war and that Utta would be safer with us. Every rumour, every crisis, every difficult international event—and there were many of them in the next year—made me more convinced than ever that Utta was safer with us.

"And then in 1939 war came. Utta was only two-and-a-half at the time. I decided that there was no reason for me to worry my conscience about Andrew's relatives until we saw whether England survived or not; and when she did, I had begun to think that Utta was ours—completely and absolutely.

"In 1945 Utta was nine. She was happy with her lessons, happy, I thought, living the quiet life that my husband and I had always lived. He was ready to retire and we moved here to St. Moritz because he had been born not far from this very house."

"And what about Utta?" Hugo asked.

"What about her?" Madame Kindschi enquired.

"Had you no thought for her? Of the life she was missing? Of the position which should be hers by right? Andrew was not only a rich man, his father had an important position in England, so Utta was entitled to come out with girls of her own age and her own class, to go to parties to meet people, to do all those things which the ordinary Society girl takes as her right."

"I know," Madame Kindschi answered. "I was brought up in just that sort of existence, and yet I was far happier married to my husband than I would ever have been had I remained with those whom you might describe as my own class."

"You were married," Hugo said briefly.

"Yes, that is true," she answered. "But I will be frank with you, Lord Roxburton. I have sometimes worried that Utta might be missing something, and yet I have thought that perhaps my husband was right. Here there are no problems, no difficulties. It is a simple life, but a happy one."

"I don't think that is quite true," Hugo said. "You have already had your problems, otherwise Utta would not today be the winner of the Swiss Amateur Championships."

"That is true. I had forgotten," Madame Kindschi agreed. "I have got to face it that Utta has been growing restless. It is a restricted life, but in disobeying my husband and letting her do what she wished to do I have reaped my own punishment. She has met you."

"That was not your fault," Hugo said. "She rescued me first."

"Yes, I remember," Madame Kindschi said. "But if she had not gone skating, you might never have seen her again. You would have forgotten her and you would never have learned that Utta was Andrew Graye's daughter."

"Perhaps that is true, but fate has a habit of creating coincidences in the most unlikely places," Hugo said. "Anyway, now it is too late. Now we have got to decide what must be done."

"Done?" Madame Kindschi echoed, her hands going flutteringly towards her heart.

"Utta must come to England," Hugo said. "You must see that. Her grandfather and her grandmother are dead, but my grandmother, who is her great-aunt, is alive, and there are innumerable cousins who will, I am sure, be very anxious to make her acquaintance."

Madame Kindschi put her hands to her eyes.

"I can't think what my husband will say," she murmured.

"I think he will accept the inevitable," Hugo replied. "I think, too, we shall find that a great deal of my uncle's fortune should come to Utta. Even if he has not left a provision for such a contingency in his Will, and I think it is more than likely that he has, I shall see, personally, that she is a wealthy woman."

"I suppose I should thank you for that," Madame Kindschi said; "and yet, instead, I find myself hating you: I gave up money and position to find happiness; I am afraid that money and position may take Utta's from her."

"Don't you think that is a personal thing that she must find out for herself?" Hugo asked.

His voice was very gentle as he spoke and suddenly Madame Kindschi got to her feet and held out her hands towards him.

"I want to hate you and I can't," she said. "There is something about you which makes me think of the men I knew in my youth. Perhaps you are right. Utta is not really fitted to the life into which we have forced her. I have often worried as to whom she will marry."

"She will have plenty of choice in England," Hugo replied.

"Yes, I can understand that. But before we go so fast I shall have to consult my husband and, of course, Utta herself." Madame Kindschi hesitated a moment.

"May I ask one thing of you, Lord Roxburton?"

"But of course, anything," Hugo answered.

"Will you never let Utta know of the suspicions I had as to her legitimacy? Of the unkindness I showed her mother? I have told her simply who her father was and that he and her mother were married secretly. She understands that that is why she must never mention her father's name in front of my husband. We have often talked of him and I have told her all I can remember of Andrew and taught her to be proud of him."

"That was kind of you," Hugo said.

"Was I likely to be anything else?" Madame Kindschi asked sharply. "Besides, I was fond of Andrew. He was a nice boy, but I should have thought too wild to make any girl happy."

"The Grayes are like that, I am afraid."

Madame Kindschi looked at him with a twinkle in her eye.

"And you?" she asked.

"But of course," he replied.

"I wonder," she pondered. "I think perhaps you are giving yourself an unnecessarily bad name."

"You are too kind, Madame," he laughed. "My friends can tell a very different story about me."

"Thank you, anyway, for listening to mine," she said.

He took her hand and raised it to his lips.

"I cannot think of anyone who would have been so frank with such grace, with such charm," he told her.

129

"Your husband must be a very exceptional man to have wooed you away from the world, and the loss is ours."

"It is a long time since I have heard such pretty speeches," Madame Kindschi answered. "And I thought it was only Frenchmen who were gallant."

"And, of course, the worst type of Englishman," Hugo smiled.

"You try to blacken yourself unnecessarily," Madame Kindschi replied.

"I think perhaps you had better call Utta." Hugo looked at his watch. "I must take her back to the rink. Poor Ernst will have a stroke if she isn't there for the finale."

"Has she really won?" Madame Kindschi enquired, as she went to the door.

"Undoubtedly! Unless the judges are blind or drunk they cannot fail to make her the Champion."

"Ernst will be very pleased," Madame Kindschi said.

She opened the door and called Utta. It was only a second before she came hurrying into the room. She looked from her grandmother to Hugo—her lips unsmiling, a sudden wariness in her expression which made her appear like a gazelle who had been disturbed unexpectedly. Madame Kindschi put out her hand.

"Ma petite," she said. "Lord Roxburton is your cousin."

"You are sure of that?" Utta asked, speaking to Hugo.

He recognised the subtlety of her rebuke.

"Quite, quite sure," he answered. "And let me say how glad I am to find you."

"Why?" Utta asked.

"Isn't that obvious?" he replied. "I have many cousins, but none so pretty, or for that matter so talented."

He was deliberately making light of the awkwardness which lay between them, and suddenly she knew that the gulf that had yawned so ominously was breached. There had been a cold tightness within her breast which melted now. It was just as if the ice of it was swept away by the sunshine of his smile. Impulsively she gave a little cry.

130

"I am glad—so glad!"

Hugo understood what she was trying to tell him.

"Yes, you are my cousin," he said quietly, "and now I am suggesting to your grandmother that you must come to England to meet your other relations."

"Are there a lot of them?"

He saw the touch of fear in her eyes.

"Quite a lot, but they are not very formidable. You needn't be afraid."

"May I go?" Utta turned to her grandmother.

"Do you want to, darling?"

"Yes, very much."

It was a blow to hear her say the words that she had so dreaded, and yet Madame Kindschi bore them bravely.

"Then it must be arranged," she said gently.

"And now we must go back to poor Ernst, otherwise he will be tearing out his hair in handfuls," Hugo said. "I promised I would take you back and I must keep my promise."

"Yes, of course, Ernst—I had forgotten," Utta said quietly.

He glanced at her sharply to see if she was pretending and realised that she was speaking the truth. There was something incredible about her, he thought, and wondered how many other girls he knew could have won a much prized championship and forgotten they must be there for the finale.

"I will bring Utta back after it is all over," he told Madame Kindschi, "and may she dine with me tonight at Suvretta House?"

"Oh, please, please, *Grand'mère,* say yes," Utta pleaded, as Madame Kindschi hesitated.

"Very well then."

"Oh, thank you!" Utta bent to kiss her grandmother then turned to Hugo and quite unselfconsciously slipped her hand into his.

"Hurry," she said. "Ernst will be worried and he has been so kind."

"I am coming," Hugo answered.

131

For the third time he raised Madame Kindschi's hand to his lips. She was trembling and for the first time he realised how much their interview, with the story she had had to tell, had upset her.

"Thank you for everything," he said quietly.

"Please bring Utta back safely." There was a significance in the conventional phrase that he did not fail to understand.

"I will take care of her," he promised. Then he was following Utta out into the sunshine, with Madame Kindschi standing on the steps, watching them go, with a smile on her lips that was a courageous effort.

The taxi was waiting and as soon as they were in it they set off back along the twisty road which led to St. Moritz.

"You were a long time talking to my grandmother," Utta said.

"A long time," Hugo answered. "But it was worth every minute of it because at the end I achieved the impossible."

"What do you mean?" she asked.

"I told you," he replied, watching her face, "that the next time I asked you to dinner you would say 'yes'."

9

Carole was worried. If she hadn't been so careful of her long crimson nails she would have bitten them; instead she tapped her teeth on their smooth, polished surface as she sat in her sitting-room, staring out with unseeing eyes at the panorama of snow and sunshine.

Since that day when Hugo went to watch the Swiss Championships instead of visiting his friend she had known that she was losing him, and she knew now that every hour that passed widened the gulf between them and made him less amenable to her wiles.

He was still charming to her in public but in private he made excuses to escape her passionate demands, and she realised that this new interest occupied his attention to the exclusion of all else.

Utta, Utta. How she loathed the name and how she hated the girl, with her fresh, springlike beauty and that strange air of untouched innocence which was harder to combat than anything Carole had ever met in her life before!

It seemed a most cruel perversity of fate that this girl, who was pretty enough to attract any man, should turn out to be a lost relation of Hugo.

"What can I do?" Carole asked herself the question.

It was almost a physical agony to feel so helpless and so impotent. She had counted on making herself indispensable to Hugo, on twining herself round him as she had twined herself around Dave, keeping him captive by sheer force of will-power and propinquity; and now she knew that she was nothing more to Hugo than another episode in his life. And yet she had been certain when they came out to Switzerland that he had intended to ask her to marry him. It was this girl who had come between them.

Carole got to her feet and walked across the room. She wanted to smash something, to beat her fists on the wall, to scream—anything to relieve the pent-up frustration of her feelings. And yet what good would it do?

"I love him! I love him!"

She said the words aloud and knew that for the first time in her life they were true. She did love Hugo; not better than she had ever loved anyone else, for she knew she had never been in love before.

Now her whole body ached with the intensity of her feelings, ached for the touch of him, for the feel of his hands, for his lips on hers.

She had wanted him originally because he had a title, because he stood for that inviolate respectability which perversely she had desired above all other things—but now she wanted him for himself.

"I would marry him if he hadn't got a penny, or a name for that matter," she told herself—and knew it was the truth. It was the man she wanted now, not the lord.

She had tried every method she knew in their moments of intimacy to coax from him the words she wanted to hear, but never, even in the most ecstatic moments of passion, had he as much as said that he loved her. His self-control was almost supernatural, she thought bitterly.

She knew that in contrast she was fast losing hers, yet what could she do?

She looked at herself in the mirror and felt that the rivalry of Utta was unfair. The frail fragility of the younger girl created the impression that she, Carole, was heavy and less attractive than she was in actual fact.

Carole was astute enough to know when she was on a losing wicket and she was well aware at this moment that she had to do something desperate or face defeat.

She put her hand to her forehead. Hugo would be down at the rink watching the International Championships, as he had watched them yesterday seated with Utta and concentrating on the competitors as though his future, and not hers, depended on the results.

By tonight they would be over, and Carole tried to make up her mind whether she wished Utta to win or to lose. It was hard for her jealousy to contemplate Utta as the victor, triumphant and elated; but yet that, in a way, might prevent her from occupying so much of Hugo's time.

Fame and success, as Carole well knew, brought their own penalties. Utta might be swept into a maelstrom of engagements which would occupy her and keep her away from Hugo. It was then, as she thought of it, that Carole gave a little exclamation.

She crossed the room quickly and picked up the telephone.

"I wish to speak to Don Carlos Jacára," she told the telephonist.

A moment later she heard Carlos' voice.

"Hello!"

"Hello, Carlos, is that you? This is Carole."

"What an honour! I am, of course, overwhelmed with delight at the sound of your voice."

134

"Listen, Carlos. I want to see you. Will you come to my room—now?"

"I shall be delighted. As I have said before, I am prostrated by this sudden attention."

"Hurry!"

Carole put the receiver down with a click.

She was tapping the nail of her first finger on her teeth when Don Carlos knocked at the door.

"Come in!"

He was smiling, smoothly and silkily, in a way that she most disliked. As usual, he wore too much jewellery and his suit was too tightly cut to give him the casual elegance which Hugo achieved so easily.

"I am here," he said simply, but his eyes were looking at her speculatively, in a manner which made her want to hit him.

"Sit down!" she said briefly.

He obeyed her, still smiling; and then at last she said sharply:

"Carlos, I think you owe me something!"

"Indeed!"

"Yes! I have often thought of the time when we first met. I was silly and unsophisticated and film-struck, but you seduced me and that is something you and I will never forget however much we may pretend.

"May I remind you that you were more than willing?" Don Carlos replied suavely.

"Only because I hoped to get something out of you," Carole retorted. "I wanted a job and you could have given me one if you had chosen to do so."

"It was not as easy as all that," Don Carlos answered.

"You did nothing," Carole said accusingly. "You took all I had to offer, all you wanted, then you threw me out and forgot about it. I was not clever or experienced enough to keep you dangling, as an older woman would have done. But you wouldn't have been interested in me then, would you, Carlos? You have always liked them young. Innocent girls are your speciality."

Don Carlos continued to smile.

"What are you trying to tell me?" he asked. "Do you

135

mind if I smoke?" He drew a cigar-case from his pocket.

"I am trying to tell you that you owe me something," Carole went on. "I want your help."

"I cannot imagine how I can be of use."

"I am not appealing to your better nature," Carole said bitterly. "God knows if you have got one. But I am asking you to pay a debt—a debt which has been outstanding for a long time."

"Very well. What do you want me to do?"

"I want you to get that skating girl out of the way."

"Utta? I thought she might be troubling you," Don Carlos smiled.

"Why should you think that?" Carole challenged him.

"It's obvious, isn't it? You wish to marry the English lord, but I wouldn't risk a penny on your chances."

"Why do you say that?"

Carlos made a gesture with his hands.

"Do oil and water mix? Never!"

"We have a great deal in common. I don't know what you mean."

"Oh yes, you do," Don Carlos retorted. "But never mind. If you think you can marry him, I wish you luck. And you think that Utta stands in your way?"

"I am sure of it. He has discovered that she is his cousin; did you know that?"

"No, but a cousin is a very comfortable relationship."

"It's not like that, you fool," Carole snapped. "She really is his cousin. The result of some secret marriage made out here before the War. He is going to take her back to England when the Championships are over."

"Well, what do you want me to do?"

"I want you to prevent it, of course. Take her to America. You are looking for a star, aren't you? She's pretty enough."

"Yes, she's pretty enough," Don Carlos agreed.

"Pretty enough for you, too, for that matter," Carole continued.

"Again I am inclined to agree with you."

"Then get her away. Offer her anything you like. If

it's a question of money I will pay the difference between what you can afford and what will tempt her."

"You are certainly very anxious to be rid of her," Don Carlos said.

"You will do this for me?" Carole enquired.

"I will do what I can—not only as an obligation, but because it would also be a pleasure."

Carole gave a little sigh of relief.

"That's settled then. Send me a bill for anything it may cost you."

"And supposing she will not come? As a matter of fact, even before I came here today and before you spoke to me I had every intention of offering her a contract. I was merely waiting to see if she won the International Championships."

"She will win," Carole said.

"Very well then, I will approach her this evening. And if she refuses?"

"She must not refuse, do you hear? Make it attractive enough for her, tempt her, make love to her. She knows nothing, she has seen no one. You can be an attractive devil if you want to, Carlos. Make certain this one doesn't escape you."

"You flatter me," Don Carlos said, "and you raise my hopes. At the same time some inner intuition tells me that this girl is not going to be easy in the way you suggest."

"Get her. You have got to get her."

"I certainly don't want to deal with Lord Roxburton," Don Carlos said ruminatively.

"There is no reason. I will introduce you to the girl myself. Let me see. I expect she will be dining here tonight, either alone with Hugo Roxburton or with all of us." Her face darkened for a moment as she added, "He doesn't seem able to contemplate an evening without her."

"I have warned you—you are flying too high," Don Carlos said.

Carole turned on him savagely.

"Mind your own business about me. I know what I

am doing. It is only where the girl is concerned that I want your help."

"Very well. You were saying?"

"I will get her to come here early. I will send a message to her house to tell her to come straight up here when she arrives. I will get one of the porters to tell Hugo that she has telephoned and will be late. I shall give you a quarter of an hour or so—perhaps longer—for you to do your stuff."

"You seem to have thought out every detail," Don Carlos said. "There is only one snag. The girl may not want fame, money or the glamour of the films."

"What makes you think she might not?" Carole enquired. "All girls want to go on the films."

"Perhaps this one is different," Don Carlos remarked.

"Why should you think that?"

"Things I have heard about her. I have made enquiries since you spoke of her before. I have even tried to speak to her, but without success. That skating instructor, Ernst Zippert, acts the part of a most effective watch-dog; and when I went to her home, an old lady with white hair—I imagine her grandmother—shut the door in my face."

"So you have tried already," Carole cried.

"Yes, I have tried. But don't worry, I am prepared to try again. If at first you don't succeed . . . That's your motto, isn't it?"

Carole stood with her back to him looking out of the window.

"I am only asking for happiness," she said slowly, in a low voice.

"That's the rarest thing in the whole world for anyone like you and me to find," Don Carlos said.

"Why do you say it like that?" Carole asked.

"Because we are of a kind," Don Carlos replied. "We are adventurers, pure and simple. . . ."

"Oh, I . . ."

He held up his hand.

"Don't interrupt. It is the truth and we might as well acknowledge it between ourselves. We are both of us

138

unscrupulous, both of us dishonest when it comes to getting what we want. But we can't cheat our way into happiness. I found that out many years ago and I think you will discover it, too."

Carole shivered.

"I have never wanted it before as I want it now," she said.

For a moment there was something strangely pathetic about her, and then she wheeled round to face him.

"I am not beaten yet, not by a long chalk—and you are going to help me."

"Yes, I am going to help you," Don Carlos agreed. "I will pay my debt. Perhaps in some way it is due to me what you are today."

"And what am I?" Carole asked defiantly, as though he criticised her.

"A very lovely woman," Don Carlos said suavely.

He rose to his feet.

"You will have the girl here about half-past eight?"

"About then," Carole promised. "You won't fail me?"

"Not if I can help it," he answered.

"Thank you!"

For a moment their eyes met, then she looked away from him.

"It is a long time since I could think of you or speak to you without hating you," she said, "but at this moment I almost like you."

"Because you think you are getting your own way," he told her with a smile. "The hard thing in life is to find we are liking people when we don't get our own way with them."

He had gone before she could think of anything to say to this, and when she was alone she felt herself shiver again at the truth of what he had said.

She was not getting her own way with Hugo. She loved him and wanted him. She was even grateful for the fact that passionately he was prepared to tolerate her. She wondered if he would want her the more if she refused to grant him the favours he accepted so casually; and then she knew she had not the strength within herself to keep away from him. She wanted him hungrily, with a desire that had something rapacious and greedy in it.

"I can't lose him, I can't." She said the words aloud then shut her eyes as if to hide even from the sunlight the yearning in them.

At the side of the ice rink Hugo thought of Carole and was thankful that she had not accompanied him that afternoon. He was well aware, though she thought she hid it skilfully, that she was desperately jealous of Utta. It showed in every word she spoke to the girl, in her whole attitude when the two women were together and in the way she tried continually to outshine and eclipse Utta.

Although the situation was not without its uncomfortable moments, Hugo could not help being amused at the way in which Utta, in her complete ignorance of the world, had no idea what Carole was about. She admired her enormously.

"She is the loveliest person I have ever seen," she told him, "and her clothes make me realise how badly dressed I am. Yet I could never look like her, not if I had all the money in the world."

Hugo, with an effort, refrained from saying that the last thing Utta should want would be to look like Carole. She was quite unselfconscious in her plain, neat dresses, which she had either made herself or which came from the local shops in St. Moritz.

The simple dinner frocks she wore, with their square necks and puff sleeves, would have been discarded contemptuously by the average schoolgirl in England; but Utta managed to endow them with a grace which made Carole, in her Paris creations, seem over-dressed and over-jewelled.

Hugo told himself, not once but a hundred times, that Utta was different from anyone he had ever met before. He had always hated young girls, finding them gauche and giggly and believing that he had nothing to say to them or they to him. Utta was so different.

She was prepared to listen and she never pretended to know anything of which she was, in reality, ignorant.

"Tell me about it," she would ask, and listen enthralled while Hugo explained something to her.

It was a flattery far more insidious, he thought, than Carole's arms creeping passionately around his neck, or Carole's lips hungrily inviting his.

She had, too, a dignity which he had forgotten existed amongst women—young ones at any rate. He recognised it as part of her grandmother's teaching and part, too, of the aristocratic blood which ran in her veins.

When anything was said that was the least way vulgar or embarrassing, Utta seemed to withdraw behind a sweet, gracious but imperturbable dignity which he could not help but respect.

She was, too, quite untouched by her meteoric jump to fame. She avoided the photographers, and had asked Ernst to see that they should not take any more pictures of her than was absolutely necessary.

"We have got to remember Grandfather," she said once.

Hugo saw that she was genuinely frightened of the thought. She had not yet realised how her life had been changed by that chance encounter with him on the mountainside.

He tried to tell her about England, about her relations, about the position which awaited her in the world outside St. Moritz; but he knew that the strength of her childhood ties were not loosened in the slightest by his advent into her life. She had only accepted him into her circle and her own attitude was unchanged.

"You are so very different from any girl I have ever known before," he said to her once.

"Am I?" she asked. "I am sorry. It must be because I have so few friends; I seem always to have been alone."

"You mustn't be sorry," he said quickly. "And try not to change. It would be a pity to spoil something that is very perfect as it is."

She smiled at that and the two dimples that he had noticed the first morning they had breakfasted together appeared in her cheeks.

"You are being kind to me," she said, "but I know how terribly ignorant I am. I expect when we go to England I shall do all the wrong things and then you will be ashamed of me. You had much better leave me here."

"Do you really think I want to do that?" he asked. "I am longing to take you to England. I want to see my grandmother's face when she sees you. I have written to her and asked her to tell the rest of the family of my discovery. To say they will be astounded is to put it mildly."

"Do you really think they will like me?" Utta asked.

"I am sure of it."

"It frightens me to think of going so far away from home; and then I remember that you will be over there and so it is not so frightening after all."

"I will try to look after you," Hugo said, and wondered why his voice sounded so solemn as he made the promise.

"You won't leave me alone with a lot of strange people, will you?" Utta asked.

"No, of course not. They won't be strange after you have met them. You must remember they were the people whom your father knew and loved and who loved him."

"Was he like you? My father, I mean."

"No, not a bit."

"I thought he wouldn't be. You don't look like a father somehow."

Hugo laughed.

"And what ought a father to look like?"

"I don't know, I never remember having one. But I'm sure it is not like you."

He had laughed again at that. She said so many quaint things that amused him. He found himself waking in the morning eager for the time when he would see her again.

He looked at her profile now as she sat beside him, watching the skaters on the rink. The great crowd of nearly three thousand people were watching the Swedish girl performing with an experienced grace which made Utta clasp her hands together excitedly.

"She is wonderful!" she exclaimed. "She will win, of course she will win."

"And what about you?"

"I am not good enough to beat her," Utta said. "But it doesn't matter—except that Ernst will be disappointed and I should hate him to be that after all the trouble he has taken."

She was speaking absolutely genuinely, Hugo realised in amazement. Not for one moment was she thinking of herself, nor was she grasping at the fame and the glittering prize which meant so much to the other competitors.

"You have got twenty minutes before you appear," he said. "Would you like something to drink?"

"No, thank you, I think I had better go and put on my skates. Ernst will be worried if I am not ready."

"Then good luck!"

Hugo put out his hand and then impulsively bent down and kissed her cheek.

"Good luck, little cousin," he said again. "Here's to wings on your feet."

He saw the quick flush in her cheeks before she turned away. What he didn't know was that as she went to the dressing-room she put her fingers up to touch her face where his lips had rested on her cheek.

"Wings on my feet!" she repeated, and then knew that he had given wings to her heart.

She loved him! She was as sure of that as she had ever been sure of anything in her life. She had loved him perhaps from that first moment when she had come upon him in the snow, swearing because he had sprained his ankle.

She loved the look in his eyes when she had come back later with Hans and Ludwig and when the light from the lantern illuminated his face as she went into the hut.

She had loved him that morning at breakfast, when, because she had never had breakfast with a stranger before, she had watched him across the table, asking questions with that quizzical look in his eyes and a teasing note in his voice.

She had loved him, too, that day by the Silvaplaner See, when she had watched him drive away with Carole at his side. There had been a pain in her heart as she saw them go, the same pain she had known when her grandmother had said she was not to see him again.

It had been love, love all the time—and yet she had not dared to put a name to that strange fluttering in her breast, that feeling as though her heart had wings.

"I love him!"

She thought the whole world was gold and the sunlight almost unbearable in its intensity.

When she went to find Ernst, he looked at her in surprise because her face was radiant and her eyes were shining like stars.

"Has anything happened?" he asked, feeling that no one could look like that unless they had good news.

"No," Utta answered wonderingly. "Oh, Ernst, I am so happy I feel I must win. I want to win for your sake —and yet I haven't got a chance against the Swede."

"You are better than she is," Ernst said, "but she has had more experience and it may sway the judges in her favour. Put every ounce you have got into it. Remember what I have told you and forget the people who are watching you."

"I will forget them all—except one," Utta thought to herself. Hugo would be wanting her to win, he would be waiting to applaud. Her cousin—the man she loved.

She gave a little sigh of sheer delight.

"You look as if you have come into a fortune," Ernst said jokingly.

"Perhaps I have," she smiled.

She was not thinking of the money which Hugo had told her would be waiting for her in England, she was thinking of the way his hair grew back from his forehead, of the grey of his eyes beneath his dark eyebrows, of the squareness of his chin and the manner in which his mouth turned up at the corners when he smiled.

"I am in love," she thought to herself, and was breathless at the wonder of it.

144

"Another ten minutes," Ernst said restlessly.

At the rink side Hugo was thinking the same thing as he looked at his watch. Then he realised that someone was sitting in the seat which Utta had vacated. It was Carole.

"Am I in time?" she asked gaily. "To see Utta, of course. She hasn't been on yet?"

"No, not yet," he answered.

"Then that's wonderful," Carole said. "We will watch her together."

She was looking very lovely in an emerald green hood edged with sable, which framed her face, and she wore a short sable fur coat over a green skiing suit. She bent towards Hugo and laid a soft hand on his.

"Darling, this is lovely—I mean being together for a few minutes alone."

"Yes," he answered absently, and she realised he had not really heard what she said.

"Are you nervous?" she enquired, quizzically.

"No, of course not," he lied.

"I believe you are," Carole accused. "You know, Hugo, that when you settle down and have a family, you will be one of those proud fathers who sit in the front row at the school concert or who attend their children's dancing class."

Hugo laughed at that, but she could see that he was watching the competitors' entrance. She felt a sudden despondency sweep over her. What magic had this girl used so that he was oblivious of everything else?

"Hugo!" she called his name softly, and when at last he turned his face towards her she was looking up at him with big, liquid eyes which seemed, for a moment, to be swimming in tears.

"What is it?" he asked.

"You are not being very kind to me," Carole said.

"Why, what have I done now?"

"You are neglecting me rather a lot."

"I am sorry you should think that."

He was looking away from her again and Carole felt herself throbbing with sudden anger. It was no use trying to divert his attention at the moment. She would

145

have to bear it, to wait, to possess her soul in patience which, as Carole well knew, was the hardest thing in the world to do.

"Will she win?" she asked at length, forcing herself to speak normally.

"I am sure of it." Hugo answered. "I have arranged a party for tonight. Ernst is coming, of course."

"And if she doesn't win?"

"She will." Hugo spoke positively.

Applause for the last competitor died away and now Utta's name was being announced over the loudspeaker.

"Fräulein Utta, representing Switzerland."

The music was the same to which she had skated for the Swiss Championship, but if she had been good then, she was infinitely more brilliant now.

It seemed to Hugo as though she was so swift that it was almost impossible to follow her movements. She sped round the Rink, she twirled, she leapt, she spun, until he felt himself breathless. And then, as the applause rang out, he felt his eyes aching from the concentrated manner in which he had watched her.

Carole was clapping languidly at his side; there was a little buzz of comment all around them. Only Hugo sat still, not moving, neither applauding nor speaking.

"Well, that's over," Carole said at last. "What time shall we know the worst?"

With an effort he seemed to pull himself together.

"Not for several hours. There are four more competitors and then the judges retire to make their decision."

"Let us go and have a drink," Carole suggested.

"I think I had better find Utta," he answered.

Carole felt like screaming but she was wise and clever enough to run up to Utta when she appeared, with a well-simulated pretension of delight.

"You were wonderful, dear, absolutely wonderful! We were very proud of you, weren't we, Hugo?" She linked Hugo and herself together intentionally. "What about a drink?"

Hugo was staring down into Utta's face.

"You know that you were good, don't you?" he asked quietly.

146

She looked up at him and longed to tell him why. Instead she answered:

"You wished me wings on my feet. I felt you had given them to me."

For a moment their eyes met. Utta drew in her breath quickly, then Carole's voice came as an interruption.

"I am sure you want something to eat or drink, you must be exhausted. Shall we go into the hotel?"

"I will go to the cloakroom and take off my boots," Utta said.

"Let me come with you and help you," Carole suggested.

"Oh, don't bother," Utta answered, but Carole persisted.

The cloakroom was empty and as Utta bent down to take off the long, white boots to which her skates were attached Carole sat beside her.

"Hugo was so nervous about you," she chattered.

"Was he?" Utta asked. "I wasn't nervous at all. I forgot the crowds, as Ernst told me to do."

"You are making poor Hugo take his responsibilities very seriously," Carole laughed. "At least it's good training for when he has children of his own."

Utta said nothing, bending over her boots, and after an intentional pause Carole went on:

"He is looking forward to taking you to England and letting you meet all your relations, and I expect you are looking forward to meeting them and to going to Rox. It is a wonderful house and we shall expect you to stay there a lot with us."

Utta's fingers were suddenly still. Then she straightened herself and looked at Carole.

"You said 'we.' Will you be at Rox too?"

Carole nodded.

"But of course. Didn't you know that Hugo and I are going to be married? No, of course you didn't. It's a secret—a dead secret which no one knows as yet."

"No, I didn't know," Utta said almost beneath her breath.

"You mustn't tell anyone, of course," Carole admonished. "And please don't mention it to Hugo—you won't, will you?"

"Not if it's a secret," Utta replied.

She bent over her boots that seemed suddenly to be very heavy, very cumbersome, weighing her feet down to the ground as though they were made of lead.

10

Don Carlos, sitting in Carole's sitting-room smoking a cigar, looked up to see Utta standing in the doorway. He had been so deep in his thoughts that he had not heard her timid tap on the door or sensed her presence until he turned his head to see her standing there with an enquiring look on her face.

"I'm sorry," she stammered. "I thought . . . I thought this was Mrs. Munton's room."

"It is," Don Carlos said, rising to his feet. "Won't you come in?"

"They told me downstairs that Mrs. Munton wanted to see me."

"She is dressing," Don Carlos explained, "and she has asked me to entertain you until she is ready."

Utta smiled.

"Thank you," she said, "but I mustn't wait long; Lord Roxburton said we would be dining at eight-thirty."

"It has been changed to nine, I believe," Don Carlos remarked. "May I offer you a drink?"

He walked towards the grog-tray where a variety of bottles proclaimed that every sort of cocktail was available.

"No, thank you!" Utta answered.

"You don't drink?" Don Carlos enquired.

"A little wine sometimes," she replied, "but I would rather wait until dinner."

"In that case you won't mind if I have a whisky-and-soda," Don Carlos said. "I must have something in which to drink your health."

Utta shook her head.

"I'm afraid I don't deserve it."

"I assure you that you do," Don Carlos replied. "It was a tremendous achievement, even though I expect you are disappointed not to be first."

"I don't mind for myself," Utta answered, "but I am afraid Ernst, my instructor, is sad. He was so convinced that I should win."

"So you ought to have," Don Carlos said. "I hear that the judges took a long time making up their minds before they finally gave it to the Swede."

"I wasn't a bit surprised," Utta smiled. "I thought she was wonderful!"

"If you ask me," Don Carlos said, carrying his whisky-and-soda across the room to where Utta was standing, "they couldn't believe that you were as good as you were. A lot of these judges are very hide-bound and conservative. They had never heard of you before and therefore they were quite certain there must be a catch in it."

Utta laughed.

"You are very kind, but the only reason I didn't win the Championship was because I wasn't good enough!"

Don Carlos' dark eyes rested on her little pointed face. There was no bitterness in her voice and none in her expression. She was, he thought to himself, that amazing phenomenon, a woman who could lose a game without losing her temper or making a complaint about it.

His eyes flickered over her, taking in every detail of her sweetly rounded figure, the whiteness of her skin, the proud carriage of her head, the grace with which she moved her arms and hands. She was lovely, he thought. Abruptly he put his drink down on the table.

"You had better sit down," he said. "I want to talk to you."

Utta's eyes widened for a moment in surprise as she seated herself on the small sofa. Don Carlos sat down beside her.

"I want to talk to you," he began, "not only because I think you are one of the loveliest girls I have seen for a very long time, but also because I have a proposition to make to you."

Again Utta looked surprised, but she said nothing. She had a quality of stillness which was, in itself, an originality.

"As we haven't been introduced, I must tell you who I am," Don Carlos continued. "My name is Don Carlos Jacára. I doubt if you have heard of me—but a large number of the young ladies competing with you this afternoon were well aware why I am in St. Moritz at this moment."

"You are something to do with skating?" Utta suggested.

Don Carlos shook his head.

"No," he replied, "I am what in Hollywood they call a talent scout. I am looking for a lead for a new picture my company is making—a picture in which the heroine must be an outstandingly brilliant ice skater."

"The Swedish girl will make a wonderful heroine," Utta said. "She is so pretty besides being so good."

"Not as pretty as you," Don Carlos replied.

She looked at him swiftly, almost as though she suspected that he was teasing her, and then she said quietly:

"Are you suggesting that you might offer me a part in the film?"

"Exactly!" Don Carlos approved. "And I am offering you the lead. You would not only look beautiful, you are exactly the right size and you skate like an angel."

"You are very kind," Utta smiled, "and of course I am very flattered, but I am afraid it is impossible."

"Impossible?" Don Carlos queried.

"Yes, quite impossible," Utta repeated. "You see, even if my grandfather would permit me to go on the films, which I very much doubt, I am going to England with my cousin, Lord Roxburton."

"And after you have been to England—what then?" Don Carlos enquired. "Are you going to lead a useless Society life with a lot of people with whom you have

150

very little in common? Or are you going to use the wonderful talents with which you have been born? Besides, you haven't heard yet what salary I propose to pay you."

"I am not interested in money," Utta answered, with a sincerity which, for the moment, left Don Carlos speechless. "I love skating and I have enjoyed going in for these competitions, but I doubt if I shall enter for any more. I skate because I love it, not for gaining notoriety, and the worst thing about it is having to perform before an audience."

Don Carlos stared at her in perplexity.

"Do you really mean that?" he asked.

"Of course!" she answered. "Why else should I say it?"

"Then you are the most extraordinary girl that I have ever met in my life," Don Carlos exclaimed. "Do you really understand what I am offering you? Fame, wealth, a place in public opinion."

Utta laughed softly.

"It sounds terrifying," she said. "If I really had to accept your offer I should be the most miserable person in the world."

"Instead of which you are now the happiest," Don Carlos said. He was too experienced in the ways of women not to notice the little shadow which passed over Utta's face or the sudden sadness in her eyes. He bent forward.

"Listen to me. Give it a trial. Come with me to Hollywood and make one film—just one. Let them see what they can do with you. See if, after all, excitement and the sensation of being a world-famous figure isn't better than just living alone with yourself in your own back-yard."

There was a note of sincerity in his voice that had not been there before. As if Utta responded to it almost despite herself, she said:

"You are very kind, I can see that. You are trying to help me, to do things for me. Please understand I can't listen to you. I know that not only is it impossible for reasons that I have already told you, but that also I

151

should hate such a life. I don't want to be famous. I want to see the world, I want to meet people, but only as an ordinary unimportant person, not as someone they stare at and criticise."

"Suppose, when you have looked at the world and met the people that you want to meet, you find it all very disappointing," Don Carlos said. "You will, you know!"

"Why do you say that?"

"Because we are all of us continually being disappointed in that things are never as wonderful as we think they are going to be," he answered.

Again he saw that shadow pass over Utta's face and he noticed that her fingers, lying in her lap, were suddenly interlocked together. "Something has upset her," he thought to himself, and his curiosity as well as an instinctive sympathy made him say:

"Won't you tell me about it?"

"Tell you about what?" Utta asked.

"What has upset you."

She turned to look at him then.

"How do you know that I am upset?"

"I have had a great deal to do with women in my life," Don Carlos answered. "And besides, there is gypsy blood amongst my ancestors which makes me very perceptive."

"It is nothing," Utta said. "Nothing I could tell you or anyone else."

"But very important to you," Don Carlos insisted.

"Isn't everything that we feel and everything in which we are disappointed important?" Utta asked.

"And it is not losing the skating Championship?" he said, knowing the answer even while he asked the question.

"No, of course not!" The quick reply was too spontaneous to be anything but the truth.

"Then it is a man who has upset you," Don Carlos suggested.

Utta got quickly to her feet.

"Please don't let's talk about it," she said. "It is silly of me to mind and not only silly, but wrong that I should reveal my feelings. My grandmother always said that private emotions should always be kept hidden. When I was a child, she would never allow me to cry in public over anything that upset me."

"Good training," Don Carlos approved, and he too rose to his feet and walked across to where she was standing.

"You are so beautiful," he said softly, "that if one man has upset you there will be a thousand more ready to console you. Could I be one of them?" He put out his hands as he spoke and laid them on her arms just above the elbows.

Utta, intent in her own thoughts and feelings, did not for a moment realise that the friendliness of his tone had changed or that the expression on his face had altered. As he touched her, some of the evil that Don Carlos kept hidden so cleverly by a superficial veneer seemed to communicate itself to her and with a little start she backed away from him. But his fingers tightened round her arms, holding her captive, and now there was a thickness in his voice as he said:

"You are lovely, far too lovely to be unhappy."

"Please let me go."

She spoke calmly enough, but he knew by the little pulse hammering in the whiteness of her throat that she was frightened.

Carole had spoken truly when she had said that Don Carlos liked only very young girls. Carole, herself, had no attraction for him now that she was polished and sophisticated and nearly thirty. As an ill-dressed, gauche, uneducated teenager she had had what was a supreme attraction in Don Carlos' eyes—youth.

It was Utta's youth which attracted him now and made him forget everything save the greedy desire rising within him like an uncoiling serpent.

"I will teach you to be happy."

She could feel his hot breath on her face, his fingers digging into the softness of her arms—and then, with a feeling of sheer terror, she knew he was about to kiss her.

With an agility which came from hours of practise on

153

the rink and a strength which he had not expected her to possess, she wrenched herself free. She moved away from him with the swiftness of quicksilver and, standing on the other side of the sofa, said in a voice which came shakily from between her lips:

"I think . . . I will see . . . if Mrs. Munton is . . . ready."

"Don't go!" Don Carlos cried. "Besides, I won't let you."

He moved a few paces backwards as he spoke and Utta, with a terror which could no longer be suppressed, realised that he stood between her and the door. With what was a heroic effort of self-control she said:

"If Mrs. Munton is not ready, then I must go downstairs. Lord Roxburton will be waiting and also the rest of the party who are dining with him tonight."

"You shall go if you will let me kiss you before you leave," Don Carlos said.

He watched with delight her effort not to show her fear. It was only the very young who could tremble like a bird caught in a trap, whose eyes appeared like those of a frightened gazelle, whose lips quivered a little even while with a superhuman effort they kept their voices steady.

"You have no right to suggest such a thing to me," Utta retorted. "I came here to this room at the invitation of Mrs. Munton. She cannot have expected that you would insult me because she was not present."

"If you think that, you don't understand our Carole," Don Carlos answered. "Never mind about her. You want to go downstairs—very well, I will let you, but you must pay your way. It is not much to ask, surely?"

Utta could feel her heart pounding in her chest. In her whole sheltered life she had never encountered anything like this. She had never imagined that a man could be so bestial.

She felt revolted and sickened at the sound of his voice, at the thought that his hands had already touched her and the very idea of being outraged by his kiss.

She wondered what she should do. To scream would

154

be to make an undignified scene. To try and force her way past him was to court disaster; he was stronger than she was.

He was smiling lewdly, with his thick lips; and she felt, with a sudden terror, that perhaps, after all, this was not Mrs. Munton's suite but his.

Perhaps she was trapped here; perhaps, whatever she did or said, it would be impossible to get away.

She was not so innocent or so stupid as not to realise that there were pitfalls in the world for girls. Her grandmother, with the practicability of the French, had brought her up to understand life, to know the truth about nature and the meaning of love between man and woman.

Besides, in her readings she had come across such situations often enough, but now that it was happening to her it was more terrifying than anything she had ever imagined.

As if Don Carlos read her thoughts, he said:

"I should not scream, the walls in this hotel are well built. It is unlikely that anyone will interfere even if they hear you. I will let you go only on the conditions I have already suggested."

"They will wonder what has happened to me downstairs, they will come to look for me."

"I doubt it. Who knows you are in the hotel except the porter? It will be a quarter-past nine, perhaps halfpast, before they will begin to wonder what has happened to you. It is a woman's privilege to be late."

"He is playing with me," Utta thought in sudden terror, "as a cat might play with a mouse"; and all the time he spoke he was smiling a smile that seemed to make every word he uttered seem sinister and horrible.

"I must keep my head," she thought, and even though her heart was hammering and her lips seemed suddenly dry, she still managed to face him proudly.

It was then that she saw her deliverance, lying on the table beside the telephone—a small, square piece of wood which held three coloured glass buttons, the bells which rang for the waiter, the valet and the chambermaid.

As Utta realised what she must do, she kept her eyes averted from the bell-push and fixed on Don Carlos. He must not guess her intentions or he might reach them first.

"You have no right to behave in such a manner," she said.

"I have the right of any man who is madly attracted by a woman."

While he was speaking, Utta leapt towards the bell-push. For a moment Don Carlos thought she was about to pick up the telephone, then, as he saw her fingers pressing each of the coloured buttons one after the other and heard the accompanying buzz, he realised what she had done.

He moved towards her and before she could get away he had caught her in his arms. She fought him wildly, stronger than even she had known she could be.

His arms were like steel bands—enclosing her, drawing her relentlessly nearer so that she felt herself becoming weak and ineffectual against the relentlessness of his hands.

His face was bent towards hers; as she twisted her lips away from him she had a glimpse of his eyes, half-closed, dark with passion, and his mouth, thick and greedy, seeking hers.

And then, even as she knew her struggle was fruitless, that she could not twist herself free of him and it was only a question of seconds before he would completely overpower her, there came a knock at the door.

"Entrez, entrez," Utta managed to gasp the words as with a smothered oath Don Carlos took his arms from her and set her free.

For a moment she staggered, losing her balance, feeling that if the back of a chair had not been near she would have fallen to the floor. Then the sight of the waiter's enquiring face waiting for orders made her pull herself together.

Without even a glance at Don Carlos she walked towards the door. Only her pride and a self-discipline which had been instilled into her since childhood en-

156

abled her to walk through the outer door instead of running.

Only as she heard it close behind her and realised that the passage outside was empty and that there was no one to see her did she start to run.

She ran wildly and without realising where she was going, passing the lift which, in her ignorance, she did not recognise, tearing down the long, carpeted corridor in search of a staircase.

Then, as she rounded a corner, she ran headlong into someone, heard him give an exclamation of surprise, then, as he dropped a stick to catch her in his arms, she realised who it was.

"Utta, what on earth are you doing here?"

It was Hugo who spoke and for a moment she clung to him, thinking only that she was safe, that he would protect her and keep Don Carlos from touching her.

"What is the matter? What has upset you?"

She heard his questions as though they came from a long way away. For a moment she could only close her eyes and let the utter relief of finding him sweep over her. She was, for a second, incapable of speech.

Her heart was pounding against her breast, the blood was roaring in her ears, and she was too breathless from the speed with which she had run down the corridor to do anything but pant, her head resting against his broad shoulder.

"What is it? What has frightened you?" Hugo asked.

In a voice that seemed strangely weak she managed at length to reply to him:

"I'm . . . all right . . . now."

She put her hand up to her forehead to press back the curls which had fallen untidily over her face.

"What has happened?" Hugo asked.

"It is . . . nothing! I promise you . . . it is nothing," Utta answered. "At least, nothing I can . . . tell you."

Her face was very pale and it struck him that her eyes were like those of an animal that has been rescued from certain death.

"I insist that you tell me the truth," he insisted.

His arms were still round her, holding her protective-ly. Now she stirred and moved a little away from him.

"I'm all right," she said. "It was . . . silly of me to get so upset."

"Upset about what?" Hugo enquired.

"It was a man," she answered, "but don't . . . don't let's talk about it."

"If someone has insulted you," he said, "I will talk about it. Tell me who it was."

For the first time she realised that he would be a for-midable person to cross or annoy; and even as she thought of it she remembered in whose room she had met Don Carlos. With an effort she tried to shake her-self free from the last remnants of her fear.

"I'm safe now," she answered. "Safe with you. I want to forget what has happened. I don't want there to be any trouble about it. Please let's go downstairs."

"But listen, Utta! I'm your cousin. I have a right to look after you and protect you. If some damned swine dared to frighten you, I will teach him a lesson that he will never forget."

"No, no, please! It won't do any good," Utta cried, "and perhaps it wasn't as bad as I thought. Perhaps other girls don't mind that sort of thing. I don't know. I am so ignorant, you see."

Hugo put his hands on her shoulders and turned her round to face him.

"Tell me the man's name."

"I won't!"

She faced him for a moment defiantly, and then sud-denly she was weak again, her hands went up to her eyes and, without thinking what she was doing, her forehead rested against his shoulder.

"I want to forget it," she whispered. "Please let's go downstairs. Let's be with the others—I don't want to be alone in this hotel again."

With a perception which was rare on Hugo's part he realised that she had reached breaking point. He re-membered then that she had had a tiring day and that she had also been disappointed in not winning the Championship. What had happened, it could wait.

He would find out sooner or later what had happened and he would give the man, whoever he might be, the thrashing he deserved. His arm tightened around Utta.

"I won't leave you alone, I promise!" he said. "I ought to have come to fetch you as I did the other night. It is my fault and you will have to forgive me."

She smiled at that, through her tears—a smile like the sun breaking through an April sky.

"That's better," Hugo approved, looking down at her. She was such a child, he thought, her fair hair against the darkness of his dinner-jacket, her eyes peeping from between her slender fingers.

"Come downstairs and I will give you a drink," he said.

"Very well," she replied obediently, and she bent down to pick up his stick to give it back into his hand.

"I'm sorry I nearly knocked you over," she managed to say.

He realised that she was making an effort and he liked her courage.

"Come along," he said.

It was then that Utta caught sight of herself in one of the long mirrors decorating the passage. With a sudden panic she put her hand up to her hair.

"Oh, please, could I tidy first?" she asked. "I wouldn't want the others to . . . guess that anything was the matter."

Carole Munton would be there, she had remembered. Carole might know what had happened.

"Yes, of course," Hugo answered. "Come to my room, it is only a few doors back. Smith will find you everything you want."

"Who is Smith?" Utta enquired.

"My valet," Hugo explained briefly.

He led the way, as he spoke, a short way down the corridor, stopped at a door and opened it with a key he took from the pocket of his dinner-jacket.

There was a small *entresol* and then, just as there had been in Carole's suite, a big sitting-room, a bathroom and a bedroom all opening off it.

"Smith!"

"Yes, my lord."

"This lady wants to tidy herself. See if you can find her everything she requires."

"Certainly, my lord."

Smith opened the door of the bedroom and Utta went in. It was a big room and although it seemed to her very luxurious it had, at the same time, an austere masculinity about it. Everything was so tidy, she thought, and except for the ivory-backed brushes on the dressing-table it might have been unoccupied.

Smith found her a comb and when she had tidied her hair, she washed her hands in the basin and smoothed down her dress. Then she went almost shyly into the sitting-room where Hugo was waiting for her.

"Do you feel better?" he asked.

"Yes, thank you," she murmured.

"I have opened a small bottle of champagne, just for you and me," he said. "What you need is a drink. It is the best cure for shock that I know."

"Do you think that is what I am suffering from?" Utta asked. She was smiling and the dimples had come back into her cheeks.

"I'm sure of it," he replied.

She took the glass he held out to her and raised it to her lips.

"You are very kind to me," she said. "I am afraid all I am being is a nuisance."

"You could never be that," Hugo answered. "I have only known you a short time, but I am utterly and completely convinced that you are the sort of person no one would ever describe in such a way."

"You are just saying that to make me feel better," Utta told him. "For one thing, I am making you late for your dinner-party."

"Your dinner-party," he corrected.

Utta shook her head.

"I don't deserve it."

"For not winning? My dear child, it is monstrous they didn't give you the Championship; but, apart from that, do you realise what you have achieved?"

"It was all Ernst's doing, not mine," Utta said, "and I'm afraid he will be terribly disappointed."

"If I know Ernst, he will have had so many drinks of congratulation already that the only thing he will be wondering is if his feet touch the floor and his head the ceiling," Hugo answered.

Utta laughed.

"I hope you are right."

"Shall we go down and see or shall we have some more champagne?"

"No more, thank you." She put down the glass out of which she had only taken a few sips. "I'm ready."

But Hugo did not move; instead he put his hand under her chin and turned her face up to his.

"I am sorry," he said, "that anything has distressed you; that it should have happened here. I don't want you to feel that the world is full of snares and pitfalls. I want you to be happy."

He felt her quiver a little beneath his hand and thought that she was still frightened about what had occurred. Her eyes had dropped before his, and now with a swift movement she moved away from him and out of reach of the fingers that had touched her face.

"Let us go down," she whispered.

"Yes, of course."

He picked up his stick and walked after her and down the corridor in silence, to stop at the lift which Utta had passed so impetuously, not knowing what it was.

When they reached the lounge downstairs, they found a crowd of people waiting for them—Carole and the Bakers, Ernst, who as Hugo had anticipated had already had as much to drink as was good for him, and the Mayfields, Hugo's friends who lived outside St. Moritz.

"Oh, there you are, Hugo," Carole said as they approached the little group. "We wondered if you had walked out on us."

"Surely I'm not as late as all that?" Hugo said sharply. "Utta, I don't think you have met Mr. and Mrs. Baker and Mr. and Mrs. Mayfield."

Utta shook hands with them while Carole watched her speculatively. What had happened, she wondered, during the time Utta had been in her sitting-room with Don Carlos? When she had finally come from her bedroom, it was to find them both gone.

She only prayed that he had been successful in persuading the girl to go to Hollywood, although, Carole thought, she had been clever in putting the position between herself and Hugo very plainly this afternoon.

She glanced at him as he stood beside Utta, introducing her to the others. "Damn the girl!" Carole thought with sudden fury. Hugo had been hers before Utta came along—she was sure of it, absolutely sure; and now he seemed almost to have forgotten her, absorbed in this new interest.

Men were all the same, the novelty of a pretty face they had not seen before made them forget everything—their obligations, their affections, even their previous intentions.

"But I will fight for him," Carole thought. "I will fight and I will win against this inexperienced brat."

Utta might be good at skating, but who cared? Hugo would find her boring enough when he got her to England and she couldn't talk about any of the things that he and his friends talked about; when he found they had no interests in common and that his gay, raffish crowd found her a bore.

Besides, Carole thought with satisfaction, she wouldn't look the same transported from her native soil. She looked pretty enough in her skating costume or in skiing clothes, but her evening dress looked what it was—a local product—and she would be laughed at if she wore that sort of thing in London.

Conscious of the beautiful fit and the exquisite lines of her own Paris gown of emerald green velvet which she wore with a necklace of rubies, Carole rose to her feet.

"Let's go and eat," she said, "I am sure everybody is hungry."

She played the part of hostess as one who has undeniable right. She seated everyone at the table, putting

162

herself on Hugo's right and Utta on his left. She would, if she had dared, have placed Utta elsewhere, but she was never quite certain how far she could go with Hugo without antagonising him.

"Have I disappointed you very much, Ernst?" Hugo heard Utta ask in a soft whisper.

"My dear, I'm as proud as if I had done it myself," Ernst answered. "And next year we will beat them, don't worry. Next year we will show the lot of them, you mark my words."

Utta said nothing, but Hugo saw the expression on her face. She didn't mean to compete again, he thought, and wondered why not. It was hard to realise that she was, in fact, second ice champion of the world.

She was so quiet and unassuming, and Hugo, who had taken part in many celebrations of athletic achievements, thought to himself that this was the strangest party at which he had ever been present.

At the same time, he knew that Utta's experience, whatever it might have been, had upset her. Tonight, for the first time, she lacked that radiant sparkle that made her different from anyone he had ever known.

She looked lovely, she was smiling and yet some inner spontaneity had left her.

He suddenly felt murderous towards the man who had upset her, spoiling, perhaps, some of her innocence and freshness so that never again could she face the world quite so untouched or unspoiled as she had been before.

"Who the hell could it be?" Hugo asked himself, but he found no answer to his question.

He did not know that Utta was not at that moment thinking of Don Carlos, but of him. She was watching Carole on his other side, leaning forward to put her red-tipped fingers on his arm possessively, looking up into his eyes with an expression that no one, however young and unsophisticated, could mistake.

"She loves him," Utta thought, "and he loves her."

There was a sudden pain in her heart that was almost like the piercing of an arrow. She had thought as she dressed for dinner that she was hungry, but now she

163

could only play with every dish that was put before her, sipping a little wine.

"Are you tired?" Hugo asked gently, and she felt a sudden warmth within her at his solicitude.

"A little," she admitted.

"I thought so," he said. "You must go to bed early."

"Yes, perhaps that would be best."

She thought how often she had lain in her little bed, longing to come to Suvretta House for dinner, longing to know more of the people, the music and the gaiety which she imagined taking place behind the lighted windows.

Now she was here and it all meant very little. She could only watch Carole and Hugo together and know that she longed, above all things, to be alone with her thoughts and feelings.

It seemed to her that, ever since Carole had told her that afternoon in the dressing-room that they were to be married, it was as if something inside herself had turned to ice. She could feel it there like a hard lump, making it impossible for her to enjoy anything in the way she had done in the past.

It was not as if in her love for him she would ask anything for herself. She had never presumed, even in her wildest imaginings, that he might marry her. She had only thought of him being there, of being able to love him.

It was the knowledge that he belonged to another woman which hurt so unbearably.

She wished now that she had never known him, that he had never come into her life, but that she had gone on living with her grandparents in the little house, knowing nothing of the heartbreaks and miseries which lurked outside.

How wise they had been, Utta thought suddenly, to keep her away from the world, to tell her she was happy! It was true! People could only bring heartache and bitterness, disillusionment and disappointment. She thought of Don Carlos and shuddered.

She looked up at Hugo and felt suddenly that she wanted to cry.

To her surprise she found that dinner was over. She did not realise that the courses were passing one by one. She had no idea what she had eaten or what had been said.

"What a fool he must think me," she thought to herself, realising that she must have sat silent, leaving Carole to do the talking. They went out into the lounge.

"Let's go to a night club," someone suggested.

"Of course," Carole agreed. "I want to dance, don't you, Hugo?"

"I am going to take Utta home," Hugo replied. "She is tired. It has been a long day for her."

"Will you join us later?" Carole asked softly. "It wouldn't be the same without you."

"I will see," Hugo answered briefly.

He put his hand under Utta's arm.

"Come along," he said. "It's bedtime, so say goodnight."

She might have been a small child being taken off by her nurse. Obediently, she shook hands all round, then her cloak was wrapped round her shoulders and a car was waiting for them at the door.

"Please don't bother to come with me," she managed to say at last. "I will be quite safe by myself."

"Don't be silly," he answered.

The porter covered their legs with a thick rug. The stars were shining above them and the moon was climbing up the sky.

"What a night!" Hugo exclaimed. "What I would like to do now would be to go for a ski run."

"Shall we do it?" Utta asked, with a sudden light in her eye.

"You forget I'm a cripple," Hugo answered.

"Oh yes, of course." The elation died away and she sat quietly in the car.

"Now that the competitions are over," Hugo said, "I suggest we leave for England the day after tomorrow. I can't do anything with this leg of mine and so I might as well cut short my holiday and take you back to introduce you to the family."

There was a sudden silence.

"I . . . I don't think I want . . . to go," Utta stammered.

"But you told me . . ." He stopped suddenly. "You're not frightened, are you?"

"I suppose I am," Utta answered truthfully. "I think really it would be much better if you went away and forgot about me. Let me stay here with *Grand'mère* and Grandfather and live as I have always lived."

"Why do you suddenly feel like this?" Hugo enquired. "When we were talking about it before, you were looking forward to coming with me, to going out into the world, meeting your relations, seeing all the things you have never seen—all the things that I can show you. I was looking forward to it too."

Utta felt her heart begin to throb again at the sound of his voice. Why, she wondered, did he talk like this when it was Carole he wanted to be with, not her? Did all men appear to be interested in every woman they met? She felt suddenly very small, young and bewildered.

"I don't think I will come," she said.

"But you must," Hugo replied firmly. "Don't be afraid, Utta. I will look after you."

"But . . . but you will be so busy." The words came out despite her resolution not to speak of what Carole had told her.

"Busy doing what?" Hugo enquired.

"I shall . . . only be in . . . the way," Utta faltered.

"Of course you won't. Whatever put such an idea into your head?"

Then Hugo, groping for an explanation as to what was troubling Utta, suddenly remembered the expression on Carole's face as she and Utta had come back from the dressing-room earlier that afternoon.

He did not know why he should think of it now, but in his mind's eye he saw it very vividly. Carole had been up to something. He knew her well enough to know when she was trying to put something over or when she had succeeded in bringing off some little coup on which she had set her heart.

He could not believe that anything she could say could upset or perturb Utta—and yet, one never knew. Women were strange creatures. Perhaps she had suggested to the child that she would be in the way. If that were the case, he could quite easily circumvent Carole's scheme.

He took Utta's hand and slipped her arm through his.

"Listen, Utta," he said. "You and I are going to have very good times together. We are going to enjoy ourselves and I'm not certain that it all is not going to be more of a treat to me than to you. I have got nothing to take up my time and so I can devote myself wholeheartedly to amusing you, to showing you your own country, which I know you are going to love as much as you love Switzerland."

"I should like that, of course," Utta said, "but . . ." she hesitated.

"But what?" Hugo answered.

"I don't want to be . . . in the way," she finished lamely, remembering her promise to Carole.

"In whose way?" Hugo enquired. "My dear Utta, when we go to London you are going to stay with my grandmother, who will be longing to see you and will be absolutely delighted to have you as her guest. When you come to Rox, I shall be your host, and I'm longing to have you too."

He felt her fingers tighten for a moment on his arm.

"But supposing . . . supposing you were married . . . or something like that?" Utta asked.

Hugo gave a little laugh. So he had been right, he thought; Carole had made mischief.

"Whoever put such an idea into your head?" he said. "I'm not going to get married, although a great many people have thought it would be a good thing for me. No! I am free, unmarried and I intend to remain that way."

He could not see Utta's face, but he felt as if a sudden quiver went through her, as if vitality and happiness flowed back into her veins.

He could hear the sudden sparkle in her voice and

guess a little at the radiance in her eyes as she said, almost breathlessly:

"It will be fun, won't it?"

11

As the aeroplane rose higher and higher in the air until finally it passed through the clouds, Utta had her last glimpse of the earth beneath.

It was her first flight; she was not frightened, but she was speechless with excitement and only the dancing gaiety of her eyes revealed the strange feelings she was experiencing.

There had been a moment of sadness when she had clung to her grandmother and found it hard to say good-bye. From her grandfather, too, she had another and more difficult moment of parting.

"Please don't be angry with me, Grandfather," she whispered as she stood on tiptoe to kiss his brown cheek.

When he had returned yesterday in response to a telegram from her grandmother, the whole story of what had been occurring, not only in the past few days but for a whole year, had to be told.

And Utta, who had feared his anger, found instead that he was hurt and surprised that both his wife and his grandchild should have contrived to deceive him.

"Why didn't you ask my permission?" he said—not once but a dozen times.

They found it hard to explain to him that the reason they had not done so was because they knew that they would never have obtained it.

For perhaps the first time in her life Utta realised that her grandfather was a very old man. He had always seemed so strong, upright and young in many ways; but now that she was no longer entirely dependent on him, she realised that he was as frail as her grandmother.

"How can I ever thank you both for what you have done for me?" she said impulsively.

The tears came into her grandmother's eyes at her words, her grandfather only shook his white head.

"We have done little," he said, in his low, deep voice. "We have only loved you."

That's what made it so hard to go, Utta thought when the moment came. The knowledge that she was in some way hurting them through their love because she must make a life of her own apart from them.

Her grandmother understood well enough; but she sensed a sort of bewilderment in her grandfather, as if he could not really understand why she was not content to leave things as they had always been and to ask nothing more than that in which he had himself found such contented happiness.

As the aeroplane left Switzerland behind and set off across Europe towards England, she had the feeling that one part of her life was closing for ever.

A new chapter was opening ahead, and though she was looking forward to it so eagerly, she was not foolish enough not to know there would be difficulties and problems, frustration and miseries in the new life just as there had been in the old.

She remembered reading somewhere that wherever one travels one takes oneself with one, and she wondered now if she was making a mistake.

Whether, in fact, she would have been wiser to stay with all that was dear and familiar.

"But I can go back," she told herself—and she had, in fact, made plans to return in a month.

Hugo had invited both her grandmother and grandfather to stay in England; but while they thanked him for the invitation, they had refused his hospitality.

"We are too old to change our ways," Madame Kindschi had said. "Utta is young; she seeks new horizons. I ask for nothing more than the view from my windows."

"That is the world in miniature," Hugo answered understandingly.

"I see you understand," Madame Kindschi smiled.

"When I go to Paris, I'm so homesick for my house here, for my husband and the life I have lived since I was a girl, that often it is hard to stay my allotted time with my family."

There was so great an understanding and so deep an affection between the two old people that Hugo could well understand that to part one from the other was to leave them both maimed and ineffective.

But Utta was different, he thought. It was time she saw more people of her own age, that she found companionship to lighten her loneliness and experience to change her ignorance of the world.

Yet even as he thought of it he knew he would not have her different. There was something so fresh, so lovely and unspoilt about her that sometimes he, too, thought it was best she stayed where she was.

Yet whenever such thoughts crossed his mind he laughed at himself for being imaginative.

"Am I very different from other girls that you know?" Utta had asked him only yesterday.

"There is a difference," he answered truthfully, "but it is entirely to your advantage."

"No, that's not true," Utta contradicted. "No one really wants to be strange, to be stared at or talked about."

"You are wrong there," Hugo said, "but I know what you mean. But I assure you that people will stare at you wherever you go because you are so pretty."

"I hope you are right about that," she answered in all seriousness, looking so like a perplexed and worried child that Hugo had a sudden impulse to put his arms around her.

He told her often enough that he would look after her, but he knew there were some things he could never do. He could not give her the self-assurance that she knew, instinctively, was lacking in herself.

He could not erase from her mind that fear of doing something wrong from a social point of view, or of making the mistakes that all who are inexperienced will make, however hard one tries to warn or protect them.

"Don't worry," he said with a smile.

170

"I don't want you to be ashamed of me," Utta replied.

He thought for one moment that he would tell her how much she was coming to mean in his life, how interested and delighted he was with her, and how he had never felt in the same way about any other woman he had known—and then he laughed at himself for being ridiculous.

Utta was only a child, and though it was obvious that she clung to him, she doubtless thought him very old and adult.

When she got to England, she would meet plenty of men of her own age—young men who would make the right sort of companions for her and whom she would doubtless find delightful and amusing.

Hugo wondered why he disliked the idea of Utta being entranced with the type of young men he had seen often enough at dances and always dismissed scathingly as callow youths.

"I am getting old," he thought of himself, and disliked the idea of that even more.

If Utta had been perturbed and a little upset by her farewells, Hugo's had not been easy.

Carole had come to his room the night before he left and what had started with passion ended with tears and recriminations.

"When am I going to see you again?" she had asked in the early hours of the morning.

"Are you coming back to England when you leave here," he asked, "or returning to America?"

"How can you ask me such a question in such a callous way?" she retorted. "Surely you want me to come to England?"

"Of course," he answered soothingly. "I only wondered what your plans are."

"My plan is to be with you," she answered, her voice softening on the words.

"That's going to be difficult," he said.

"What do you mean?"

He reached for a cigarette.

171

"Have you forgotten that I am to play chaperon to Utta?" he asked. "I pledged myself to look after her and I mean to take her round and show her everything."

"Good heavens, haven't you got any female cousins to do that sort of work?" Carole enquired.

"Plenty," Hugo answered. "As a matter of fact I want to do it."

"So that's it," Carole said.

"I don't know what you mean by that," Hugo replied.

"Oh yes, you do," Carole answered, "but I should have thought you would have been too sensible to go in for cradle-snatching. Besides, you are not giving the girl a chance. You're the first man she has ever seen. Of course she thinks she is infatuated with you. When she has had a proper look round, she may think very differently."

"I quite expect that," Hugo said. "And as for my being besotted, I assure you that my interest in Utta is principally because she is Andrew's child."

"You may be able to put that nonsense over with a lot of people," Carole snapped, "but not with me."

Hugo shrugged his shoulders.

"Very well, have it your own way."

Carole bit her lips for a moment and then she said:

"We are not quarrelling, are we?"

"No, of course not," Hugo answered.

"I love you, Hugo! You know that, don't you?"

"You have told me so," Hugo replied. "But love has a lot of different meanings to a lot of different people."

"I doubt if anyone has ever loved you as much as I do," Carole answered.

"You flatter me," he replied. "You are a very sweet and generous person."

"I think we suit each other very well," Carole said.

He realised what she meant by that and stirred uneasily. There was no way he could think of at that moment to stop her from what she was about to say.

"I don't want to leave you," Carole went on. "I want to stay with you, to be with you. Oh, Hugo, can't you understand?"

He understood well enough and was deliberately blind.

"My dear, if you are coming to England, we shall see each other very shortly. You must come down to Rox and I expect I shall be in London a great deal."

"That isn't what I am asking," Carole replied. "Oh, Hugo, don't be obtuse. Why don't you marry me?"

"Marry you!" Hugo's eyebrows went up as though he had never heard of the idea. "My dear, I should make an abominable husband. No one would put up with my moods and bad temper for more than a week and I have an instinctive abhorrence of divorce."

"There wouldn't be one if you married me," Carole said. "I would make you a good wife. You know that we both like the same things and the same people. I'm rich, Hugo, very rich, as you know; and though you have money too, there is no one in England today who doesn't want American dollars. Marry me and I know we will be very happy together."

In answer Hugo put his arm around her shoulders and kissed her cheek.

"Dear Carole," he said, "you don't know what you are asking. I'm an inveterate bachelor and I doubt if I shall ever settle down as my grandmother has always asked me to do. Besides, I have the feeling that if I did I should become a bore."

"Oh, Hugo! How can you be so stupid?" Carole cried. "You could never be a bore and I promise you that whatever you do I would never divorce you. Marry me and I know we shall be crazily happy together."

Slowly Hugo disengaged himself from the arms she had flung round his neck.

"I am sorry to sound so selfish," he said lightly, "but I want to feel free."

Carole dug her finger-nails into the palms of her hands to prevent herself screaming out and raging at him.

"Think about it," she pleaded. "You will miss me next week before I come back to England. Think about what I have said and think how happy we could be together. Do you promise?"

173

"Yes, I will think about it," Hugo promised.

When at last she had left him, he found himself breathing a sigh of relief, as if he had passed through some unexpected danger, but not entirely unscathed.

He saw now how mad he had been to consider for a moment marrying Carole. He had never loved her. She had only seemed desirable before she surrendered to him so easily.

"Man is the hunter!" He found himself repeating the old words.

He thought that when he did find a woman whom he wanted to marry, he would seek her out for himself. Whatever he had said to Carole about freedom, he knew that one day he must have an heir for Rox.

It was impossible to think of Eddie living there, arranging his precious china in the cabinets and mincing about the place in the affected manner which always made Hugo want to hit him.

No, he wanted children—strong sons whom he could teach to fish and shoot, daughters who would decorate the house with their prettiness. It was a delightful picture!

Then Hugo laughed out loud to himself. How pompous he was getting! Yet all this talk of marriage made him feel serious. After all, it was of paramount importance to him, at any rate, that he should not marry the wrong woman.

Carole had been a near squeak. He had, after all, considered her seriously; he had come out to Switzerland fully expecting that, when he returned home, he would be engaged. Perhaps knowing Utta had saved him from making a fool of himself.

If he had not been so interested in her, he might have been more concerned with Carole, might have found the way she tried to twist herself round a man and her passionate love-making irresistible.

Yes, it was Utta to whom he must be grateful, Hugo thought, and he did not know that in her own room Carole was thinking the same thing with very different emotions.

174

"It's that bloody little skater," she said. "But I am not defeated yet."

She said the last words defiantly, staring at her reflection in the mirror. Hugo would miss her, she told herself.

These nights of love and passion must have meant something to him. When he had Utta with him day after day, he would find out how boring the unformed and empty mind of a young girl could be.

Carole looked back at herself at the same age, remembering the platitudes she had spouted so confidently as if they were new and original, the way she had found it impossible to concentrate on arguments or even follow intelligently a serious conversation.

She had only been happy when people were making a fuss of her; and she could remember now how, as Dave's wife, she had craved for compliments as other women would crave for sweets or drink.

"He will soon be bored by her," she said with a twist of her mouth.

She was trying to bolster up her own morale, trying to convince herself that the refusal that he had just given her was not final.

"He can't do without me," she thought, remembering Dave, who had found it impossible to get away from her.

But Hugo was a very different character from Dave. She had never met a man who was so independent despite a reputation for being a roué where women were concerned.

What Carole could never understand was that Hugo accepted women as part of the good things in life. They were a delight just as a bowl of beautiful flowers was a pleasure and delight when one found them on a table.

He enjoyed women; he might wish to possess them for a short time—but he had no desire to own them. He did not feel that they must be his to the exclusion of everyone else.

"If only he would be jealous!" more than one woman had said where Hugo was concerned; but it seemed that

175

that particular emotion had been entirely left out of his make-up.

"I will get him yet," Carole said again to her own reflection.

Then she turned away from the sight of her own eyes lest she should see there the sharpness of fear and the dullness of despair.

High above the clouds Hugo thought, with relief, that he was free of Carole for ever. He had no intention of renewing their acquaintance on the old footing when she returned to London. There was nothing more dead than a love affair that was over. As far as he was concerned, his affair with Carole had been over for some days.

It was only her resistance which kept it alive and a feeling within himself that he must not be too harsh or too unkind to her, because he had, for one moment, had very different thoughts about her.

As far as he was concerned, this had been good-bye for ever. He settled himself more comfortably in his seat and thought that women were a curse. Then a movement beside him made him glance down at Utta.

She was looking very lovely in her travelling clothes —a plain tweed coat and skirt with a little blue hat which fitted closely to her fair curls. Her clothes were simple and inexpensive and yet she had inherited her grandmother's knack of making anything she wore seem elegant.

"Enjoying yourself?" he asked.

She smiled at that and her eyes were sparkling as she replied:

"I was so afraid I might feel sick, but instead I feel wonderful."

"That's good!"

"I won't talk in case you want to go to sleep," Utta said. *"Grand'mère* is always telling me there is nothing so tiresome as women who talk in railway trains or on long distance journeys when men want to sleep."

"I am not in the least tired, thank you," Hugo said a

176

little stiffly. Utta's words had unconsciously conjured up a picture of him as being old or at least middle aged.

"She is very young," he told himself—and was to repeat the same words a hundred times before twenty-four hours had passed.

While they were flying, not only Utta's grandparents and Carole were thinking of them and regretting their departure, each in their separate ways, but Ernst found himself taken away by Don Carlos Jacāra from a crowd of congratulatory friends who wished to stand him drinks.

"I want to talk to you," he said.

Ernst put down his beer reluctantly and followed Don Carlos to a corner of the room which was out of earshot of those grouped round the bar.

"What is it, sir?" he enquired.

He knew Don Carlos well, both by sight and reputation; and though it was part of his business to keep in with such men, he had an instinctive dislike of the American.

"I want to talk to you about that girl Utta," Don Carlos replied.

Ernst said nothing, but waited. He was well aware that Don Carlos had tried to get Utta to accept a film contract. He had also learned that in some way that had not been explained he had offended and upset her.

"You know that I offered her a big part in Hollywood?" Don Carlos said.

"Yes, I heard that," Ernst answered.

"She refused; but I have reason to believe one day she will change her mind. I shall be seeing her in England, but when she comes back here to visit her grandparents I want you to let me know. It is quite easy for me to fly over from America or wherever I may be at the moment. I will leave you my card."

Don Carlos drew one from his pocket and taking a gold pencil wrote his telegraphic address on the back. While he was doing this, Ernst scrutinised him carefully and what he saw was apparently not pleasing, for his eyes were hard and his expression somewhat surly as he took the card.

"This is for yourself," Don Carlos said, drawing some notes from his pocket.

"No, thank you, sir," Ernst replied.

His refusal seemed almost to startle Don Carlos.

"But of course, you must take them—why not? Besides, I am one of the few people in the town who have not bought you a drink."

"I would rather not take your money, thank you, sir," Ernst insisted.

"I see!" Don Carlos said. "You are willing to do what you can for little Utta because you are so fond of her. That is the right spirit and I commend you for it. She is a very lovely girl and she will go far—very far—I promise you, if she will only trust herself to me.

"Perhaps I approached her too quickly. It is the first time she has competed in the Championship. In a little while she will be only too eager, you will see, to consolidate the advantage she has just gained—then, if she comes to me, I will arrange everything."

"I don't think she will come to you," Ernst said quietly.

"Why do you say that?" Don Carlos replied.

"I think you know the answer as well as I do, sir!"

Ernst put the card into his jacket pocket and turned away and went back to the bar.

Don Carlos stood staring after him, an ugly expression on his face. In that moment he almost hated Utta. The very mention of her name seemed to make people unpleasant to him.

"A stupid, clumsy bungler," was what Carole had called him and the words had hurt his vanity much more than anything else she could have said.

He was not clumsy and he was not a bungler. It was just that in the whole of his life he had not come up against anyone quite like Utta before.

He thought of her frightened loveliness and he felt again that strange excitement that had swept over him that night when he had her cornered in Carole's sitting-room.

Perhaps he had been too impetuous. Perhaps it had been a blunder to frighten her—and yet her confusion and fear had given him a thrill such as he had not known for years.

There was no reason for this upstart skating instructor to be offensive to him. The man was swollen-headed, that was what was the matter with him.

They were all the same; the heady draught of success went to their heads far more quickly than wine.

Muttering some very ugly words beneath his breath, Don Carlos left the bar and went in search of Carole. He knew just how she was feeling at Hugo's departure and he thought somehow between them they might be able to evolve a plan to retrieve what they had lost.

It was raining when the aeroplane came down at London Airport and Utta hugged her overcoat around her as the wind sweeping across the aerodrome seemed to penetrate right into her bones. She was used to cold, but this was very different from the crisp, dry cold of Switzerland.

"It's very grey, isn't it?" she asked Hugo, as after going through the Customs they set off in the big, comfortable car that had been waiting for them outside with its uniformed chauffeur.

"Grey?" he questioned. "Yes, I am afraid it is rather a dull day."

Utta thought of the sunshine, bright and golden, shining in at the windows of her home, and then she gave herself a little shake. How ungrateful she was to be comparing already the new world with the old!

She sat forward in her seat to see more of the streets through which they were passing.

"Is there no countryside?" she asked after a little.

"Not here," Hugo answered. "This is all really part of London."

"It's very big," she said with a little sigh.

She added to herself that she was very small. It was a feeling she was to find repeating itself again and again in the days that followed.

The house of Hugo's grandmother, for instance, seemed to her enormous, although Hugo had told her that the Dowager Lady Loth lived very simply.

179

It was a tall, ugly house in one of the streets off Berkeley Square, with a narrow staircase and high rooms, one front, one back, ascending for five floors.

Lady Loth was waiting for them in the drawing-room. It seemed to Utta rather a dark room with not one decisive colour about it. At first she could hardly see her hostess for the mass of small tables, high-backed chairs and cabinets filled with china which seemed to fill the room almost to the point of suffocation.

And then, in a chair by the fireplace, she saw an old lady. She was not in the least like her grandmother. She was rather large and shapeless and her hair, which was grey, was caught untidily into a bun at the back of the neck.

She wore a black dress which had no pretensions of elegance, and round her neck were several rows of what had once been exceedingly valuable pearls but which, with Japanese competition, had fallen to about one-fiftieth of their value and were practically unsaleable.

On fingers swollen with rheumatism, Lady Loth wore innumerable rings of good stones but in old-fashioned settings, all of which were badly in need of a cleaning.

"So this is Andrew's daughter!" she said in a firm voice as Hugo bent to kiss her.

Then Utta found herself looking into the sharpest and most penetrating pair of blue eyes that she had ever encountered in her whole life.

"Yes, Andrew's daughter, Grandmother," Hugo repeated.

"You are not the least like him," Lady Loth said in a tone which sounded to Utta almost accusing.

"How do you do?" Utta held out her hand politely.

The old lady put her hand on her shoulder.

"Why have you kept yourself a secret all these years? It was somewhat inconsiderate of you, wasn't it?"

"Now, Grandmother, don't start harrying the poor child before she has even sat down," Hugo said. "We have had a long journey and we hope you've got some tea for us."

"If I know you, you are expecting something stronger than tea," Lady Loth answered with a chuckle. "Ring the bell. I can't think why Baxter hasn't brought it up already."

Even as she spoke, the old butler, who seemed to have shrunk until his clothes were much too big for him, came staggering into the room with a heavy silver tray. Utta watched fascinated as a table was laid at the old lady's side.

She had never seen so much silver—a hot-water kettle, a huge teapot, milk and cream jugs and sugar basin. The cups and saucers were the most delicate and beautiful china imaginable.

But with all this fuss there was very little to eat—a few slices of rather tasteless bread-and-butter, a cake with a surprising scarcity of currants and some biscuits which had not been kept in an airtight tin and had therefore gone soft.

"How are you, Baxter?" Hugo asked.

"As well as can be expected, m'lord," the old butler replied in a quavering voice.

"There's nothing wrong with Baxter except that he will keep thinking about his age," Lady Loth said. "He talks of wanting to retire. I tell him it's stuff and nonsense. He's two years younger than I am."

"You'll be eighty next month, won't you, Grandmother?" Hugo asked.

"I suppose so," Lady Loth replied. "I make no secret of my age—but I don't think about it either! A whisky-and-soda for his lordship, Baxter."

"Very good, m'lady." The old man tottered from the room while Utta watched them with wide eyes.

She was to find out later that Lady Loth was what was known as a "character".

"If I can't say what I think at my age, when can I say it?" she would remark, and would then say something shrewd and penetrating which went straight to the point or got uncomfortably under someone's skin.

She had been married three times. The first, when she was young, to an impecunious young cavalry officer. The second to Hugo's grandfather, to whom she was devoted; and thirdly, when she was over sixty and a widow, to Lord Loth, a Field Marshal of great reputation who had now been dead for over ten years.

"I live here very simply; you mustn't expect too many fal-de-lals," she said to Utta.

Hugo smiled:

"I wouldn't, of course!" Utta stammered.

She was finding this shabby old house, which had not been changed or renovated in any way for the last thirty years, both impressive and awe-inspiring.

Hugo had a sudden longing to show her Rox, to watch her face when she saw the beautiful grey stone house with its magnificent furniture, painted ceilings and beautiful pictures.

But it was important that Utta should first meet the family and it was more convenient for most of them to come and see her in London. As if she guessed his thoughts, Lady Loth said:

"Your sister, Pamela, is coming up from the country tomorrow. She came round here and made a great to-do about offering Utta a bed in their flat. 'You know how cramped we are, Grandmother,' she said, 'but Utta could sleep in Walter's dressing-room if you find it is too much for you to have a young girl in the place.'"

"What did you reply?" Hugo asked.

"I told your sister that when I was in my dotage I would let her know. If there wasn't room for Andrew's child in this house, it would be a poor thing," Lady Loth replied vehemently. "Besides, it is good for the servants to have something to do. They are getting lazy; I don't entertain like I used to do."

She paused for a moment and then added:

"The truth is, Hugo, so many of my friends are dead. If I want to have a dinner-party, I don't know whom to ask unless it is ghosts." She spoke sharply.

She had had no intention of inviting sympathy, but Hugo bent forward to lay his hand on hers.

"Come on, Grandma, I bet really you've got a couple of young men up your sleeve."

She chuckled at that.

"There's always the General," she said. "But he's so

deaf he can't hear a word I say. I don't like wasting my pearls of wit!"

Hugo threw back his head and laughed.

"You're incorrigible, Grandma. The only thing that worries me is whether you are the right sort of chaperon for Utta—she has been brought up very strictly. You will shock her to death if you're not careful."

"Not if she's been in your company for long, I won't," his grandmother retorted. And then smiling a little at Utta she said in a more kindly tone: "If you find it too dull, you have only got to say so. There's Walter's dressing-room, although that will be uncomfortable enough."

"I'm sure I shall be very happy here," Utta said quickly. "It is very kind of you to have me."

Lady Loth watched her speculatively.

"There's a certain likeness to your father when you smile," she said. "He was a dear boy."

"I wish I had known him," Utta told her.

"I wish you had," Lady Loth agreed simply. "It was very naughty of him to go off and get married in that hole-and-corner manner. I can't think what he was thinking about."

"Merely getting his own way," Hugo said. "You will remember, Grandmother, it's something we have all inherited."

"It would do you good not to get yours for once," Lady Loth retorted. "What have you done with that American woman?"

"Are you talking about Carole Munton?" Hugo enquired.

"You know very well I am," his grandmother said. "I hear you were in her party, or she in yours."

"Yes, that was true," Hugo agreed. "We joined up, but naturally she has remained on in Switzerland."

"Nothing natural about it," Lady Loth said. "Have you finished with her?"

Hugo looked a little uncomfortable. He was well aware that Utta was listening, her eyes very wide but full of interest as they moved from one face to the other.

"You are getting too curious as well as being indiscreet, Grandmother," he replied evasively. "Can I take Utta up and show her her room?"

"Certainly not!" his grandmother snapped. "Ellen will do that when she has finished unpacking. It is no use pushing us about in this overcharged modern manner. Ellen will take her own time, you know that."

"Very well then, I will leave Utta with you and I will come back and fetch her at dinner-time. We're going to dine out and see the sights of London."

"Oh, how lovely!" Utta exclaimed. It was the first she had heard about this and her face was suddenly radiant. "Please, what must I wear?"

"You have an evening dress?" Hugo enquired. "Yes, of course you have! You wore it at St. Moritz."

"I have got that one and a short one too; *Grand'-mère* told me everyone was wearing short frocks in Paris. It is new and very pretty, I think."

"Well, wear the short one then," Hugo smiled. "Have you got an evening wrap? I dare say Grandmother will rake up some sables for you, which, although they smell of mothballs, are worth a king's ransom."

"Smell of mothballs, indeed!" his grandmother snorted. "Ellen would have a fit. She hangs them out on the roof garden at the beginning of every winter and then puts them in my drawer with bags of lavender. Mothballs! Get along with you. You are getting too impudent to be funny."

"Sorry, Grandmother, but lend them to Utta all the same. We are going to all the smartest places and we shan't be back until the early hours of the morning, so it's no use waiting up for us."

"You needn't flatter yourself that I should do anything of the sort," his grandmother replied. "But I am glad you are taking Utta out. You are a good boy— when it suits you." Their eyes met and hers were twinkling with a shrewd understanding.

He put his hand on Utta's shoulder as he passed her and smiled down into her rather anxious little face.

"Don't be frightened of my grandmother," he said.

184

"Her bark is much worse than her bite." And with that he left the room.

Utta looked apprehensively at Lady Loth. She was, she thought, the most formidable old lady she had ever imagined.

"Have something else to eat," Lady Loth told her, "and tell me about your life in Switzerland."

Lady Loth was, Utta discovered, an excellent listener. She had a very definite curiosity about everything and everyone. It was, in fact, that which kept her so young. She had never lost touch with the world; and though she might not approve of some modern innovations, she was far too inquisitive to ignore them.

Utta told her about her grandparents and how she had found Hugo on the mountainside with a sprained ankle.

"A romantic beginning," the old lady chuckled. "And after that you told him your name and he found out you were Andrew's child."

"No, it wasn't a bit like that," Utta said, and she related what had really happened and how Hugo had recognised the signet ring she had worn in the competitions.

"So you are an ice champion," Lady Loth said.

"I was only second," Utta explained.

"And do you intend to take it up as a career?"

"I don't really know," Utta replied. "I don't think my grandfather would approve."

Lady Loth gave a little snort as if she thought that Nicolaus Kindschi's opinion did not matter one way or another, but she said nothing and after a moment Utta went on:

"I think perhaps Hugo will decide what I had better do. He wanted me to come to England and meet my relations."

"Are you letting him run your life for you?" Lady Loth enquired.

"Yes!" Utta answered. "He arranged everything with my grandparents and has promised to look after me while I am here."

"The role of nursemaid must be a new one to Hugo,"

the old lady muttered almost beneath her breath, and then with a look of inquisitive speculation in her eyes she added, "It might be the saving of him."

12

"We are going to Rox for the week-end," Pamela said.

Utta felt a little thrill of delight go through her. However, she said nothing to Pamela, for she found Hugo's sister rather difficult to understand.

She was not like anyone she had ever met before in her life. Good-looking, although too like Hugo to be really feminine, she had a brisk, somewhat sharp manner which in reality belied her kind heart. But she was hard to know.

She gave everyone she met a superficial friendliness, but one always felt that she put a barrier between herself and any close intimacy with other people.

Utta tried to explain this, faltering over her words, when Hugo asked her how she got on with his sister; but little though she had been able to say, he understood.

"I know exactly what you mean," he said. "If you ask me, it's the frustration of living with Walter. Wait till you see him—he's the biggest bore in the House of Commons and that's saying something!"

Utta could understand his point of view; at the same time, when she met Walter, she found it easy to get on with him.

One only had to listen to him, to give him an undivided attention as he droned on about world economics or the sinister machinations of the Communist Party. At the same time he was a clever administrator.

"He is one of the props of the Party," someone once said to Hugo, who exclaimed:

"Good Lord! Is that what's wrong with it?"

Hugo's other relations Utta found somewhat bewildering. There were innumerable cousins of every age, but *en masse* they all seemed to look very much the same.

The women were dowdily dressed and appeared to be mostly of uncertain age and the men were either very stout or unhealthily thin, but they all laid down the law dogmatically as they warmed their behinds in front of the fire.

What was much more amusing than meeting them was hearing Lady Loth's comments on them.

"George was inclined to be a bully until he married when he was nearly forty. His wife looks as though butter wouldn't melt in her mouth, but she rules both George and his house with a rod of iron. They tell me the servants are too terrified of her even to give in their notice."

"Hetty! Oh, she's always been a misfit. My poor father used to say that he thought she had been changed on the seashore as a child. She likes to think she's arty, but the only thing she would be capable of drawing would be her old age pension—and then someone would have to go with her and show her how to do it."

"And then there's Eddie. . . ." Lady Loth paused with a mischievous smile on her lips.

Utta had already seen Eddie and found him preposterous. There was something about his neat, dapper figure, his white, carefully manicured hands, which he waved as he spoke, which made her want to laugh.

Then he had such an affected, mincing way of speaking and accentuating the words in his sentences so that one could almost visualise them standing out in italics.

"I was *absolutely astounded,* yes, *astounded,* my dear, when I heard that Hugo had discovered Andrew's daughter. Who would have *imagined* such a thing? I *thought* secret marriages and undiscovered heirs went *out* with Marie Corelli."

Yes, Eddie was like someone out of a book, Utta thought—but then she might say the same of others of Hugo's relations and, of course, hers.

She found herself forgetting that she belonged to them or they to her, and she found it hard, at times, not to resent their intense curiosity at what she had done and where she had been before she came into contact with Hugo.

"I feel as if you ought to put me in a cage," she said to Hugo. "They don't think of me as a human being, but as an exhibit, something strange that you have dug up on your travels."

He laughed at that. He was beginning to discover that hidden beneath the surface Utta had a surprising, and often rather wicked, little wit.

He led her on to tell him what she thought about people and things and places; but though she did not realise it, he delighted in watching her face when he showed her something new or unusual.

The emotions would chase themselves across her expression and, if she was shocked, as she was quite frequently, at some rather broad remark, the song of a cabaret singer or even the nakedness in many of the theatres, a blush would spread slowly up her white skin in a manner which Hugo never failed to find entrancing.

"You are showing the girl too much at once," Lady Loth grumbled. "You will give her mental indigestion— if she hasn't got the other sort with the beastly food you eat in those so-called smart restaurants of yours."

"She has got to grow up sometime," Hugo replied laconically.

Utta had interrupted to say:

"But I want to see everything, oh, please don't stop him. I want to go everywhere. You don't know how ignorant I feel when people are talking about things I didn't even know existed."

"You don't know really when you are well off," Hugo smiled, but he continued to take her about.

She went to cocktail parties, which she found intolerably hot and unpleasant and which frightened her because, as she said to Hugo:

"One might be invisible. No one listens to anything one says and they all appear to be talking at once at the very tops of their voices."

He took her to several smart dinner-parties and to a small dance given not for the débutantes but for what were popularly called "the young-marrieds". This she enjoyed, for she loved dancing; but when Hugo asked her her impressions afterwards, she was devastatingly frank.

"The men were so funny!" she said. "They either told me how boring everything was or paid me compliments."

"They were trying to flirt with you, I expect," Hugo said.

"Is that flirting?" Utta enquired wide-eyed. "I think it's awfully silly."

He had laughed again and then Utta had added:

"I know they are your friends, so I don't like to be unkind about them, but why do you like them so much? They don't seem to have any brains like you have, and when they talk it is all about nothing."

"What do you want people to talk about?" Hugo enquired.

She knitted her brows together.

"About real things. Things they have done or want to do; things they like or people of whom they are fond."

"You must be thinking of the French," he said, recognising that what she expected must have come from some suggestion or idea of her grandmother's. "The English are very reserved. They talk about nothing because they don't wish to reveal their real feelings, especially to a stranger."

"When does one cease to be a stranger?" Utta asked.

"I do not know the answer to that question," he replied. "Do you feel that you and I are strangers?"

The dimples appeared at that.

"No, of course not. I feel we are friends, real friends." She looked away from him or he might have seen some deeper emotion than friendship shining in her eyes.

"I hope you will always think in that way," he said solemnly.

She was so young. He remembered it every minute of the time he was with her and almost all the time they were apart.

She spent her first week-end in London because it

189

was the only time that Lady Loth could have the majority of the cousins to tea.

"Some of their husbands actually work!" she told Utta. "Or think they do, which comes to much the same thing."

"I thought they would be too rich for that," Utta said innocently.

"My dear child! Get into your head that nobody is rich in England today," Lady Loth answered. "When I was young, it was different. I remember at Rox there used to be a footman behind every chair and we usually sat down twenty-five or thirty for shooting parties.

"My brother-in-law used to have his own private coach on the train running from Paddington to Rox every Friday for the guests who were going down to stay for the week-end. There would be his own men-servants in attendance to serve the food and wine which was sent up specially in hampers. When one arrived at the station for Rox, there would be perhaps a dozen carriages and wagonettes waiting for the travellers, their servants and luggage.

"Things took longer, but we did them in style. There was none of your ceaseless rushing or the vulgarity of being in so much of a hurry that one has no time for good manners."

Lady Loth, Utta had discovered, had very strong ideas not only on manners, but on how people should behave and speak.

It made her wince when anyone referred to the " 'phone" or a "photo". She herself always spoke punctiliously of the "chimney-piece" and she corrected Utta sharply when she asked what time lunch was.

"If you mean luncheon," she said coldly, "it is at one o'clock. Lunch is what the staff have at eleven."

"Your grandmother looks old," Utta said to Hugo, "but she is very young in the way she takes so much interest in everything. She likes to know exactly what is going on and every time we go out she questions me about every detail of where we have been and what we have done."

"She likes to keep up to date," Hugo smiled. "As a

matter of fact, I believe she was fascinating when she was young and all the men in the county were madly in love with her. My grandfather was so jealous that they used to say it was a miracle that he had never murdered any of his wife's admirers."

"It seems funny to think of that now," Utta said— and then more seriously she added: "Are you afraid of growing old?"

"Not particularly," Hugo answered.

She gave a quick little sigh of relief.

"I thought perhaps you were."

"What made you think that?"

"It was something your sister Pamela said. Perhaps I shouldn't have been listening as she wasn't speaking to me, but she said to a friend: 'Yes, Hugo must be getting old, you can see that he's terrified really and yet he is too fascinated to cut and run as he would have done a year ago.' "

Utta looked up at Hugo when she finished repeating Pamela's words.

"I didn't know quite what she meant by that. I thought perhaps it must be old age of which you were frightened."

"I promise you that I look forward to having grey hair and hobbling along on two sticks," Hugo teased.

He was smiling, but at the same time, unknown to Utta, he was swearing because Pamela had been so perceptive. He had thought she had been deceived into thinking that Utta's interest in him was only that of a child who had an affectionate trust for someone older and wiser than herself.

Now he knew that Pamela was well aware that Utta thought herself in love with him. So she also thought that he was in danger. He smiled at the idea.

The child was sweet and quite the most fascinating little creature he had seen for a long time, but, at the same time, she was far too young for someone like himself.

As he had thought often enough, she would find someone of her own age.

"I shouldn't believe everything Pamela says," he said

to Utta. "She talks a lot of nonsense at times, as do her friends and all the people you meet milling around London."

Utta had begun to think that it was true, for only that morning Pamela had said:

"It's a pity you had to arrive at this time of the year. There is absolutely nobody here at all—they are all in Switzerland, Nassau or the South of France."

It was a ridiculous statement, Utta thought, when every party they went to was packed with people, the restaurants were crowded and it was difficult to get a seat for any of the plays that Hugo particularly wanted her to see.

She had been so much alone or with older people such as her instructors, who usually spoke pedantically, that she had found it hard to credit such exaggeration and impossible to force herself to speak in the same way.

She found herself continuously slipping into verbal pitfalls or saying things which brought a shout of laughter from those who heard her.

She had an instinctive longing then to run to Hugo's side, to hold on to him as though he and only he could protect her.

Every day made her realise more the manner in which she relied on him, the importance he was assuming in her life. She faced the fact in Switzerland that she loved him.

Merely to see him or talk to him made her feel as though her heart had wings; and every day they were together this feeling deepened into something more than rapture, something stronger than joy.

If she went for long without him, she found herself feeling empty and longing, with an intensity such as she had never imagined possible, for the sight of his broad shoulders filling the doorway.

As if Pamela guessed a little of what she was feeling she said to her on the morning they were leaving for Rox:

"You must be longing to see your father's home."

"Yes, I am," Utta answered a little shyly.

"And now it belongs to Hugo! I suppose you realise that if you had been a boy Hugo would have had to clear out?"

Utta's eyes widened.

"I never thought of that."

"Yes, he would have had to give up the title and, I suppose, pay back all the money he has spent," Pamela said. "But Hugo always was lucky and you are a girl."

"If I had been a boy, I would not have let him find me."

"Why ever not?"

"Because he would have hated me. Can you imagine what it would be like to have to give up your home, your position, everything you care for, to some stranger?"

"But you wouldn't have been a stranger, you would have been Andrew's son."

"I would have been a stranger to Hugo," Utta persisted.

"He is a very lucky person and the situation does not arise," Pamela remarked a little tartly.

"I expect he deserves to be lucky," Utta said softly.

Pamela laughed, unkindly it seemed to the girl listening.

"You have got a glorified idea of Hugo," she said. "I am devoted to him, but I am not so blind as not to see his faults. He has got a great many, I can assure you. But I suppose you are like all the other women who lose their hearts to him. I believe it was Eddie who said once that the road to Rox was paved with Hugo's broken love affairs."

Utta went very white, but she said nothing. Pamela busied herself with some letters she was putting away in her bag. She felt as if she had been mean and almost despicable in striking Utta what she knew herself was a blow beneath the belt.

At the same time she felt she had to warn the child. What was the point of being idealistic where Hugo was concerned?

Already people were talking, asking who was his latest conquest, and wondering how long Utta would last

193

when the charms of the rich and sophisticated Carole had paled so quickly.

"Let her know the truth before it is too late!" Pamela said to herself.

She did not realise how much too late it was already for anything she might say to do the slightest good.

"I love him!"

She did not know that Utta whispered that to herself now and disbelieved everything that she might say or insinuate. She had never seen Hugo as anything but charming and gentle save for that one moment when he had regarded her with suspicion when he first saw Andrew's ring. But he had apologised for that and always she was remembering how she had fled to his arms when she had been frightened by Don Carlos.

He had seemed then so strong and reliable, someone to whom she could trust herself absolutely, someone to whom it seemed instinctive to turn in trouble.

That was how she thought of Hugo; and she loved him, not only because she could not help it, because everything about him seemed to foster and increase that love.

She was content to sit without speaking at his side on the journey to Rox. They went down in two cars because Pamela said that Walter, who was joining them later, might wish to leave early on Monday morning.

She did not know how delighted Utta was to have the opportunity of being alone with Hugo.

She wished, above everything else, that she could have been alone with him the whole week-end, to have seen his home without anyone else there, to have explored the place without any interruptions from Pamela, Walter or anyone at all.

If she had hinted at such ideas to Pamela, she would have been scandalised.

"I wonder if there will be a party at Rox," Pamela had said when they first knew they were going.

"A party?" Utta echoed in dismay. "Oh, I hope not!"

There was such a note of horror in her voice that Pamela looked in surprise.

"Why do you say it like that?" she enquired.

"I wanted to be at Rox alone with Hugo," Utta replied. "He promised to show it to me and he has talked about it so much; I just thought there would be nobody else there."

"My dear child, you must be mad!" Pamela exclaimed. "Do you imagine that even in these modern times an unmarried girl can stay alone with an unmarried man? And especially with someone of Hugo's reputation."

Utta blushed and said no more. She had not thought of anything like that and Pamela's scorn made her feel ashamed, and yet she had known that nothing anyone could say would make her feel afraid of being alone with him.

"He is not like that," she told herself.

Sitting beside him in the car, she longed to snuggle a little closer to him and tell him how happy she was that they were going together to Rox.

As if he guessed her thoughts, he said as they drove out of the traffic of London into more open country:

"I have asked no one to stay this week-end. I didn't think you would be bored."

"I want to be with you all the time," Utta said. "I want you to show me everything—the house, the garden, the park. I don't want to miss anything."

"It's a tall order," Hugo smiled, "and you will see why when you see Rox."

Strangely enough, when she did see the great house standing against a background of the dark green trees which protected it as though it were a jewel, Utta was not overcome by its vastness.

It seemed to her as if it was just as she had expected it to be—lovely, gracious, yet warm and welcoming.

The winter sunshine was sparkling on the windows as they came in through the great stone gates and saw, lying ahead of them, the long drive which sloped down to the three ornamental lakes. On the other side of the valley Rox gazed over its green parklands and yew-hedged gardens.

Hugo slowed down the car and as they moved down the drive he watched Utta's face. She said nothing for a long time and then, as they reached the balustraded bridge over one of the lakes, he stopped and switching off the engine turned round in his seat.

"Well?" he enquired.

"I knew it would be like this," she said in a low voice.

"How did you know?"

"From what you have told me. Because it is the house you should have."

"I am very proud of it," he answered.

"But of course," she replied.

He watched her eyes as she looked at the gables silhouetted against the sky, the twisted chimney-pots and the flag, blue and white, flying in the wind.

"What would you have felt if I had been a boy?" she asked.

He knew instinctively what she meant though he had no knowledge of Pamela's remarks on the subject.

"I should have hated to give it up to you," he said, "and yet I would rather you had it than a great many people—Eddie for instance."

"He must never live here," Utta said. "It would be wrong, horrible. He wouldn't understand."

She did not need to supplement her words. Hugo nodded his head.

"No, Eddie would not understand."

He looked down at Utta as he spoke and for a moment there was a flicker in his eyes and he half-opened his lips as if to speak. Then he closed them again, turned round in his seat and started up the engine.

Another woman would have exclaimed and perhaps cried out at the beauty of the Marble Hall. Hugo was tired of the gushing platitudes of those who viewed the Adam furniture in the Silver Drawing-Room for the first time.

He knew by heart exactly what people would say when they entered the Long Gallery, and yet somehow he was not astonished when Utta said very little.

Her feelings were shown by the excitement in her eyes and the tenseness of her hand when sometimes she would lay it on his arm and draw his attention to some particular object about which she wanted to ask a question.

He thought then, as they moved round the old house, how perfectly she fitted in there; how, if he had never known her before, he would somehow have guessed that by her blood she was part of the place.

Only when he brought her at length in front of her father's portrait in the Long Gallery did he feel, for a moment, as if he, himself, were the intruder and the newcomer while Utta had more right to Rox than he.

Andrew had been painted by a famous artist while he was still at Oxford and there was some indefinable likeness between him and Utta, even though in features they were completely opposite.

She stood for a long time looking at the portrait and then she turned to Hugo with a little smile.

"I feel that he is glad for you to have Rox if he cannot have it himself," she said.

On an impulse Hugo picked up her hand and raised it to his lips.

"No one could have said anything more gracious than that," he answered.

"Show me more," Utta begged. "Is there time to see the garden before it is dark?"

"That must wait for tomorrow," Hugo replied. "I haven't half-finished the house. There is the Music Room and the Observatory, the Chapel where your grandparents are buried, the State bedrooms and the Orangery."

"How wonderful!" Utta exclaimed. "I keep thinking each room will be the last, and I feel, too, that though it is so big I could never be lonely here."

"Why do you say that?" Hugo enquired.

"Because it is full of people who have been here before. They have lived and loved, been born and died here. They can never be forgotten as long as Rox stands."

He stopped suddenly and looked at her. She was wearing the soft blue coat and skirt that she had worn when she left Switzerland; she had pulled off her hat and her hair was like flames of dancing gold against the dark panelling.

"Do you feel that you belong here?" he asked in a low voice.

"Of course I do!" Utta answered. "That is what I have been trying to tell you. I knew it from the first moment as we turned down the drive—I am sure of it now. It is home to me as it will always be to all those who bear the name of Graye."

"Then listen," Utta . . ." he began.

At that moment Pamela's voice called to interrupt them.

"Tea is ready," she cried, "and I can't wait any longer for either of you."

"We're coming," Utta replied, and added in a low voice to Hugo: "Poor Pamela, she hates waiting for her tea. I'm afraid we had forgotten all about her."

They hurried to the Small Drawing-Room where tea was laid in front of a blazing log fire.

"They telephoned to say that Walter has caught the four-thirty train and will be here by six o'clock."

"Did you tell them to send the car to meet him?" Hugo enquired.

"Yes," Pamela replied. "I hope Walter remembers to bring the evening paper. I want to see what they say about the party we went to last night."

"You are an inveterate reader of the gossip columns, that's what's wrong with you," Hugo teased his sister.

"Everyone enjoys gossip as long as it's about their best friends and not about themselves," Pamela replied.

When tea was over, Utta saw a little more of the house.

Now it seemed that everywhere they went there were people, either in the rooms they visited or coming in search of Hugo with a message to say the Agent was waiting to see him or that the Head Keeper had called in the hope of an interview.

Twice he was fetched to the telephone and finally, before they had seen half there was to see, it was time to go upstairs and dress for dinner.

"I feel I want to stroke this balustrade," Utta said to

Pamela as they went up the wide oak staircase about which there was a legend that one of the mad Lord Roxburtons had, for a bet, driven a coach and horses up it.

"It looks to me as though it wants a good polish," Pamela said critically. "The servants get awfully lax if Hugo is away for any time. The old ones are all right, they have been here for years and adore the place; but the new ones don't care and if someone isn't at them all the time, they get slack and lazy."

"It must cost an awful lot of money to keep a house like this going," Utta remarked.

"It certainly does," Pamela replied. "It's lucky that your grandmother was American—Hugo is a rich man! Not that he couldn't always do with more, if it comes to that." She was thinking of Carole as she spoke and regretting a little that the Munton millions would not contribute to the glory of Rox.

"Of course," she reasoned with herself, "it may not be over."

Yet it was unlikely that Hugo would seem so devoted to Utta if his heart was engaged elsewhere. All the same, you never knew where he was concerned. He was an extraordinary person.

She often thought she understood her brother less than any other man she knew.

Utta's bedroom had a small four-poster which delighted her and embroidered curtains which had been done by skilful fingers in the eighteenth century.

"It must have taken them years and years," she said to Pamela, looking at the tiny stitches which so skilfully portrayed birds and flowers with tiny cupids flitting amongst them.

"I expect they had plenty of time on their hands in those days," Pamela said. "How Walter would have enjoyed himself if he had lived then! He is always grumbling about the way the housemaid darns his socks and he thinks I ought to do them. He really considers it a wifely duty. He has never really got round to acknowledging the emancipation of women."

"I will darn them for him if you like," Utta said.

Pamela laughed.

"You will do nothing of the sort. If you do, you will spoil him and he will expect me to do the same for the rest of my life. Besides, men have no respect for anyone they can treat like a door-mat."

"Would darning be being a door-mat?" Utta asked.

"Of course it would," Pamela replied. "A man respects a woman when she is independent, just as he only wants her when she is hard to get."

She spoke lightly, but when the bedroom door had closed behind her Utta stood thoughtfully in the middle of the room. She wondered if that was true, and then she knew she could never pretend to be what she wasn't.

She was never clever or subtle enough to be anything but herself. If she loved anybody, she loved them with her whole thoughts and being, with her heart and her soul.

"That is how I love Hugo," she told herself.

Then she stretched wide her arms with a sudden gesture of ecstasy. She was here at Rox where she longed to be. She was here under his roof with nothing to interrupt them save Pamela and Walter.

She felt suddenly that there was an urgency about everything. It was as if a tidal wave was carrying her forward and onward almost quicker than she could breathe, and yet at the same time she gloried in the speed of it.

She was riding on the crest of a wave and ultimately it would submerge her in deep waters from which she could not escape if she would.

And yet she was not afraid—this was love, this was life, this was what she had always wanted, and now it was hers.

She was in such a hurry that she could not dress leisurely but almost scrambled into her evening dress and slipped downstairs long before the others were ready and while the housemaids were still tidying the drawing-room and making up the fire.

She went to the piano which stood in the corner and began to play it very softly. Hugo came to the door and stood watching her for some minutes before she realised that he was there.

She had chosen a Chopin waltz and she played the rippling notes as if they came from the very depth of her heart. Then she saw him and suddenly her fingers were still.

The lights in the corner of the room were low and for a moment, as she rose to her feet, he thought that she looked like a ghost of the past—one of her own ancestors.

She wore a dress of silver lace which Pamela had bought for her in London and which was, in reality, almost too grand for a quiet evening at home with just three members of the family. But Utta had wanted to wear her best at Rox.

It was not only for Hugo she wanted to appear beautiful, but for the house itself. It was as if she paid it the compliment of giving it herself, even as she took comfort and pride from its beauty and grandeur.

"I was just trying the piano," Utta said, a little shy on finding that Hugo had been listening to her.

He walked across the room to her side.

"Don't stop; you play well."

"Not really. My teacher said I was born idle because I always wanted to be outside instead of practising as I should have been doing."

"Play me something else," Hugo commanded.

"I am afraid I know no modern music."

"If, by that, you think I am asking for jazz, you are very much mistaken," Hugo said.

She smiled at the note almost of asperity in his tone and then her fingers began to play a crazy, haunting little tune which he recognised as one of the Swiss folk songs.

It was not very subtle and yet it seemed to linger in one's mind, evoking pictures of spring in the mountains, of flowers growing up to where the snows began, of blue skies and sunshine and the sound of cow bells coming across the valley.

"Thank you!" he said as she finished, "and now another."

She got to her feet and walked away from the piano.

"You will make me vain. I am no pianist and yet somehow this house calls for music."

"We will give a ball here for you," Hugo said. "I knew there was something I wanted to do. A ball in the summer when people can walk out on the lawns. We can have lights round the lake as they did in my grandfather's time, the fountains lit up and the house itself floodlit."

"It sounds wonderful!" Utta exclaimed. "But actually I wasn't thinking of that sort of music."

"What were you thinking of then?"

"I don't quite know," she said dreamily. "It is as if there was some hidden melody throbbing around us as we move about, as we open one door and go through another."

"Are you being psychic or only imaginative?" he enquired.

"I don't know," she answered. "I only feel that the house is full of melodies. It is a happy house—you will be always happy here, I am sure of that."

"Alone?" he enquired.

"Whether you are alone or with other people, you will still be happy," Utta said positively.

"I don't think any man is particularly happy alone," Hugo insisted.

She looked up at him when he said that and her eyes were held by his.

For a moment she dare not breathe; and then, as they stood there lost in some strange enchantment of their own, they heard Pamela's voice talking to Walter as they came down the stairs together.

13

"Why have you been so long coming to see me?" Carole asked the question with deliberate sweetness.

But there was a certain hardness in her voice that she could not entirely disguise.

Hugo smiled at her disarmingly.

"I have been very busy."

"Going places with your little cousin from all I hear."

"Then you have heard right. Did you enjoy yourself after we left?" he continued, deliberately changing the conversation.

Carole shook her head.

"You know I didn't. It all seemed very flat after you had gone. I missed you, Hugo." Her voice softened seductively as she bent towards him, her eyes very soft and tender and her mouth invitingly red.

It seemed as if Hugo did not notice. He was intent on choosing a cigarette from his case and, as he shut it with a click, he looked round the be-flowered sitting-room.

"Got a match?"

"There is one by your side," Carole replied a trifle sharply. "Now listen, Hugo! We have got to make plans."

"Plans for what?"

"You know the answer to that—to see each other; to be together."

She knew that she was taking a risk in deliberately forcing his hand, and yet after all that had happened she was still so sure of herself that she felt he would not deliberately refuse her.

He had not written to her when he left Switzerland and though she had expected that he might meet her at the airport after she had telegraphed her time of arrival, there had only been a great bunch of carnations at the Ritz to welcome her.

She had telephoned him, not once but several times a day, yet always it seemed she was unfortunate in finding he had just gone out, left for a theatre, or else no one knew where he had gone or when he was expected back.

Finally, it was only by arousing herself much earlier than her usual time in the morning that she managed to catch him when he was having his breakfast.

"I have got to see you," she said, ignoring even to herself the fact that he did not seem very keen.

Now that he was here, sitting opposite her, looking so handsome and so distinguished in his quiet, well-cut

London clothes, she felt a sudden surge of emotion and it was with difficulty she did not rush to him, fling her arms round his neck and beg him for his love.

She had just enough pride left to keep control of herself in spite of the fact that Hugo's calm detachment was a provocation which she felt might drive her to any insanity.

He put down the match with which he had been lighting his cigarette, arranging it with an almost precise care in the middle of a glass ash-tray before he said:

"I am not good at being tied, Carole."

"What do you mean?" she asked, conscious of a sudden fear.

"I think you understand," he said, and then he smiled in his irresistible manner which made it almost impossible for any woman not to smile back.

"My dear, we have had a wonderful time together—don't spoil it."

"But, Hugo . . ." Carole began.

"There are no buts," he interrupted. "We are both grown-up people; we both knew what we were doing and we both enjoyed every moment of it—but it is over, my dear, and you have got to face the fact."

"Do you really think . . ." she began furiously, springing to her feet, but Hugo was too quick for her.

He had risen too and before she could say anything he walked across to her, put his arms round her and pressed his lips against hers.

For a moment she resisted before she went limp in his arms, feeling the ecstasy of his touch flood over her, surrendering herself to the flames of rising desire which flickered within her body.

Then, so quickly that she could hardly credit it, he released her.

"Good-bye, my dear, and thank you!" he said.

Before she could collect her scattered senses, he had picked up his hat and rolled umbrella and had gone from the room, shutting the door of her suite quietly behind him.

It was only as she heard his footsteps die away down the passage that the paralysis which seemed to have held her motionless and almost without breathing passed and she came to life.

She ran then to the door, but even as she reached it she realised that it was too late; she could not go chasing after him down the corridors of the Ritz, someone they knew might see her. No, she had to let him go, there was nothing she could do about it.

She stood for a long time with her face to the door, her forehead resting against it, then she walked back to sit on the sofa, tapping the tip of her finger-nail against her teeth, a dark and brooding expression on her face.

In that moment it seemed to her that all she had tried to run away from in the past came back to haunt and taunt her. She could hear those voices over again:

"No, nothing today!"

She could hear her own sobs in the small, airless back room which had been her only sanctuary in the boarding house; she could hear Dave's voice coarse and drunk, shouting insults at her; and she knew that her wealth had brought her nothing but emptiness, nothing but heartbreak.

She loved Hugo! She loved him as much as her shallow, empty little heart was capable of loving—and yet he had left her.

Outside the Ritz Hugo drew a deep breath of relief. It had been an uncomfortable interview, as he had expected it to be.

It was not the first time women had been uncomfortably persistent in their pursuit of him, and each time it happened he wondered why he had been such a fool as to encourage their affections in the first place.

He almost envied the men who had no attraction for women, who had to plead and cajole or bribe their way into favour.

As always when some women of whom he was tired tried to cling possessively to him, he felt ashamed, not only for her but of himself.

"Damn it!" he said out loud. "I want a drink."

He walked down to his Club in St. James's Street. Round the bar he found a number of his friends and as he drank and joked with them he tried to forget Carole, to forget the maddening sense of guilt which lingered at the back of his mind.

Utta spent the day shopping with Pamela. She found herself astonished at the number of things Pamela thought absolutely necessary for her wardrobe. There were day dresses, cocktail dresses and evening gowns, besides suits and tweeds, overcoats and underclothes.

"We're spending an awful lot of money," she said once or twice in awed tones.

"Don't worry about that," Pamela answered. "Hugo said you were to have everything that was necessary and until some arrangement is made with the lawyers he will pay the bills."

"Are you quite sure he won't be horrified at the amount they come to?" Utta asked.

"No, of course not! Hugo is a rich man. Besides, you have got to be a credit to the family." Pamela was teasing, but Utta took her quite seriously.

"Of course!" she said. "I wouldn't like any of you to be ashamed of me."

To her surprise Pamela, who was never demonstrative, bent forward and kissed her cheek.

"As though we would be," she exclaimed. "You are quite the nicest and most attractive relation we've ever had."

If Utta was surprised at Pamela's effusiveness, anyone else who might have heard that conversation would hardly have believed it possible.

Pamela had grown used to keeping her feelings to herself and it was very seldom that she paraded her affections or showed the world anything of her innermost feelings.

No one knew how greatly she regretted that she and Walter had no children. They had been married now for fifteen years and had given up hope.

Sometimes Pamela dreamed of holding a baby close against her breast, of hearing her children call for her, of knowing that maternal love which nothing else in the world could equal.

206

It seemed to her at times that Utta was like the daughter she might have had, or perhaps a younger sister she had never known.

She enjoyed taking her round the shops, introducing her to their friends, having someone else to think about besides Walter, with his chronic indigestion which came from long hours in the House of Commons and irregular times for meals.

The last night they had stayed at Rox, when Utta was dressing for dinner, Pamela had come into her room with a worn, velvet box in her hand.

"I have brought these for you," she said a little abruptly.

"For me!" Utta exclaimed. She took the velvet box from Pamela's hands, opened it, then gave a little exclamation of surprise and delight. A two-row pearl necklace lay on the white satin which lined the box.

"Pearls!" Utta exclaimed. "Are they really for me?"

"Yes, and they're real," Pamela replied briskly. "None of your rubbishy cultured stuff which everyone wears now. They belonged to my mother. She gave them to me when I was twenty-one."

"But you can't really mean me to have them," Utta said.

"Yes, they're a present," Pamela insisted. "They are too small for me now. It's a young girl's necklace and it will suit you beautifully."

As Pamela rightly said, they did suit Utta. The soft, iridescent sheen of the pearls showed up the purity of the skin that encircled the base of her neck. She was very conscious of them as she went downstairs to show Hugo.

"They were your mother's," she said softly, putting up her long fingers to touch them.

"I remember Pamela wearing them," he smiled, "and I'm glad that she has given them to you."

"I've never had such a wonderful present," Utta told him. "In fact, I've never owned any jewellery before."

"We shall have to see what else we can find you," he said carelessly. "There is a tremendous amount of family jewels kept in the Bank—it would do some of them good to have an airing."

He said no more although he thought how wonderfully Utta's fair skin would show off the emerald necklace or the set of aquamarines, which had been his mother's favourite stone.

He was well aware that Pamela was hoping that he would ask Utta to marry him, but some perverseness in himself would not let him really consider it.

"The child is too young," he said; and even while he watched her with pride, he forced himself to ignore another feeling fighting its way into recognition within his heart.

"There is plenty of time," he thought.

He would not be hurried; and deliberately, because, although he would not admit it, he was half-afraid of himself, he avoided being alone with Utta in the great romantic rooms at Rox, which seemed somehow impregnated with the atmosphere of love.

He did not know how much Utta had longed to be alone with him or how disappointed she was when at Hugo's invitation both Walter and Pamela had gone with them on the tour of the gardens.

She rebuked herself for being so selfish and yet she could not help it. The mere fact that Hugo was beside her gave her a thrill as if every nerve in her body responded to some secret chorus of beauty and music.

Everything was so right when he was there; everything seemed flat and empty when he was absent.

As she chose her new clothes with Pamela, she judged each by the standard of how it would seem to Hugo. "Will he think that I look pretty in that?" "Will he admire me in this?"

That was the only criterion for her choice, and although she had so little experience, her instinctive good taste made her want all that was simple and classical and discard everything that was vulgar and gaudy.

"I'm exhausted!" Pamela said at length. "We must go home and have a cup of tea. I can't walk another step."

"There is something about shopping that is much more exhausting than skating," Utta confessed. "I never

208

feel tired when I am skating, but now I shall be glad of a rest."

"Not half as glad as I shall be," Pamela said. "Come on, don't let's look at another thing."

She led the way from the shop and drove Utta back in her small Austin, which was easy to negotiate in and out of the traffic. Lady Loth welcomed them in characteristic manner.

"Have you had a good afternoon—wasting time and money?" she asked tartly.

"We've spent a great deal of the latter, if that's what you mean, Grandmother," Pamela replied. "But Utta at least has something to clothe her nakedness."

"You're spoiling the child—making her like you and all the rest of your dolled-up friends, who think of nothing but the latest fashion. Look at me! I've worn the same style for twenty years and it hasn't done me any harm."

"You wouldn't have said that at Utta's age," Pamela replied; then she laughed. "If you want to know the truth, Grandmother, I think you're as vain as any of us when it comes to going anywhere. Look what a fuss you made about your robes for the Coronation."

"Did you go to the Coronation?" Utta asked wide-eyed.

"I did!" Lady Loth answered. "I was a Lady-in-Waiting once and they haven't forgotten me."

"Can I see your coronet?" Utta enquired.

"Yes, child, if you want to. It's upstairs in a hat-box; I will get Ellen to bring it down after tea."

"That would be lovely!" Utta exclaimed.

"You'd better get Ellen to bring down the tiara as well and your diamond necklace," Pamela said. "You looked magnificent when you went to the Abbey and it is no use pretending that you weren't aware of the fact."

"I didn't want you to be ashamed of me," Lady Loth said; and hearing almost the same words that she had used herself, Utta's eyes met Pamela's and they both smiled.

Baxter came tottering in with the tea.

"You are wanted on the telephone, Miss Utta," he

209

said. "I can't get the lady's name, she speaks too strangely."

"You're getting deaf, that's what is wrong with you," Lady Loth said severely. "Look at me, I can hear everything that is said to me."

"I can hear well enough except on the 'phone," the old man grumbled. "These new-fangled instruments are a curse, that's what they are!"

Utta ran downstairs to the library, the uncomfortable, cold front room of the house, which was seldom used except by those who wished to telephone. She picked up the receiver from where it lay on the table.

"Hello!"

"Is that you, Utta?"

It was Carole speaking, she recognised the voice at once.

"Yes, Mrs. Munton."

"I want to see you. Can you come round now? It's very important."

"I don't know," Utta replied. "I have only just got back from shopping."

"It's urgent!" Carole insisted. "I want to see you and you are to come alone."

"Very well," Utta agreed. "I will do my best. Where are you speaking from?"

"The Ritz. It isn't far, you can walk round if you can't get a taxi."

"I will come as soon as I can," Utta promised.

"Don't fail me!" Carole spoke sharply and put down the telephone.

Slowly Utta replaced the receiver. She didn't know why, but she had an uncomfortable feeling of repugnance. She didn't want to go and see Mrs. Munton.

She had been jealous of her; and though Hugo had made it quite clear that there was no reason for such an emotion, she could not help herself feeling both unfriendly and a little shy towards the beautiful, poised woman of the world who was so familiar with him.

"I don't want to go!" she said aloud and shook herself impatiently.

She was being morbid and fanciful. Besides, as Mrs.

Munton was a friend of Hugo's it would be rude of her to refuse an invitation which had been so pressing and so insistent.

That she was Hugo's friend should be enough to ensure Carole Munton's respect and politeness, Utta thought. She ran upstairs to the drawing-room.

"Who wanted you?" Lady Loth asked curiously.

"Mrs. Munton, a friend of Hugo's. She wants me to go round and see her at the Ritz."

"Now?" Pamela enquired.

"Did you tell her you were tired? We've had a long afternoon."

"I'll feel much better when I have had a cup of tea," Utta said, "and besides, as she asked me so particularly, it would be rude if I didn't go."

"If it's a cocktail party you had better change into one of your new dresses," Pamela suggested.

"A party!" Utta echoed. "I hadn't thought of that, but I don't think that it is a party. She didn't say so anyway, and she said particularly that I was to come alone."

"Well, you certainly needn't change if it's just a woman-to-woman chat," Pamela said. "It's annoying not to be certain—but that's people all over. They never tell you what's happening. I was dining with some friends of Walter's last week and the hostess said 'just a little party', but when I got to it there was the most enormous crowd, everybody dressed to the nines, and I had gone in quite a simple dinner-frock with hardly a jewel. I could have cried with fury."

"Nowadays women do such things on purpose," Lady Loth said. "But in my day it was considered very ill-bred not to do everything in one's power to make one's guests feel comfortable and happy. A hostess took trouble in those days and didn't just herd a collection of people she hardly knew into one room and fill them up with a nauseous mixture of drinks which would ruin any decent digestion."

"Which is just one way of saying, Grandmother, that you don't approve of cocktails," Pamela remarked.

"Approve!" Lady Loth exclaimed. "I don't disapprove of anything you do these days, I merely think the lot of you are vulgar and ill-bred."

Pamela laughed. "Don't listen to her, Utta. Cocktail parties are a cheap and easy way of entertaining. We can't all afford to give balls with champagne suppers and powdered footmen."

Utta got to her feet. "Perhaps I had better tidy myself and then go along to the Ritz," she said.

"Shall I drop you?" Pamela suggested. "It won't be much out of my way."

"No, don't worry," Utta answered, "and thank you very much for choosing me all those lovely things this afternoon."

"You've got a fitting tomorrow morning," Pamela said. "I'll call for you about eleven. I had better come and see that they have got the things right."

"Oh, please do!" Utta said, with such sincerity that Pamela's eyes were very soft as she watched her go from the room.

"She's a sweet child," she said aloud as the door closed behind Utta.

"Do you think Hugo will marry her?" Lady Loth enquired.

Pamela looked at her grandmother in surprise.

"What made you think of that . . .?" she began, and then she stopped and laughed. "It's no use trying to keep anything from you, Grandmother. It's what I have been hoping for, but who knows where Hugo is concerned?"

"If you ask me, he's as pleased as Punch with the girl," Lady Loth remarked.

"But I am not sure if he realises it himself," Pamela said. "I was watching him at Rox this week-end. She amused him; he is gentler with her than I have ever seen him with anyone, and it is obvious that she's in love with him."

"Wears her heart on her sleeve," Lady Loth ejaculated.

"That's just it. It's all too easy." Pamela gave a little sigh. "I would love to have Utta for a sister-in-law and she seems to belong to Rox, which, of course, in fact she does."

Upstairs in her bedroom Utta powdered her nose and, because she was afraid of Carole, put on a hat which she thought was slightly more sophisticated than the others. Then running downstairs, she set off towards the Ritz.

It was only five minutes' walk, but it seemed to her longer. The nearer she got, the more she felt depressed at what lay ahead of her.

Why should Mrs. Munton want to see her? Why had she been so pressing on the telephone and why had she told her to come alone?

She had grown used to entering big hotels since she came to London, but she felt very shy, small and insignificant as she went up to the reception desk and asked, in a low voice, for Mrs. Munton.

"The page will take you up, madam," the clerk told her.

Utta followed the boy across to the lift, which carried them to the second floor.

It was a long walk down a red-carpeted corridor to where Carole's suite overlooked the Green Park. She was sitting in the window, and as she walked across the room Utta thought, with a sinking of her heart, that she looked more beautiful than ever.

She was wearing a dress of black satin. There were five rows of pearls round her neck and a huge diamond brooch sparkled on her slim shoulder.

"Oh, here you are," Carole ejaculated. "I was beginning to think you must have lost your way, you were so long in coming."

"I walked," Utta replied simply. "I am sorry if I kept you waiting." She stood expectantly in the centre of the room. Carole had not shaken hands with her, but now with a gesture of her hand she indicated a chair.

"Sit down."

Utta did as she was told, sitting on the edge feeling very young and very vulnerable and, at the same time, unaccountably afraid.

Carole took the lid off a white onyx cigarette-box and helped herself to a cigarette.

"You don't smoke, do you?" she asked.

"No, thank you," Utta answered.

Carole lit the cigarette and sat down on a chair facing her.

"I'm going to be very frank and straightforward," she said. "I want you to be the same with me."

Utta clasped her hands together but said nothing.

"Has Hugo asked you to marry him?" Carole enquired. Her voice was harsh and seemed for a moment to echo round the room.

"No," Utta said. The answer came out spontaneously before she had time to think. Even as she spoke she wondered why she had not told Mrs. Munton it was no business of hers.

"Do you expect him to ask you?"

"I don't know why . . . I should answer these questions . . ." Utta began, stammering a little over her words.

"There is a very good reason for my asking, I can promise you," Carole told her. "I want to know the truth. I want to know exactly how far things have gone between you and Hugo."

"I don't know what you mean," Utta replied.

"Of course you know what I mean," Carole said impatiently. "Do you deny that you love him?"

Utta went very pale; she did not reply.

"Answer me!" Carole insisted angrily. "Tell me the truth or are you ashamed?"

"I have got nothing to be ashamed of," Utta answered. "Yes, I love Hugo."

"And he loves you," Carole added, "or thinks he does."

She spoke bitterly and did not look at Utta as she spoke or she would have seen the sudden light in her eyes. Carole stubbed out her cigarette.

"Listen to me," she said. "I have only just come back to London, but already everyone is talking of you and Hugo. He intends to marry you, they say, and I'm quite certain that you intend to marry him. But before you make up your mind I have got something to tell you, something that I think you ought to hear."

"What is it?" Utta asked in a low whisper.

"I told you in Switzerland that Hugo and I were engaged," Carole went on. "I told you only what I believed to be the truth. I thought I was dealing with a man who was honourable, a man who would keep his promise, a man whom I could trust. I was mistaken. I think he meant to be all these things until you came along. You took him away from me."

"It is not true," Utta cried uncomfortably. "I have never taken him away from you. He came into my life by chance and later he discovered who I am, and it was obvious, wasn't it, that he should bring me back to England to meet my relations?"

"You were in love with him before that," Carole said accusingly. "Oh, I don't blame you—Hugo is very easy to fall in love with, as a great many women besides us have found."

The hurt in her voice was so poignant that Utta said nothing.

"But don't think that I have brought you here to reproach you for being deceived by him. You are too inexperienced to know what you are doing in dealing with a man like Hugo."

Utta got to her feet.

"I don't think I want to stay here and hear you saying such things about him," she said. "I'm sorry if you are unhappy or if he has hurt you, but it is not my business."

"It is your business, you little fool!" Carole cried roughly. "Sit down!"

"I think I had better go," Utta replied, with a calmness she was far from feeling inside.

"Sit down, I tell you!" Carole commanded. "You have got to hear what I have to say first."

Utta hesitated and then, wondering if she was doing right, sat down again on the edge of the chair.

"I told you that Hugo and I were engaged," Carole said. "He promised to marry me and we lived together for some months. Do you understand what I mean by that?"

Utta's lips were dry.

"Yes, I understand," she whispered.

"He was in love with me," Carole continued. "Madly and crazily in love with me—until you came along. It is you who have spoiled our happiness together, you who have taken him away."

"I'm sorry, but it isn't true."

"But it isn't as easy as you think," Carole went on, ignoring the interruption. "It isn't just a case of being off with the old and on with the new where I am concerned. Hugo is not going to get away with that—not this time."

She got to her feet, walked to the box on the table and took out another cigarette. "Hugo has done this sort of thing often enough before," she went on. "There were plenty of people ready to tell me of his reputation—besides, I'm not a fool. But this time he is going to play the game whether he likes it or not. He is going to marry me and not you."

"I don't think you will be able to make Hugo do anything he doesn't want to do," Utta said in a quiet voice.

Her heart was hammering, but she had kept control of herself. Perhaps it was because Carole was obviously so on edge that she found herself growing less afraid of her, yet at the same time she was panic-stricken by the suffering and harshness in her voice.

"That's what you think," Carole retorted, "and that's what Hugo thinks too, but you are both mistaken. Do you hear me? You are both mistaken."

She spoke the last words very slowly, lit the cigarette and sat down again.

"So you think you are going to marry Hugo?" she went on with a sneer in her voice. "And if you do, shall I tell you what will happen? You will marry him, go to Rox and have your children there. Children who will inherit the house, the title and all that Hugo possesses, but the child who is the real heir to it all—Hugo's eldest child—will be born without a name, without a father. Does that mean anything to you?"

Utta was very still, but she could feel her fingers biting into each other as she held them clenched in her lap.

"What are you trying to tell me?" she asked in a voice hardly above a whisper.

"I am telling you that I'm having Hugo's child," Carole answered. "Now, will you decide whether he should marry me or you?"

Utta looked away from her and out through the window over the Green Park. For the moment she saw nothing, everything was swimming before her eyes, and then, unsteadily, she rose to her feet.

"I . . . must . . . go," she stammered.

"Not before you have answered me," Carole said.

Utta looked at her.

"I shall not marry Hugo," she answered quietly.

"I thought you would say that," Carole replied. "Go now, if you want to."

Without looking back Utta walked across the room, opened the door and passed into the corridor. It seemed to her endless as she walked down it, feeling as though her legs would hardly carry her.

When she reached the lift, she was forced to sit as it descended to the ground floor.

"Are you all right, miss?" the attendant's voice enquired.

She came out of her reverie to find he was staring at her with concern on his face.

"Yes, quite all right, thank you," she answered, and walked from the lift across the hall and out into the street. She felt as if nothing was clear—not even her mind.

For the moment she could not think, could not feel, she was dazed as though someone had hit her on the head and she was not yet fully conscious.

When she reached the house, she crept upstairs, tiptoeing past the drawing-room lest Lady Loth should hear her and call her in for a chat. In her own bedroom she locked the door and flung herself down on the bed, her face hidden in the pillow.

It was then as she lay there that the feeling of being dazed and semi-conscious passed away. Her brain became clear again and the pain within her heart seemed to throb with an agony which she had not believed it possible for her or anyone else to feel.

"Hugo's child!" It was still hard to credit that the words that Carole had told her were the truth, and yet she knew she could not disbelieve them. Hugo and Carole living together, loving each other!

It was only right and proper, she thought miserably, that, as Carole had said, the child of their union should have its chance, should live at Rox, should know its father, should have the security and the protection of his name.

How could anything else possibly be fair or right? What a fool she had been not to realise from the very beginning that there was something between Carole and Hugo!

She had known it perhaps, deep down in her heart, by the possessive way in which Carole had laid her hand on his arm and looked up into his eyes and in the manner in which she had coupled his name with hers in her conversation on all possible occasions.

Carole was right, she had been the interloper coming between them, separating them and interfering by her very presence. And yet, how could she have helped loving Hugo?

It happened before she even knew who he was, that moment on the mountainside when her heart had known what her mind would have denied.

"I love you!" She said the words aloud and felt guilty even as she said them.

She remembered that moment at Rox when she had looked into his eyes and thought she had found an echo of what was leaping and burning within herself.

How stupid she had been to think for one moment that happiness could come so easily with so little effort! And yet the pain of knowing it was denied her was too terrible to be endured.

Utta sat up suddenly on the bed: Knowing what she knew now, how could she see him again? How could she feel as she felt and speak naturally or without revealing the horror and misery of her knowledge?

218

She must get away.

She jumped to her feet and going to the big old-fashioned mahogany wardrobe took from it her suitcase. It was covered with the labels of the Swiss airways and for a moment she felt the tears prick her eyes as she remembered her excitement and her joy at travelling beside Hugo towards England.

Everything had seemed so wonderful, everything had seemed so perfect.

This was not the moment for tears. She had very little time. Whatever happened, she could not meet him, could not explain, could not let him guess the humiliation she felt of loving him and knowing how hopeless it was.

Swiftly she pulled open the drawers and threw the first things that came to her hand into the case.

In the bottom drawer she found her skating boots and her costumes—the ones she wore for practising with Ernst and the one her grandmother had given her for the competitions.

She put them in too; they might be useful. After all, it was the one thing that she could do well, the one talent by which she could earn her own living.

It was then that Utta stood still and put her hands to her face. She knew that she was not going to return to Switzerland. She could not face her grandparents, could not explain at this moment why she had come back. What could she say? How could she tell her grandmother and her grandfather that she had fallen in love with a man who had betrayed another woman?

They would not understand, they would be horrified, shocked and disgusted.

She could never be disgusted with Hugo because she loved him too much. She took her hands from her face.

"I shall love him till I die!" She said the words out loud and knew they were a vow—a vow she would never break.

Yet in the meantime what was she to do? She must be alone, she must have time to think. She had a sudden horror of being cross-examined or questioned as to her feelings, as to what Carole had said to her of the predicament which lay ahead of Hugo.

She wanted to run away, run so fast and so far that no one would ever find her.

"I must be alone, I must." As she spoke the words, she ran to the wardrobe.

She took down her travelling coat, wrapped it round her and pulled a little plain knitted cap over her curls. She took up her handbag. Pamela had given her ten pounds only yesterday.

"You can't walk about with nothing in your purse," she said, "and when that's finished, ask me for some more."

Ten pounds would solve the problems of the immediate future. Utta picked up her suitcase. She went to the door, opened it a crack and listened. It was seven-thirty; Lady Loth would be in her bedroom changing for dinner.

It was unlikely that Baxter or any of the other servants would be on the stairs or in the hall. Her case was heavy, but she managed to hurry down the stairs at almost a run.

There was no one about, the house was very quiet.

Opening the front door she went out into the street and pulled the door to behind her.

It closed with a slam of irrevocable finality.

14

Hugo arrived at eight-thirty to take Utta out to dinner.

They were dining with some friends of his at their house in Regent's Park and planned to go on later to the Café de Paris to hear the latest cabaret singer who had just arrived from America.

Lady Loth was at dinner when Hugo walked into the dining-room looking excessively dashing in his dinner-jacket with a red carnation in his buttonhole.

"Have you got a glass of wine for me?" he asked as

he bent to kiss her cheek. "I know you've got the most delectable vintages stored away in your cellar for all that you never bring them up for any of us."

"What's the use of wasting good port and delicate wines on people who ruin their palates with vitriol and vinegar?" Lady Loth enquired spiritedly.

Hugo laughed.

"A perfect description of present-day gin."

"You needn't soft-soap me into bringing up my best bottles," his grandmother went on. "There aren't many of them left and you'll have them when I die."

"By that time they'll be too old to be palatable," Hugo retorted.

"You needn't think you flatter me," she replied sharply; at the same time he could see that she was pleased.

Baxter brought a glass, set it by Hugo's side and came back with a decanter of sherry.

"It's a good year, m'lord," he said as he poured him out a glass.

Hugo tasted it appreciatively.

"Very pleasant," he approved.

His grandmother snorted.

"There you are, you see. I might just as well give you the stuff they sell at the grocer's for all the difference you would notice."

"Where's Utta?" Hugo asked. "Have you been teaching her fashionable ways and that it's correct to keep a man waiting? I have never known her unpunctual before."

"It would be a good thing if she wasn't always ready to come at your beck and call," Lady Loth remarked.

"Tell Miss Utta I'm here, Baxter, will you," Hugo said to the old butler.

"Very good, m'lord."

Baxter withdrew from the room. Hugo leant back in his chair.

"I was thinking, Grandmother. We ought to give a dance for Utta at Rox this summer."

"A dance?" Lady Loth queried. "I thought perhaps you were planning a different sort of ceremony."

221

"What's the hurry?" Hugo asked, not pretending to misunderstand her.

"She's a pretty girl and it would be a surprise to you to find you were not the only pebble on the beach."

"It certainly would," Hugo replied, with an impish complacency which he assumed deliberately because he knew it would annoy his grandmother.

She snorted at him, but before she could speak the door opened and Baxter returned.

"Ellen says, m'lord, that Miss Utta has not yet returned."

Hugo stared at him in amazement.

"Not returned," he ejaculated.

"Are you quite sure?" Lady Loth enquired. "She went immediately after tea."

"Where did she go?" Hugo asked.

"Someone rang her up. Baxter took the message. Now who was it, Baxter?"

"I didn't get the name, m'lady."

"Oh no, of course I remember now, it was that American woman, Mrs. Munton. She asked Utta to go and see her, and the child set off immediately she had had something to eat."

"Carole asked Utta to go and see her?" Hugo questioned.

"Yes, yes, I've just said so," Lady Loth replied impatiently. "Don't keep repeating my words."

"But it seems so extraordinary," he said. "And she hasn't returned since?"

"That's just what we have been telling you," Lady Loth said somewhat tartly.

Hugo got to his feet.

"If you will excuse me, Grandmother, I will go and telephone."

"Perhaps she stayed to dinner, forgetting that she was going out with you tonight," Lady Loth said maliciously.

Hugo did not answer this but crossed the hall to the library. It took him a few seconds to find the telephone number of the Ritz.

Finally he dialled it and having got through he asked

222

to speak to Carole. He could hear the telephone ringing in her suite before finally Adèle answered.

"Hello, hello!"

"Is that you, Adèle?"

"Who is it?"

"Lord Roxburton speaking."

"Oh yes, my lord. Shall I tell Madam you wish to speak to her? She is in her bath."

"No, don't bother. Is Miss Utta Greye still there?"

"Oh no, my lord. Miss Greye left a long time ago. Let me see, I went in to Madam just after she had gone —it must have been six o'clock."

"She's not come back. You are quite sure she's not there now?"

"Absolutely sure, my lord. Shall I call Madam?"

"No, thank you, Adèle, that's all I wanted to know."

Hugo put down the receiver. He could not understand it. Why had Utta not come home? Then he thought perhaps she had gone to Pamela. He dialled another number and this time he only had to wait a few seconds before his sister's voice said sharply:

"Hello! Who is it?"

"Is that you, Pamela?"

"Oh, Hugo! I was just rushing out of the door, we are dining with the Prime Minister and I'm terribly late."

"Is Utta with you?"

"Utta? No, of course not, she's dining with you."

"Yes, I know, but she isn't here."

"What do you mean by 'she isn't there'?"

"Exactly what I say."

"But I can't understand it," Pamela said. "She knew quite well you were fetching her at half-past eight because she talked about it and we discussed what dress she was to wear. What do you think has happened to her? I know—I remember now, she went round to see Carole Munton at the Ritz. I offered to drop her but she preferred to walk. She must be still there."

"I have just been speaking to Carole's maid and Utta left the Ritz about six o'clock."

"Good Lord! What can have happened to her? She can't have lost her way."

"No, of course not!"

There was a pause, then Pamela said:

"You don't think she's had an accident? After all, she isn't used to traffic."

"I will ring the hospitals and if necessary the police," Hugo said.

"Shall I come round?" Pamela offered, then added hastily: "No, I must go to the P.M.'s. Walter will be simply furious if I fail at the last moment, but ring me if you have any news. I am terribly worried, Hugo, but I can't believe it is anything serious."

"No, of course not," he said soothingly. "I expect there is some quite reasonable explanation."

"Of course, but you will telephone me?"

"Yes, as soon as I find out what has happened!"

He put down the receiver and picked up the telephone book. Half an hour later he went upstairs to the drawing-room, where Baxter had informed him his grandmother was waiting for him. She was sitting by the fire holding out her thin, blue-veined hand towards the flames.

"Well?" she queried, as he came into the room.

"The hospitals have no one answering Utta's description and the police say there have been no accidents reported between here and the Ritz during this evening."

"Then what could have happened to the child?"

"That's what I am going to find out," Hugo said grimly.

"Where are you going?" Lady Loth asked.

"To the Ritz," Hugo replied, and was gone before she could ask him any further questions.

Carole was having cocktails with several friends in her sitting-room when Hugo was announced. She glanced up at him in astonishment and moved swiftly towards him with outstretched hands.

"Hugo, what a wonderful surprise . . ." she began, but stopped abruptly when she saw the uncompromising grimness of his face.

224

"I want to speak to you alone."

She glanced towards the chattering group of men and women around the cocktail table.

"It will have to be in my bedroom then."

"It doesn't matter where so long as we're alone," Hugo answered.

"That sort of remark would have made me very happy a week or so ago," she replied.

He did not speak and she led the way into the next room, her dress of sequin-embroidered tulle rustling as she walked. He closed the door behind them, then turned to face her as she leant nonchalantly against the foot of the bed.

"Well?" she said enquiringly.

"What did you say to Utta?" he asked.

"So that's why you have come," she said without surprise. "I wondered if she would have the guts to face you with it."

"Face me with what?" Hugo enquired.

Carole looked at him.

"You mean she hasn't told you?"

"I'm the one asking questions," Hugo said. "Utta came here to see you at your invitation. I don't know what you said to her but, knowing you, I can have a good guess that it must have been something unpleasant. Whatever it was, she has not been seen since."

"Not been seen . . ." Carole began. "Do you mean to say she hasn't come home?"

"Exactly! I went round just now to take her out to dinner and found that nobody has seen her since she left to visit you."

"I can't understand it," Carole exclaimed, and then she stopped.

"I think you can understand it very well," Hugo said. "And now tell me what you said to Utta when you invited her here this evening."

Carole stood upright and took a deep breath.

"I told her the truth."

"And what was that?"

"That I am going to have a child—yours."

225

"I had a feeling it might be something of that sort," Hugo remarked.

He walked past Carole to the bedside table on which rested the telephone.

"What are you doing to do?" she asked curiously.

"I am going to telephone Sir William Bartlett," Hugo replied. "In case you have not heard of him, he is the leading gynaecologist in the country."

"Do you think he will be able to help you? It's too soon for that."

"On the contrary. Science today leaves very little to chance and this is where scientific investigation can be of great assistance. I wasn't born yesterday, my dear Carole, nor am I frightened by this type of blackmail.

"If the tests such as Sir William will make are conclusive and the paternity of the child by the comparison of the blood and various other modern methods is assured in due course, then I shall consider marrying you."

He raised the receiver as he spoke.

"Give me Sir William Bartlett," he said to the telephone clerk who answered.

"Wait!"

The word seemed to force itself between Carole's lips.

"Cancel that call," Hugo said into the receiver.

He put down the telephone and turned to look at Carole.

"It isn't true," she told him weakly. "You'll find out sooner or later, so I might as well confess now. I'm not having a baby because it is impossible for me ever to have one."

"And yet you told Utta those damnable lies to distress and frighten her."

"Why should she have everything her own way in life?" Carole asked furiously. "Why should she be protected, cherished and cosseted, while I have had to fight and struggle for everything I have ever wanted, for everything I have ever got?"

She was trembling as she spoke, half with anger and half with self-pity, but Hugo's eyes as he looked at her were hard as agates.

"I never believed before, Carole, that you were a

226

wicked woman," he said scathingly. "Now I am ashamed, not only of you but of my own stupidity that I was ever deceived into thinking you not only desirable but decent."

She cried out at that and her arms went out towards him, but already he had turned away; then the door slammed behind him and she was alone with the darkness of her despair.

When he reached the ground floor, Hugo hesitated and finally, after some thought, he went into a telephone booth. For the next twenty minutes he telephoned every aerodrome from which there were aeroplanes leaving for Switzerland.

All had the same answer—there were no bookings for anyone in the name of Greye and no one of Utta's description had left on 'planes departing that evening.

Finally, baffled and feeling more apprehensive than he showed outwardly, Hugo returned to his grandmother's house. Baxter, when he opened the door, told him that Pamela had rung up twice asking if there was any news.

"If Madam rings again, will you speak to her, m'lord?"

"Yes, if I am still here," Hugo answered, and went upstairs to the drawing-room.

"Well, where is she?" Lady Loth greeted him.

"If I knew that, I should have gone to fetch her," Hugo answered. He sat down in the chair and put his hand to his forehead. "I can't think of any place she is likely to go to except one. She has no friends except people she has met in the last week. It seems to me obvious, if she is thinking of running away, that she will return to Switzerland."

"There are more ways of going to Switzerland than by air," his grandmother remarked.

Hugo sat upright.

"You are right," he exclaimed. "I was a fool not to think of it. She may have gone by train to Dover or Folkestone and crossed by boat. You are sure that she had her passport with her?"

"Quite sure," Lady Loth replied. "I asked Ellen to

have a look after you had gone. I had the feeling that this might happen. When children are frightened or homesick, they run home."

Hugo looked at his watch.

"It will be too late now to catch anything but a morning train. It would be quicker for me to go by 'plane."

"So you are going after her?" his grandmother questioned.

"Of course," he replied.

"What did Mrs. Munton say to upset her?" Lady Loth enquired.

Without mincing his words Hugo told her the truth.

"An ill-bred woman," Lady Loth remarked tartly. "At the same time, this should be a lesson to you."

"It is one I won't forget," Hugo assured her. He rose to his feet. "I shall tell Baxter, when Pamela rings again, to say that Utta has gone home to Switzerland and that I'm going after her tomorrow morning. I'm certain that's where she will be, but if Pamela thinks there is any doubt she will worry quite unnecessarily."

"I will keep the truth to myself," Lady Loth promised. "And Hugo—bring Utta back with you if you can. I have grown fond of the child."

"We will come back together," Hugo said confidently.

He did not sleep well that night, which surprised him, for always in the past he had never let anything, however worrying or however unsettling, interfere with his own sense of well-being.

But he found himself lying awake thinking of Utta being distressed and perhaps made unhappy by Carole's lies. For the first time Hugo found himself condemning the looseness of his life and the instability of his morals.

Before, he had always thought that whatever he did concerned only himself and one other person. If they were both of an age and blessed with a knowledge of the world, he had always felt that what they did was nobody else's business and nobody else's concern.

But now he realised that Utta, in her innocence, had been involved and hurt by both him and Carole.

He was honest enough to take part of the blame on

himself. Carole was Carole; she did not conform to English standards of decency.

Whose fault was it but his, who had entered into an affair with no thought of anything save his own desire and the gratification of his own senses? Now he was reaping the harvest he had sown and if he didn't like it he could still not deny that he was just as much to blame as Carole.

He found himself remembering so many things about Utta which he had never thought of before.

Her little hesitation at times when she was not quite certain what to do; the way she would look up at him for guidance; the sweetness of her smile when she was happy or when something touched her heart; the manner in which her eyes would light up when he appeared; the little pulse in the whiteness of her neck which would beat when he knew that she was excited.

He remembered the softness of her when he had held her in his arms that night in the corridor because something or somebody had frightened her. He remembered the terror in her voice.

The last thought brought him from his bed and he walked up and down his bedroom, smoking cigarette after cigarette until the ash-trays were full and the floor was scattered with the butts of them.

Then finally he cursed himself for being a fool and threw himself down determined to sleep, only to hear every hour strike; and he was unutterably relieved when six o'clock came and Smith called him with an already packed suitcase.

"Are you quite sure you don't want me to come with you, m'lord?"

"No, but if I stay longer than a night or so, I will send for you."

There was always a chance, Hugo thought, that he might have difficulty in persuading Utta to return with him, and yet he felt sure that she would not really be difficult—not where he was concerned.

It was bitterly cold on the airport and he wondered if Utta was warm enough, travelling more slowly across Europe by train.

He reckoned that she would reach St. Moritz about the same time as he did, provided she had started last night—and then again she might have had to wait until this morning, in which case he would be there first.

High above the clouds he made plans. He would not go blundering in on the Kindschis in case Utta had not got there. It would only upset them, he thought, and they were old people.

He did not realise that for perhaps the first time in his life he was thinking of others rather than of himself. If Utta had taught him nothing else, she had taught him consideration.

The journey by train from the airport seemed insupportably long. The sun was shining, glittering on the snow and the train climbed higher and higher, and yet Hugo had no eyes for the scenery. He was all impatience to arrive.

He wanted to see Utta, he wanted to get over what he knew would be an uncomfortable moment in which he had to explain to her about Carole.

How he wished now he had never set eyes on the American woman! How he wished he had never gone to her party with the Duchess of Melchester, or let himself become inveigled into an affair which he had never wanted, except for a few half-hearted moments, to be anything but transitory!

He wondered now how he could have been so mad, so blind, as to think, even for a split second, that she might be his wife and the chatelaine of Rox.

He thought of her clinging, possessive passion with horror and hated himself because he had been prepared to accept what she offered him.

By the time the train reached St. Moritz he was feeling in a surprisingly humble state of mind.

If he had told the truth, he was even a little afraid of the moment when he must look into Utta's honest, straightforward eyes and tell her what a fool and a beast he had made of himself.

The porter put his suitcase into a taxi and he directed it to go to Suvretta House. The manager greeted him with open arms, delighted that he should return so soon.

"I regret we cannot give you the same suite that you had before, my lord. It is unfortunately engaged. We have another almost exactly similar on the floor above."

"Yes, yes, that will do," Hugo said impatiently. "I don't expect to be here more than a night or so. Send my luggage up to the room. Do you know if Ernst Zippert is in the hotel?"

"He may be in the bar, my lord. If not, shall I send a porter up to his house to say you wish to see him?"

"Yes, find him for me," Hugo said, "and ask him to come to my sitting-room. I will dine up there, by the way."

"Very good, my lord."

Hugo walked swiftly through the lounge to the lift. He had no desire to be seen. Although Nicolaus and Madame Kindschi were out of touch with the people in St. Moritz there was always the chance that someone might carry tales.

He did not want them to know that he was here until he was certain that Utta was with them.

When he reached the sitting-room, he rang for some drinks, then waited restlessly until Ernst appeared. He came hurrying into the room, red-faced and smiling, delight written all over his countenance at seeing Hugo again so soon.

"I could not believe it was true, my lord, when they told me you were back!" he exclaimed. "Is Utta with you?"

"That is what I wanted to ask you," Hugo said, and seeing the astonishment on Ernst's face, he added: "Sit down and have a drink."

"A small one, if you please," Ernst replied, then added: "You thought that Utta was here; how was that?"

"Listen, Ernst," Hugo said. "What I am going to say to you is entirely in confidence. I trust you and I know that you have been a good friend to Utta."

"I love that child as if she was my own," Ernst answered. "Has anything happened to her? You are not trying to tell me that?"

"No, no, nothing I'm sure," Hugo reassured him,

231

"but I have reason to think that she may be with her grandparents."

"But that's impossible," Ernst replied. "I was with Nicolaus Kindschi only this afternoon. We spoke of Utta and he said he had had a letter from her saying how much she was enjoying England and telling him of all the places she had visited and the people she had met."

"Then I must have arrived before her," Hugo said.

"What is all this about, my lord?" Ernst asked.

Hugo hesitated for a moment and then he told the truth.

"Utta was upset and distressed by a pack of lies which Mrs. Munton told her. That was yesterday evening after tea. She did not come back to my grandmother's house, where she was staying, and we came to the conclusion that, being unhappy, she would naturally go home to her grandparents."

"Yes, yes, I see that," Ernst said. "But she should be here by now."

"Remember she has never done any travelling," Hugo replied. "She may only have been able to catch a morning train from Victoria."

"Then where would she have stayed the night?" Ernst enquired.

"At a hotel, I suppose," Hugo answered, and put up his hand to his head. "Damn it all, man, do you suppose I haven't been worrying all the time? The child is so young, so inexperienced—and yet what else could she do? She must be coming here."

"Yes, yes, my lord, I am sure you are right," Ernst soothed him. "If she does not arrive tonight—I think there is one more train after yours—then it will be to-morrow morning."

"This is what I want you to do," Hugo said. "I want you to find out when she gets here and let me know at once. On no account distress or upset the Kindschis by letting them know what has happened. I will have my meal up here tonight so that no one will see me, and to-morrow, I feel sure, Utta will be home."

"I can only pray that you are right, my lord," Ernst replied. "If anything should have happened to Utta . . ."

"Nothing will have happened to her!" Hugo shouted, then added: "I'm sorry, Ernst, but I'm worried, as you can imagine."

"That's all right, my lord, I know how you feel. Mrs. Munton was not the type of woman who should mix with Utta. There are women and women, as you and I know, and we get all types and sorts out here. Utta was different; she had never been spoilt or touched by the things which ruin so many of her sex."

Ernst stopped short, then with a note of emotion in his voice, he added:

"Sometimes it seemed to me as though she were not really of this world but part of the mountains and the snows and the very sunshine itself."

There was a long silence before Hugo got to his feet.

"Find her for me, Ernst," he begged.

For a moment all differences of position and breeding were forgotten—it was man speaking to man, crying for help.

"I will do my best," Ernst promised.

Hugo put his hand into his pocket and brought out two five-pound notes. He would have passed them to Ernst in the quiet unobtrusive way in which it was usual to tip a man of Ernst's position, but the Swiss waved the money away with a gesture of his hand.

"I want none of that, my lord," he said. "What I do I do for Utta. You are the second person who has asked me to keep track of her movements and offered me money which I wouldn't touch, not if I was starving in the gutter and down to my last sou."

"The second person?" Hugo enquired.

"Yes," Ernst replied. "That Hollywood fellow, Carlos Jacára, approached me after you had left and asked me to let him know when Utta returned home from England."

"What did he want to know that for?" Hugo asked sharply.

Ernst shrugged his shoulders.

"He spoke of Hollywood contracts. I dare say he had one in his pocket, but he is a menace where any decent girl is concerned. He has been here before and I have

233

seen what happened to the girls to whom he takes a fancy. If I came across him on a dark night when there was a hole in the ice and no one was about, I would drop him into it. The world would be a better place without him. As it was, I had to keep my temper, although he realised that I was not very co-operative."

"I will wring his neck if I find him making himself unpleasant to Utta," Hugo said grimly.

Even as he spoke he guessed what had upset her that night when she had fled down the corridor into his arms.

He had half-connected her fear with Carole, because Carole's suite was on the same floor and she was coming from that direction; and yet it would have been hard to understand what Carole could have said at that moment to distress and frighten her so that she had been white and trembling and very near to tears.

Now he knew, and there was murder in his heart as he thought of that slimy-looking creature to whom Carole had introduced him that day when they were lunching at the Palace.

And even as he thought of Don Carlos and Utta, he knew, for the first time, not only a terror as to what was happening to her, but the first bitter yet poignant pangs of jealousy. Utta was his, utterly and completely his.

That any other man should look at her, should approach or insult her, was something beyond his toleration, something which he could not even think of without longing for violence.

He was so deep in his thoughts that it made him start when Ernst spoke again.

"I will make some excuse to go up to the Kindschis' house after supper, my lord," he said, "and I will call in on my way back and tell you if Utta is there."

Hugo held out his hand.

"Thank you, Ernst. You realise that there is no one to help me, except yourself."

"I shall do everything that is in my power, my lord," Ernst promised.

Hugo ordered some dinner, but when it came he could not eat it. He was not hungry and even drink

234

could not assuage the chaotic feelings within his mind or the worry which seemed to hover around him, croaking dismal forebodings and suggesting a thousand terrible things that might have happened to Utta between London and here.

He found himself visualising railway accidents, sinking ships, crashing aeroplanes—anything which might prevent her reaching home, and always the terror at the back of his mind was that she might have done something desperate.

He had never known what it was to feel like this about any woman. He who had never known fear before was afraid because he loved.

It was then, like a brilliant light, the truth was there for him to see. He was in love—in love with Utta—as he had never been in love with anyone before.

He loved her—loved her little sweet pointed face, her fair hair, her gentian blue eyes, those two dimples in her cheeks. He loved her.

Small, exquisite, fairylike, she had twisted her way into his heart and now he could never be rid of her.

He knew now how blind he had been not to realise this sooner, not to grasp at his happiness with two hands when it had stood and waited for him.

He had, indeed, thought of speaking to Utta last week-end at Rox, but somehow the thought that Pamela and the family were waiting to hear of his engagement made him hold back defiantly and become obstinate, simply and solely because the obvious was expected of him.

Now he cursed himself for worrying for one moment as to what they thought or said. Only Utta mattered: Utta who loved him as he loved her; Utta who trembled at his approach, whose eyes lit up at the sight of him.

How could he have been so proud, so ridiculous as not to have realised then and there that he was not worthy so much as to kiss the ground on which her feet had walked?

She was far too good for him. In her innocence and purity it was she who must condescend to him not he to her.

He had thought himself so important with his title, his position, his wealth and Rox, yet what had he to offer in exchange for an untouched heart and the innocence of a child's mind?

Hugo pushed the dinner-table away from him. He was not hungry, he only wanted one thing and one thing only and that was Utta.

It was eleven o'clock before Ernst returned. As he came into the sitting-room, Hugo sprang to his feet.

"She is there!" he said.

It was a statement rather than a question, born out of the fullness of his heart.

Ernst shook his head.

"The last train got in at ten o'clock," he said. "I made enquiries and stayed with Nicolaus until it was certain that Utta had not come by it or she would have arrived at home before I came away."

He saw the expression of disappointment on Hugo's face.

"She will be here tomorrow," he added consolingly.

"Yes, tomorrow!" Hugo said. "But I am just wondering how I will get through the night until she comes."

There was a sudden silence after he had spoken, then Ernst's voice, low, respectful and yet hesitating, said:

"Forgive my presumption, my lord, but do you love her?"

There was no pause before Hugo answered him and his voice seemed to ring out triumphantly.

"Yes Ernst, I love her with all my heart!" he replied.

15

Utta skated round and round the small Ice Rink.

No lights were lit and the pale light from outside could hardly penetrate in winter through the dingy windows high up on a building which had once been built for storage.

Yet she did not see the shabby walls with their peeling paint, the empty bar with its kicked and battered cocktail stools or the spectators' seats of torn plush which had been bought from a dismantled cinema.

Instead, she saw the sunshine and the snow and the tops of the mountains silhouetted clearly against a blue sky.

In spirit she was back in Switzerland, skating when all the fashionable visitors were fast asleep and there was only Ernst watching her critically to rebuke or command.

It was seven o'clock in the morning and it was at this time of the day, when she could have the rink to herself, that she was happiest.

She spun, leapt, twirled and double O'd, and in the back of her brain some disinterested part of herself knew that she was skating better than she had ever skated before.

Here on the ice rink she could forget everything save that her feet had wings. It was over a fortnight now since she had left Lady Loth's house, carrying her heavy suitcase, too dazed, too bewildered to know anything except that she must get away.

She had walked some distance until she found herself in Park Lane and realised that her arm was aching from the weight of her case. Then she hailed a taxi.

"Where to, miss?" he asked.

For a moment Utta hesitated and then, not realising how pathetic her white face and wide eyes looked, she said:

"Can you take me somewhere cheap where I can stay for the night?"

"What do you call cheap?" enquired the driver, looking at her expensive coat with its fur collar.

"I don't know what one has to pay in England," Utta answered limply.

He seemed to size her up.

"Get in," he commanded gruffly, and he drove her to one of the narrow, mean streets around Victoria Station. He stopped at a door.

"They won't rob you here," he said, "but she may be full up."

It was a tall, shabby house with broken railings and peeling paint and the lace curtains covering the windows were badly in need of a wash, but the woman who answered Utta's ring of the bell was not unfriendly.

"Yes, I have got a room left," she said. "It's a top, mind you, and not very large, but I see you haven't brought much luggage with you."

"No," Utta replied. She was not disposed to argue or be choosey. She would have taken the room whatever it had been like. Fortunately it was comparatively clean, if sparsely and poorly furnished.

She gave the landlady an advance for two nights and then, when at last she was alone, she sat down on the bed and stared blankly at the wall in front of her. She must have sat there for some hours.

She heard a bell ring in the distance; it was apparently a call for supper, for she heard footsteps hurrying down the linoleum-covered stairs, but she made no move and no one troubled about her.

It grew dark and, at length, when it was quite dark, she undressed and got between the coarse cotton sheets of the hard bed.

She lay for a long time with her eyes wide open, staring into the darkness until, just before dawn, the ice round her heart seemed to melt, the paralysis which had numbed all her faculties began to ebb away and at last the tears came—at first slowly and then faster until, in an irresistible flood, she was sobbing as though swept by a tempest.

All the next day she stayed in her room, her eyes red and swollen, feeling that she could not bear to speak to anyone, could not force any word, however trivial, from between her lips.

At lunch-time someone thumped on her door and asked her if she would be down for a meal. With an effort she replied that she was not hungry and whoever it was went away.

In the afternoon she wept again, the hopeless, de-

spairing tears of one who finds the world dark and deso-
late without a flicker of hope anywhere.

But youth is elastic; when it has reached the depth of
suffering, it rises again, unconsciously, of its own volition. The following morning Utta awoke dry-eyed and,
for the first time since she left Lady Loth's house, she
felt hungry.

She dressed and went downstairs, meaning to creep
out of the house to find breakfast somewhere in the
neighbourhood, perhaps at the station, but the landlady
saw her and called her into the dining-room.

"I thought you must be ill," she said. "Are you better
today?"

"Yes, thank you," Utta replied.

"Then sit down and I'll get you a bite of breakfast.
The others have all finished. I think the kippers are finished too, but I'd spare an egg if you'd eat it."

"Thank you very much," Utta said.

The egg, when it came, had travelled a long way and
was not too appetising; the tea was strong and black.
But she was hungry and, as she told herself severely, she
could not afford to be particular.

"Are you leaving today?" the landlady asked conver-
sationally.

"As a matter of fact," Utta replied, "I was wondering
if I might stay on."

"Glad to have you so long as you let me know," the
landlady replied. She paused a moment and then, overcome by her curiosity, asked: "Are you looking for
work?"

"Yes . . . I am," Utta told her, and was suddenly
aware that her answer was the truth. Of course she had
got to find work. The ten pounds would not last for
ever.

"Well now, and what sort of thing are you looking
for?" the landlady asked.

She rose from the table and started stacking the
plates together, a cigarette hanging out of the corner of
her mouth as she worked, the long sleeves of a shabby,
much washed jumper showing beneath the short sleeves
of her printed overal.

"I . . . don't exactly know," Utta replied.

"Ought to be easy for you to get a job in a shop," the landlady remarked. "Had any experience?"

"No, none."

"Pity! Jobs aren't as easy as they were. Anything you can do like typing or book-keeping?"

Utta shook her head.

"I'm afraid not. I can skate."

"You don't say! Can you really? Well?"

"Yes, quite well I think."

"Then that's all right. With your face they'll take you on in the chorus of one of these ice shows—though perhaps it's the wrong time of year. Christmas is the time, with all the pantomimes on ice they were fair shrieking for girls."

"I don't think I want to be in an ice show," Utta said hastily, remembering that she wouldn't want to be seen.

"Well, there's always the clubs," the landlady went on. "I tell you what!"

She slapped one of the dishes down on the table with such a clatter that it made Utta jump.

"Pop along to the ice rink in Albert Street. It's just round the corner, about two minutes from here—the Splendide it's called—and ask for the chappie who's the Secretary—Ted Walters is the name. Tell him I sent you; he might know of something. He's not a bad sort, I meets him in the Coach and Horses on a Saturday night. Beautiful dart player he is."

"You think he might be able to suggest something?" Utta said.

"No harm in trying, is there, dear?"

"No, of course not, and thank you very much."

"That's all right. Thank me when you get something. And by the way, if you are staying another night it's pay in advance."

"Oh, yes, of course," Utta said, blushing a little.

She brought out her purse and paid for two nights. As she replaced her note-case she thought that her money was dwindling fast and that it was urgent that she should get a job as soon as possible.

She went upstairs to put on her coat and hat. Her face in the mirror gave her a shock.

For one thing she looked immeasurably older, for another her white face and dark-ringed eyes seemed to belong to a stranger. With powder and lipstick she tried to make herself look more presentable.

No one would want to employ a ghost or a girl who looked so tragic that she was likely to depress anyone with whom she came in contact. There was not much improvement when she had finished.

Impatiently Utta turned away from the looking-glass and went downstairs.

"Best o' luck!" the landlady called to her as she passed through the hall.

"Thank you," Utta replied.

It was a cold, grey day and the pavements were dangerous from a frost the night before. Utta found the Splendide Ice Rink without much difficulty. The outside was not very prepossessing.

She was to learn later that it belonged to two or three tradesmen who had thought to cash in on the ice-skating craze without spending more than the minimum amount of capital.

By cutting their prices so as to compete favourably with other rinks, they managed to attract a certain number of poor customers, mostly teen-age boys who concentrated more on ragging than on skating.

There were only two or three people practising when Utta arrived that first morning.

The Secretary, Mr. Walters, was a cadaverous-looking young man who was likely to be bald before he was thirty and whose brisk, somewhat efficient voice completely belied his movements.

"Mrs. Horrocks sent you, did she?" he said to Utta's timid introduction of herself. "She's a good sort, though I can't say I've much of an acquaintance with her outside the Coach and Horses."

"I thought you might be able to advise me as to where I can get a job skating," Utta said.

"Do you skate well?" he enquired.

241

She nodded and touched the brown paper parcel under her arm.

"I thought perhaps someone would want to see what I can do."

"Right-o," he answered; "but if you're good, you're too good for here; and if you're bad, we don't want you." He smiled at his joke, but Utta said quickly:

"You mean you might be able to offer me a job?"

"Well, there's one going," he told her. "Lady Instructress—the last one walked out three days ago. I ticked her off for larking about at the bar; she didn't like it and she left."

"I wouldn't do that," Utta said. "I mean . . . do you think I could take her place?"

"Better ask the salary first. We're not one of those posh rinks that can pay the earth. Here it's five pounds a week, you bring your own boots and you pay for your own food—no perks and few privileges."

"I would be very glad to take that," Utta said.

"Are you sure?" he replied doubtfully. His eyes took in the cut of her clothes, the expensiveness of her leather handbag and suede gloves.

"Please may I show you what I can do?" Utta pleaded.

"O.K."

He opened the door of the office and they went out into the rink. There was a smell of cold and of dirty ice, there was an acrid stench of stale tobacco and of dirt, which seemed to pervade everything despite the fact that now there were two women on their knees scrubbing the entrance hall.

Utta sat down in one of the plush chairs and put on her boots.

"I haven't brought a proper skating costume," she told Mr. Walters.

"That doesn't matter," he replied. "You don't wear them here except on gala nights and for exhibitions. I don't suppose you will want to be giving any of those."

"No, of course not," Utta answered because it seemed expected of her.

She took off her coat and put it down on a chair beside her. Her dress had a full, pleated skirt and as she stepped on to the ice she knew it would not impede her movements.

For the first time since the horror of that moment in Carole's sitting-room at the Ritz when the world seemed to have fallen away from her leaving her numb and alone, she felt more like herself.

There was the joy of movement, the wonder of feeling her feet carry her rhythmically through complicated movements and figures. She forgot, for a moment, how much depended on her performance and remembered only that she was on ice again and that skating was as much a part of her as breathing.

She must have skated for nearly a quarter of an hour before she remembered that Mr. Walters was watching her and that her future depended on his opinion. She spun round a dozen times and skated back towards him.

He was sitting where she had left him and as she reached the side of the rink and held on to the rail he rose to his feet.

"What's the idea?" he asked roughly.

"The idea?" she questioned.

"You wanting a job here."

"I've got to have one. As I explained to you . . . I want work."

"In the Splendide, when you can skate like that?" he asked. "Go on, there's something behind it."

"There's nothing—really there's nothing," Utta said quickly.

"Then why don't you go to the Westminster or any of the other big ones? They'd jump at you."

"But I would rather be here, really I would," Utta told him. "It is . . . it is near where I'm living and it's quiet."

"So that's it, is it?" he said. "Are you hiding or something?"

"Perhaps," Utta replied.

He stared at her for a moment and then he shrugged his shoulders.

"Well, it's none of my business, but if you want the job it's yours."

"Thank you!" Utta exclaimed. "When do I start?"

"Now, if you like," he said. "There's a woman over there been asking me all the morning for lessons. I haven't been able to fix her up until now." He turned to walk back into his office and then he stopped. "By the way, what's your name?"

Utta hesitated. She was well aware she must not give her own name. She had seen copies of *The Skater* lying about Mr. Walter's office. There was certain to be a photograph of her in it, for innumerable photographs had been taken of the first three in the International Championships.

"Gadner," she answered, "Nita Gadner."

It was the first name she could think of and she remembered the girl to whom it belonged—a wide-eyed child in the village of Silvaplaner who had asked for her autograph the last morning when she had been practising there with Ernst.

She had a sudden pang of homesickness at the thought. How happy she had been that morning and how excited at the thought of what lay ahead!

She could go back; why did she stay here miserable, alone, in this sordid, smelly Rink when the sunshine, the snow and the love of her grandparents were waiting for her in Switzerland?

And then she knew that she could not bear to face them, could not tell them what had happened or confess her own misery at the knowledge of Hugo's treachery.

Her grandmother had known she loved him, known it as she had packed with shining eyes, as she had been unable to prevent her love for him being written all over her expressive face.

They had said nothing, but that was not to say they did not understand each other, *Grand'mère* and herself. They had been so close for so many years that there was often no need for words.

That last night before Utta left for England Madame Kindschi had come into her bedroom when she was already in bed. She bent down to kiss her granddaughter and then, with her lips against the softness of Utta's cheek, she whispered:

244

"I shall miss you, *ma petite!*"

"I shall miss you, *Grand'mère!*"

Madame Kindschi smiled.

"Yes, my love, but not so much. You see, you are growing up, you are reaching out into new worlds, you are discovering new joys, new people. My life is finished! I have done all the things that you are starting to do now and that is why I understand, that is why I know what you are feeling."

Utta reached up to put her arms around her grandmother's neck.

"You always have understood, *Grand'mère.*"

"I have tried to, my darling; that is why I want to say one word of warning now. Don't expect too much from people. If they are giving the best of which they are capable, that must be enough, you must not ask for more."

"Do I?"

"Yes, my dear, sometimes. When you love a person, I think that you expect them to be perfection. If they cannot live up to that, you must not be too hard on them, not be too disappointed."

How vividly that conversation came back now; but yet, Utta thought, she had not asked for perfection, only decency and truth.

She put her hands to her eyes and then, as if she ran away from her own thoughts, skated across the rink to the woman floundering by the rail who had asked for lessons.

Teaching other people, Utta found, was hard work. She who had never been tired when she was skating got very weary when she was instructing others.

The ones who could skate a little were not so difficult, it was the beginners, who clutched at her, who were too frightened to do what she told them and often too stupid even to make the simplest effort.

It was after three days of struggling round and round that Utta felt that she must skate by herself or go mad. She went to see Mr. Walters in his office. She had learned by this time that Mr. Walters did very little but sit in his office reading the newspapers for the majority of the day and evening.

He locked and unlocked the bar, counted the skates to see that no one had gone off with a pair, and that, in effect, was the sum total of his efforts to make the Splendide Ice Rink a success.

"Hello, Nita, what is it?" he asked, as Utta stood in the doorway.

As she was one of the staff, he made no effort to take his feet off the table and he only dropped his newspaper low enough to enable him to look over the top of it.

"I want to ask you if I can come here early and skate before anyone else arrives," Utta said.

"Good Lord, whatever for?" he asked.

"I never get a chance during the day," Utta replied. "There is always someone wanting lessons, asking questions or doing something which occupies my time. Can I come very early before the rink is opened?"

"What time do you mean?" Mr. Walters asked.

"Oh, about six-thirty—seven if you like."

"You must be crazy, that's all I can say," he remarked. "Here you are on the ice all day and half the night and you want to come at that unearthly hour! Well, have it your own way. I'll give you the key after I've locked up and hold you responsible. If anything happens, I'll get into a hell of a mess with the Board."

This was only talk, as Utta well knew. The Board's only interest in the rink was how much money they made out of it. All the internal arrangements were left entirely to the discretion of Mr. Walters.

"Thank you very much," she said.

"Thank me for nothing," Mr. Walters retorted. "You're mad, as I have told you before, or you wouldn't be here."

Utta smiled and left the office. She was well aware that Mr. Walters, like everyone else at the rink, was incessantly curious about her. She gave no confidences and they were forced to invent their own explanations as to why she was there.

"Ever thought of going in for a competition?" one of the male Skating Instructors asked her.

"Yes," Utta replied.

"What happened?"

"I didn't win."

He looked surprised.

"Can't understand it," he said, "unless you're the type that goes to pieces in front of an audience. I used to be like that myself when I was a kid, otherwise there was a chance I might have won a pot or two."

"I don't want to compete with anyone," Utta told him.

"It might be worth your while," he called after her as she skated away from him.

As the days went by Utta found the agony and misery departed a little.

Now she could think of Hugo without being stabbed with a pain that was almost unbearable and she could even whisper his name to herself without bursting into tears. She found herself wondering what he must be thinking of her disappearance and she even felt a little ashamed in case Lady Loth was worried or perturbed by her disappearance.

Then she told herself that Hugo would know the truth. Carole would have told him that she was going to have a baby and he would have understood from that the reason why Utta had found it impossible to stay under his grandmother's roof.

"I still love him," Utta told herself, not once but a hundred times, in the darkness of her cold little bedroom, when she found it impossible to sleep and would lie awake hour after hour hearing Big Ben boom the hours.

"I love him!"

Nothing could alter that. He might belong to Carole, he might be wrong, wicked and many other things, but she still loved him. That, in itself, was the real reason why she knew she could never go back, could never see him again—because she dare not.

If she saw him, she thought, she would forget everything and want to run close to him, to hold on to him, to hide her face against his shoulder as she had done that night at Suvretta House when she had been frightened by Don Carlos.

She loved him and nothing he could say or do could really alter her feelings towards him. She began to understand now so many of the books she had read and which had seemed so utterly incomprehensible to her.

Why, she had asked herself in the past, did women married to really bad men go on loving them whatever they did or however they behaved?

Now she knew that love was something too great and perhaps too divine to depend on circumstances or logic or reason or anything except love itself.

"I love him!"

The ice round her heart had melted, and the fire had come back.

She could feel herself aching in every limb of her body for Hugo's presence. She could feel herself yearning with mind, body and soul for the sight of him again, for the knowledge that he was there, that his eyes were seeking hers and his lips were smiling.

Sometimes she dreamed that she was with him, and then she would wake with a sudden singing happiness that would only gradually disappear as she opened her eyes to see the stained ceiling, the peeling wallpaper and the curtainless window.

Sometimes she felt as if she moved in a dream, that everything she did and said during the day was unreal, a kind of horrible fantasy from which she would awake to find it a nightmare.

Slowly the days went on. She lost count of them, feeling that tomorrow would be like today and exactly the same as yesterday.

The only moments to which she looked forward were those times when she was alone on the rink, when she could skate and forget, when she could go through all the movements that Ernst had taught her and feel her muscles co-ordinating with her will to achieve a perfection greater than she had ever achieved before.

At the end of the first week she found that almost her whole salary was swallowed up in paying for her food and lodgings.

At the end of the second week she had to draw on the tiny store of notes that were still left to her—and then she began to get frightened. She was not foolish enough to think that her clothes would last for ever; there were things that she wanted—small things it was true, but which must be bought and paid for.

She began to think that perhaps Mr. Walters was right and she would be wise to seek a better-paid job elsewhere—and yet she was afraid, afraid of chancing her luck once more in a world where she knew no one, had no contacts and no friends.

She liked Mrs. Horrocks; she felt in some strange way at home in the squalor because it had become familiar.

She learned how to handle the rough youths who rushed shouting about the rink, knocked each other over in boisterous horseplay, who were inclined to drink too much when the bar was open and became truculent when told to behave themselves.

She learned how to encourage people who were shy and how to snub and subdue those who were inclined to be flirtatious—and yet in everything she did she felt as though it was a stranger who moved and talked within her body.

A stranger who had very little in common with the young, joyful and happy Utta who had lived in St. Moritz.

Then one morning it was raining as she walked through the streets for her early morning practice. She had no umbrella and the rain beat down on her defenceless head.

She ran the last hundred yards and arrived breathless at the door of the Splendide. She drew the key from her pocket, opened the door and went in.

The usual indefinable smell greeted her and the place seemed almost dark, so that defiantly, knowing she was not entitled to do so, she turned on some of the lights.

As she looked about the dingy, dirty building, she felt a sudden distaste and disgust that she had never known before. Was she to spend the rest of her life in places like this?

She had only to get on an aeroplane and in a few hours she would be back in the sunshine. She could almost see her grandmother's arms outstretched towards her, the gladness on her grandfather's face.

At the thought she put her hands up to her eyes. How could she bear to tell them?

How could she creep back beaten and defeated from her first encounter with the world? And then she knew it was not herself and her own feelings that was troubling her, it was because, in spite of everything, she wanted to protect Hugo.

She could not bear to tell anyone, to see the contempt and anger in her grandfather's eyes when he learned what had happened, to endure the sympathy her grandmother would show her.

No, it was Hugo she was trying to save; and even while she knew it was absurd of her to feel like this, she knew, too, that she could not help herself.

In an effort to forget her feelings and the headache which seemed to press agonisingly against her forehead, she threw off her coat and stepped on to the ice.

For a moment the magic was not there, not even that was left to her now, and she moved desolately feeling that the spirit had gone from her and only emptiness remained.

Slowly, however, like a melody stealing its way into her consciousness, the wonder and thrill came to her as it had always come before.

She leapt in the air and felt the exhilaration as she spun round. The ice rink was forgotten, there was the sunshine and snow again.

Her heart began to beat, her lips parted, she was coming alive. Her unhappiness and her headache were forgotten, her arms were outstretched, her feet seemed to carry her without any conscious volition on her part.

And then suddenly at the end of the rink she saw—him.

The whole world seemed to turn topsy-turvy and everything vanished, save the fact that he was there waiting for her. Her feet carried her to his side and she put out her hands and found that he was real.

"My darling, I have found you at last!" It was Hugo's voice, low, deep and astonishingly broken.

She looked up into his face in amazement and saw there were tears in his eyes.

He looked thinner and much more drawn than when she had last seen him, and she began to tremble, for he was holding on to her hands as if he would never let her go.

"Where have you been?" he said. "How could you have been so cruel as to go away like that? I have been crazy, utterly and completely crazy, wondering what had happened to you."

"I have been here," she answered in a very small voice, but there was starlight in her eyes.

"The very last place I should have thought of looking," Hugo exclaimed. "I have been to all the others. I have searched every Ice Rink in London. It was only by chance that I saw this place and walked in because the door was open."

"You were looking for me?" Utta asked.

"Looking for you!" he ejaculated. "What do you think I have been doing these past sixteen days?"

His hands tightened on hers. The barrier was between them and he was a step higher than she was so that she must look up to him; and then as she tipped back her head, he said hoarsely:

"My darling, I love you so!"

Utta tried to remember that she must not listen to such words. At the back of her mind she thought that she must take her hands from his, and yet she was powerless against the wave of ecstasy which ran over her.

She felt herself quiver and tingle, she felt her lips part and her breath come quickly; and then, as she looked into his eyes, the world stood still.

For the first time she knew the glory of loving and being loved. There was no mistaking what she saw in his eyes, no misunderstanding the magnetism of the magic which passed between them.

Everything was forgotten—they were just alone, two people who were meant for each other, two people who had found each other after a long time.

At last Hugo spoke again.

"Oh, my sweet!" he said hoarsely. "Come somewhere where we can talk. We can't just stand with this rail between us."

Trembling but obedient, Utta skated along until she came to the entrance; but Hugo was there before her and as she stepped from the ice on to the rush carpet he took her in his arms.

He seemed to lift her off her feet against his heart, his lips were on hers and she was lost in a kiss which seemed to draw her very soul from between her lips.

"I have found you . . . I have found you!"

He was repeating the words over and over again, triumphantly, possessively. Then he was kissing her wildly —her lips, her cheeks, her eyes, her hair, the softness of her neck where a little pulse beat excitedly. . . .

"How could you have done it? How could you have done anything so cruel, so unbearable?" he asked a little later as they found themselves sitting side by side on the red plush seats.

His arms were still round her and her head against his shoulder. And then, suddenly, she stiffened and tried to draw away from him.

"What is it?" he asked.

"It's . . . it's Mrs. Munton," she whispered.

In answer he put his hand beneath her chin and turned her face up to his.

"How dare you not trust me? How dare you believe such lies? Didn't you know even then that I loved you?"

She felt her tenseness vanish beneath the touch of his fingers.

"It isn't . . . true then?" she asked.

"It was a lie, my darling. A damnable lie."

"Oh, I'm glad."

He could hardly hear the words, her lips were so close to his.

"You forgive me?" he asked. "Forgive me for all that I did before I met you? I've been punished—God only knows how cruelly I have been punished these last weeks, thinking that I had lost you, thinking that I should never find you again."

She heard the raw sincerity in his voice and knew it was the truth. He had suffered—she was to find later that it had made a finer and better man of him.

"I didn't want to hurt you," she murmured.

"And so, instead, you hurt yourself! My foolish little love, never leave me again. I can't bear it, I can't live without you. You are mine—mine for all time and I will never let you go."

His lips held hers at the last word. Now they were joined together, joined in the wonder and glory of a love which knew no barriers.

Closer and closer he held her until she could feel a flame flicker within herself to respond to the fire in him.

Only when she felt she could bear no more of a happiness that was too glorious, too brilliant and too overwhelming did he let her go.

Then, as he looked down at her shining eyes, at her flushed cheeks and her lips parted with ecstasy, he gave a little sigh of utter contentment.

"I have found you again, my darling," he said softly. "I have found what I have been looking for all my life. This, my sweet, is what I have been waiting for although I didn't know it—Love!"